THE LINE BETWEEN US

Kate Dunn

SAPERE
BOOKS

THE LINE
BETWEEN US

Published by Sapere Books.

20 Windermere Drive, Leeds, England, LS17 7UZ,
United Kingdom

saperebooks.com

ISBN: 978-1-912786-73-2

To my son Jack,
who could read maps from an early age and set the course for both of us.

ACKNOWLEDGEMENTS

I owe profound thanks to my husband Steve whose unstinting generosity gave me the time, space and encouragement that I needed to keep on writing; to my agent Laura Longrigg who never gave up on me, to my editor Amy Durant for having faith in my book, and to my mother for being utterly inspiring and holding me to account as a writer.

I'm also indebted to Zita Adamson for the intuition that she brought to early drafts, to Carole Pugh for her sustaining friendship, to the poet Deborah Harvey for her advice about autism, and to Dr Simon Robbins, Senior Archivist at the Imperial War Museum, for giving me access to invaluable first-hand accounts of the sinking of the *Lancastria*. Jonathan Fenby's book *The Sinking of the Lancastria* was an invaluable resource as well.

Finally, I'm grateful to my father, staunch advocate, bedrock and sometime proof reader, who died in 2004 and would have loved to have read *The Line Between Us*.

PART ONE

Chapter One

Western France, June 1940

I used to dream that one day I would call you by your name: Ella, I would say, my Ella, but I've had all the dreams knocked out of me. Only people who have never been to hell can say they've been to hell and back. There is no return journey, as far as I can see. They are calling what happened at Dunkirk a re-embarkation. It didn't feel like that to me. Why can't we call things by their proper names and not use pretty phrases? My unit managed to get as far as Abbeville, while the rest of the British Expeditionary Force was falling over itself to reach the coast. Retreat is what I call it. That's the view from here.

Not everyone managed to re-embark. Our lot received orders to evacuate westwards across France. Progress was painful and slow because the roads were jammed with refugees. Women and children mostly, and the elderly. Some had prams or wheelbarrows piled with their belongings, some had suitcases, a few just had bundles tied with cloth. The whole of Brittany was clogged with people on the move, trailing their belongings and all that was left of their old lives past abandoned buildings, looted homesteads and villages in tatters. When we got to the outskirts of St Nazaire we were ordered to disable all our vehicles and proceed on foot.

The War Office sent two liners to bring us home. They were moored out in the estuary and a couple of destroyers ferried troops out to them, but they had to leave stern first as there wasn't much room to manoeuvre and they were held up by the tides as well, so it took a heck of a long of time. Two of the men in my platoon — Cadwalladr and Sweeney — and me, were some of the last to leave shore and when we pulled up alongside, one of the crew shouted down to us that they were overloaded and couldn't take anyone else. The captain of the destroyer we were on called up that a couple of hundred more wouldn't make any difference either way, and as it was hardly the time or place for a lengthy conversation, in the end they agreed to let us on. We clambered up the netting on the side of the boat. I haven't much of a head for heights, so I counted the number of rivets in the metal as I climbed, not looking down at the water, which seemed a long, long way below.

The atmosphere on board was so merry. An RAF chap just ahead of us knelt down and kissed the deck. It was like the start of the summer holidays; everybody was so excited at the prospect of seeing home again. We were assigned places on the aft deck — there wasn't room for us anywhere else.

The *Lancastria* was one of the Cunard fleet. She'd been taking holidaymakers to the Bahamas when the war started. I'd never seen such luxury. Cadwalladr and I dumped our kit and went off to explore. It was difficult to get around in the crush, but we made it to the dining-room, which had arches and columns and waiters doing silver service with damask napkins on their arms. We had bangers and mash. After a month of sleeping in school halls and cellars and sometimes in ditches, with only scanty army rations, it was like heaven on earth.

Things got a little jumpy while we were eating — some Jerry planes flew over and let loose a couple of bombs and one of the crew told us that the other liner we were to sail with, the *Oronsay*, took a direct hit that knocked out her bridge.

I remember thinking how lucky I was to be on the *Lancastria*. I remember thanking my lucky stars.

After that we expected to be under way at any moment, but there were rumours of U Boats further out to sea and the captain wanted to wait for an escort, so there was a slight delay. Cadwalladr went off to find the ship's barber. I remember him saying he wouldn't feel human until he'd had a haircut and a shave. He was laughing as he wandered off.

I never saw him again.

I'd heard they were giving out chocolate at the Purser's office, so I went and joined the queue for that. There were some refugee children waiting in line and I got talking to an old lady whose husband had been a chocolatier in Vienna before the war. She said he was Jewish and that they'd been arrested trying to leave on forged papers. He bribed the guards to let her go. The last time she saw him he was being marched away from her at gun-point.

She was telling me all of this when there was an almighty crack and the ship rocked. I felt a flush of absolute terror run through me and broke out in a sweat, but there was a large cheer and the lads up on deck shouted, "They couldn't hit us if they tried!" The bomb, or whatever it was, had fallen in between us and the other liner, the *Oronsay*.

I knew I had to get some air. My heart was pounding and I couldn't breathe. I made my apologies to the old lady and started to shoulder my way out of the queue. I hammered up the stairs, pushing my way past people who were coming down. Somebody grabbed me by the arm and said, "Don't go up there, there are six German planes in the estuary, we've been ordered below because it's safer."

I didn't stop to let him finish.

There was a bren gun mounted at the back of our ship — the only one we had — and as I flung myself out on deck, it started firing.

"Got the bastard," somebody shouted.

But they were wrong. They were wrong. The bastard got us.

He erupted out of the sun, a lone airman. The rest of his squadron were banking back up, having dropped their payload near the docks, but he set his plane in a dive straight at us. I thought he was coming for me, that he was zero-ing in on me. I felt like an insect pinned to the deck of that ship. At the last second, he reared up out of the dive and spilled his bombs all over us.

I wouldn't have thought a boat as big as that could shudder. But she did. She shuddered for all of us, for what was about to become of us all.

From where I was standing it looked as though a bomb had gone straight down the funnel; another hit us in the side and the third and fourth landed on her bows. Smoke and flames started belching out further down the ship, and straight away she began to list. I was standing close to a ventilation shaft and I grabbed the rim of that to save myself. I could hear men screaming. One of the bombs ruptured the boilers in the engine room and the men down there were being scalded alive. The screams I heard from inside that shaft have been sounding in my head, filling every silence.

Somebody shouted an order for everyone who could to rush to the port side of the boat to try and right her, and I managed to make it to the rail. Already I could see men in the water. They were jumping from portholes below me. The horizon was crooked now, smoke blotting out the sight of land. My feet skidded out from underneath me as the deck lurched further. I hung onto the rail as if it was the only thing left that mattered.

I didn't have a life jacket and I couldn't swim, anyway.

13

The lifeboats were hanging at an awkward angle as the ship tilted; they didn't look as if they would be much use at all. The fellow next to me removed his spectacles and put them in his pocket and then he jumped, his legs bicycling the air.

That started it. Lots of the men around me started to jump, some of them hitting the hull lower down as it heaved itself up from the sea. I couldn't make myself, I just couldn't. I was frozen with fear, and bewilderment; and nothing that was happening seemed real. I knew I had to do something, but the thought was like an echo of something urgent, like something important that I had forgotten to attend to. The only thing that mattered was gripping the rail.

And then I let go. I didn't give it much consideration; it was almost as if my fingers decided for me. I skimmed down the first few feet of the deck, which must have been sloping at about forty-five degrees. All kinds of objects were bouncing and falling around me, somebody's kit bag clobbered me across the back, slamming me into a stanchion. I edged my way round it. I was frightened that I would be flipped right off the deck and over the side, so I pitched myself in the direction of a bench, from the bench to a locker and from the locker to the starboard railing.

Fifty feet below the iron cliff of the deck, the water was like molasses. A fuel tank had been hit and black cataracts of oil were filling the sea. One of the lifeboats, crammed to the gunnels with women and children, was being winched down; people were climbing over each other to get into another. A chain of men were manhandling life rafts over the side, careless of the knockout blows they dealt to the fellows already in the water. The first lifeboat jammed halfway down and there was panic as the children started screaming. I saw the white face of the old lady from the chocolate queue. She was trying to calm the little girl sitting next to her as the boat swung back and forth. Crew members were hanging off the rope, struggling to free it. In the end they gave up. Someone slashed the line with a knife and the boat plummeted vertically into the sea. None of those terrified kiddies stood a chance.

It was every man for himself after that. The stern of the *Lancastria* was rising as the ship twisted further into the water. Someone had lowered a rope over the side and it hung straight as a plumb line a dozen feet beyond my reach. Around me, men with life belts were hurling themselves over. I think I saw Sweeney go. He was holding his rifle as he jumped, though I don't believe that in the circumstances he'd have been court martialled for leaving it behind.

I leapt from the vast slant of the ship. I thought I was going to die. I don't know how I reached the rope, but I did. I slid down so fast I took the skin right off my hands. I dropped the last twenty feet, smashing through the waves, down through the oil; I could feel the abrasion of bubbles stinging my face, the heaviness of my clothes, the relief...

Down I went, and down, and down, and down. I could have gone on falling through the water forever, the weight of it pressing me lower and lower, pressing the breath from my body, squeezing the strength from me, dragging the life right out of me. I felt I was plunging to a place that had no prospects and no memories.

But then I started to remember...

Chapter Two

I remembered those cheese-paring early years when our little family was cut to the bone, then cut to the bone again: that scraped feeling of loss, the sting of the graze when a telegram came from the War Office, our Glyn first. I was standing on a stool by the draining board turning the handle of the mangle for Ma. She was over by the copper, wielding a pair of wooden tongs almost as big as me, hauling the washing from the scalding water then plunging it back. I remembered the hold the steam had on our clothes and how Ma used to break off from churning the laundry round and round to wipe her forehead against the skin on the inside of her forearm. She must have been wiping at the very moment the post boy propped his bicycle against our wall. I saw him look up at our house and roll his lips tight between his teeth. I kept on turning the mangle, leaning into the handle with as much of my nine-year-old strength as I could muster, watching Mrs Parry's sheets fall in folds like beaten cream. I could hear the fume of the washing boiling in the pan and a bluebottle doing somersaults along the windowsill, but there was no sound from Ma. I glanced over my shoulder. She'd abandoned the wipe halfway through, but her arm was still pressed against her face as though she were shielding her eyes and counting to ten the way that Delyth and I did when we played murky. The wooden tongs dangled in her other hand. She set them down upon the table and a long-drawn breath seemed to get lost somewhere inside her.

There was a single knock on the door.

She stood gripping the back of one of the chairs.

"Shall I answer it?" I said, but I didn't jump down from my stool. We never got letters in our house.

Ma made her way across the room as though she were wading against the tide in slow, reaching strides and, as she laboured past me, I yearned for the comfort of her, so that I stretched towards her without knowing what I was doing, a reflex action to prevent her from answering the door, receiving the envelope from the post boy's hand, accepting his strangulated offer of condolence, then closing the door and leaning against it. She held the letter in both her fists.

"Open it, Ma," I said in my ignorance. "Go on."

"I —"

"Ma?"

"I can't —"

"Go on, Ma."

"It'll be our Glyn," she said. "I know it will —"

She did open the letter, though, and a moan came out of her, a sound I never want to hear again. I leapt from my stool and flung myself at her and she pushed me away. That's what I remembered. She brushed me to one side. I was her baby and it was her boy she wanted. She made an empty circle of her arms and wouldn't let me in.

Private Glyn Griffiths was killed in action during the Somme offensive, 1st July 1916, the telegram said. *Lord Kitchener expresses his sympathy.*

It was a cruel thing to take my brother first and let my Dad go after.

I remembered how my sister Delyth, the middle one of the three of us, went on being Delyth and I went on not being Glyn. They never found his body, so there was no grave, not even some corner of a foreign field to fob us off with. Ma was absent for weeks and weeks after the news came — she was in the kitchen at home with us and at chapel and she kept up the daily round of things, more or less, but she wasn't really there and the further away she seemed, the more my heart hurt with the love of her.

When Ianto Price was married, and he and his new missus threw coppers for the village children waiting at the church, I made sure I caught far more than my fair share. Then I went to Wilkes's in Front Street, the window screened in mysterious yellow cellophane, and I bought three lace handkerchiefs.

"For the crying," I said in a timid voice, handing her the brown paper package that Mrs Wilkes had wrapped up specially. She tied it with a length of gingham ribbon when I said who it was for. Ma opened the package and she fingered the handkerchiefs, staring at the embroidered corners, then she nodded her thanks, but her lips stayed pressed together with a tremble that was always there. Later that week, I put the hankies through the mangle with the rest of the washing, so at least I knew she'd used them.

When I thought of it, coming back from school, I picked some of the wild flowers growing in the verges of the lane: cornflowers and meadowsweet and loosestrife, then I'd run the rest of the way home, so that they weren't too wilted, and get them into a jam jar good and quick. Sometimes she'd notice and say something, mostly she'd fall into a deeper silence; once, she looped her arm around me allowing me a whiff of the serge and carbolic scent of her that I missed so much and she said, "You're a good boy, Ifor," which I thought was a hopeful sign and I considered myself well rewarded.

We were all of us better when there was laundry to do — it took the place of the conversations that we used to have. Delyth and I would trail our way round to the back door of every house in Morwithy, "Any washing today?" we'd chant, and we'd sing out our price list: flannels for a farthing, towels a penny, sheets tuppence, then Delyth would say "Smalls a ha'penny," in a loud voice to make me blush. The winter after Glyn was taken, we'd drape ourselves in the linen for the warmth and walk home like ghosts of the children we had been before.

My sister didn't inherit the good looks of either of our parents, but she had a spirit that lit up her blunt, workaday features and gave her an — air, I suppose you'd call it. When she turned fourteen, she left the board school and went to work as a kitchen assistant in the munitions factory in Newport, and all of us felt a little richer.

"I'm having the time of my life," she whispered one evening soon after she started, "But don't you go telling Ma."

She was more like a neighbour than a family member after that. Although she still slept in her room upstairs, it was as though she dropped by at the end of her shift if she happened to be passing, to give us the benefit of having our tea with her. She was full of talk, suddenly. She gave me a thrupenny bit from her wages and said I could spend the whole lot on sweets if I wanted, just to underline the fact that she was one of the grown-ups now. She told us about the canaries, the girls at the factory who handled the high explosives and were turned yellow all over by the chemicals and before you could say knife, she'd joined the union and was borrowing a copy of *Das Kapital* from the library. Just for show, mind you. I don't believe she read a single word. That's sisters for you.

I remembered our Dad coming home soon after we got the telegram. He had two days of compassionate leave on account of Glyn and arrived before the notification that he was due. I wasn't around, but Ma told us how she went out to hang some blankets on the line in the yard and there he was, standing by the gate and she said, "Are you coming in then?" and he helped her hang the wash.

I don't believe they knew where to start with the talking. They were careful with themselves, wary almost, as though a stray word might set something off. A lot of what needed to be said they routed through me: tell your father about, ask your mother if.

"What do you do in France?" I enquired. "Actually?"

Ma had shooed us into the parlour. She wanted the kitchen to herself, she said, while she made tea. I had no idea that sadness could be a kind of internal exile. I thought it was supposed to bring you all together.

"Why don't you ask your mother if she'd fill a bowl with some of the hot water when she's done with it?" he said stiffly. "My feet could do with a bit of a soak." He was stretched out in his chair, his body braced with discomfort as if there wasn't a part of him that didn't hurt. "There's a lad," he said.

Dutifully, I went back to the kitchen and Ma filled a basin with hot water and added some mustard powder and some baking soda and stirred it round and round more than it needed, so that a lot of the heat was lost and I started to wonder what on earth was going on. It was like living in a house with someone else's parents. And then I twigged. I was living with Glyn's parents, that's what.

I carried the basin into the parlour without spilling a drop and set it down in front of our Dad.

"Digging," he said. "That's what I do. I'm a sapper. It's like gardening up at the big house," he said, "only different." He rested one foot on the other knee and started peeling off his sock. The skin was yellowish and lifted from the flesh, as though it had been blistered and the pus had gone. It looked as if it might come away with the wool and the smell of it made me feel queasy, so I hurried off to find him a flannel. When I came back, he was easing both feet into the basin.

"Here you are, Dad," I said, holding out the flannel. A tremor, like a slow flinch, travelled through him and he leaned forward and put his huge hands on my shoulders so I could feel the weight of them.

"Get yourself an education, son," he said and the flinch seemed to be working at his features and I glanced anxiously at him, at his black brows and his black moustache. He had a face as wild as a hedgerow with fierce green eyes to match and the tang of hemp and nettle prickled round him. I could see how it stifled him to be at home, though I guessed he didn't want to be anywhere else. "That's the thing," he said, and the words must have been brewing for some time. "Not like Glyn," he burst out, and a nerve at the corner of his mouth came unravelled so that the skin kept snagging.

"Is it the mustard stinging?" I asked nervously.

After a pause, he nodded. He leaned back and gripped the arms of the chair with his hands, braced again. He closed his eyes and the snagging spread up his cheek.

I knelt down in front of him and I wet the flannel and I washed his knobbly old feet, one and then the other, wiping his rindy heels clean, patting them dry, doing one toe at a time.

"There," I said. "Is that better?"

He said my name — Ifor — and it came out as a shudder, under his breath, and then he said it again and I'm glad, now, that we had that moment together, while Ma cooked up a storm in the kitchen, banging away with the pots and pans as if she could dent her grief with them. It was the last afternoon I ever spent with him.

The next day he went trudging off down the lane back to the war, the morose hunch of him a dark outline in the July sunshine, and the three of us stood at the front watching him go. He never turned round to look at us; he didn't wave, although I'd sketched half a one ready, which I managed to snatch back and change into a scratch of my head, fearing that Delyth would notice.

"That's that, then," said Ma. "I must get a load on. I can't stand about —" Abruptly, she covered her mouth with her hand and, when that wasn't enough, she pressed a corner of her apron over it too. "I must —" she said. Her voice was full of breakages and the tremble was all over her. "I'm sorry," she said, hurrying up the path. Delyth went bustling after her, shooting me a look that made me feel I was to blame.

I stayed staring down the lane long after Dad rounded the corner. They'd taken our old iron gate to make guns with, or I'd have clutched at that hard enough to leave rust stains on my hands. I was waiting to see if he would turn around for one last sighting of me: the youngest, the overlooked one. That's what I was waiting for. I pictured him scrambling back along the lane, his pack jouncing about, stooping to be on a level with me, throwing his arms wide. I thought of what he said about me getting an education. The last lesson he taught me was how to remain behind.

He was killed in the spring of 1917. The post boy propped his bicycle against our wall, but he didn't look up at the house. He walked up the path with his head bowed and handed Ma the telegram without lifting his eyes to her face.

"He was an artist, your father," Ma said. "More than a gardener. The Herbar he planted up at the big house was a work of art. I'll take you to see it one day."

She stood up. At one end of the over-mantel shelf stood a photo of my brother in his uniform. Beside it was a candle that she always kept burning. At the other end of the shelf was a snap of our Dad dressed in his work clothes, cut from a larger, formal photograph that must have been taken up at Nanagalan. She reached into a drawer and took out another candle which she fixed into a pewter candlestick. She lit one from the other. A thread of smoke curled bluely upwards and I was cast into the shadows outside the halo of light.

I peered at the telegram on the table, wet with the suds from her raw, red hands. His death didn't touch her like my brother's had; if anything, it brought her back to herself. When I had done with being brave for her and had made it upstairs without letting myself down, when I had washed and said my prayers and was lying clenched in my bed sobbing my heart out, she crept into my room and slipped in beside me. She tucked the sheets around us both and made a nest of our sorrows and slept with me under her wing.

I remembered how Ma and I apportioned our losses for they were too much for a single soul to bear: the grief for Glyn belonged to her, the grief for Dad belonged to me, and I made the burden of his melancholy my own — his lumbering walk away from us, the utter emptiness of the lane when he was gone — as though the weight of his hands was pressing on my shoulders still. Night after night, I sat in his chair in the parlour, stretching myself out to fill the space that he had left, as braced as he had been. There's wanting, then there's needing and longing, and then there's yearning. I yearned for my Dad, and I yearned for my brother too. I was insatiably sad.

The three of us got along with a kindly incomprehension of each other's anguish. One evening, when Delyth was out at a factory meeting and Ma and I had done the dishes after tea, she folded the dishcloth and then on an impulse, she took my hands and held them against her cheeks, pressing my palms close. I looked at her face and she looked at mine. Her skin was still tight and shiny and pink, her eyes were the faraway blue they had always been and her hair had that curl from the steam in the kitchen — our house was as misty as a Scottish moor — and I could almost believe that nothing had changed. The hollowing happens on the inside, though. We scanned each other for signs of landslip and erosion. She kissed the top of my head with some of her old briskness and released my hands back to me.

We kept being waylaid by our bereavement so that life lost its predictability: we took one another by surprise. Delyth started courting — Delyth! — though she wouldn't admit it. She began reading poetry and colonising the tin bath on a Friday night and she asked Ma to cut her hair into a fringe, and that's how we knew.

Then, without warning, we received a small parcel full of Dad's belongings. Ma untied the string and folded back the paper. I watched her steady herself: she smoothed her apron; she took a short breath which choked off at the end. She eased the lid from the box apprehensively. Inside lay his pay book, his Bible, his wristwatch and his penknife. She ran her fingers over each as though there was a Braille for memory that she could read.

"You should have his penknife," she said. "Being the boy. I'll let Delyth have the Bible." She picked up the knife and made a study of the handle. "He was a great one for whittling — do you remember?"

I nodded, eyeing the penknife. I could see him sitting out the back with a cigarette adhering to his lip, paring a stick through the green wood to the white until it had the pale contours of bone, the smoke from his ciggie like a wreath in the air around him.

"There," she said. "It's yours." She closed the lid of the box and made a clumsy attempt to wrap the paper round it once again, until, with a spurt of anger that erupted from nowhere, she gave up and sat down abruptly in her chair. After a minute or two, she dragged the box towards her and her palm hovered over the rough cardboard without quite touching it. "Oh for goodness' sake go and — do something, Ifor. Will you just — ?" she snapped, waving me away.

I found a stick in the lane and went trailing home with it. I sat on the back step with my arms clasped round my knees and waited. There was silence inside the house, but not a good kind. I peeled some bark from the stick with my nail and snapped the twigs off one by one until my fingers were sticky with cobwebs and sap and silvered with insect wings and such a flow of misery was in me.

All at once, the door was ripped open and Ma stood there with the ambushed look she had when the sadness was on her. "Where's that knife?" she said, her voice rising and I hung my head thinking she'd changed her mind and wanted it back. Perhaps she would give me the watch instead, but it wouldn't be as good as having the penknife, not by a long chalk. I fished it out of my pocket, but kept a hold of it and she lunged forward and snatched it and tried to open it, but it was worse than trying to wrap the paper round the parcel because her fingers were trembling and I could see her face was streaming wet. She kept fumbling with the knife and her thumbnail bent right back to the quick, making her sob out loud, but she unsheathed the steel blade, "Give me your hand."

I put my hand in my pocket, but she seized my wrist and pulled it out. "Give it," she said.

"I'm sorry," I stuttered, thinking that this was some kind of punishment, that I was to blame for the box and Dad and everything and that if it had been me and not Glyn, things would have been different, they'd have been better and she'd have been happy. "I'm sorry Ma —"

"I don't ever want you to carry a gun. I don't ever want you to go for a soldier," she said and she had hold of my forefinger in one hand and the knife with its glittering blade in the other and she raised it. She raised the knife. "Not you," she said. "Not again." She was weeping catastrophic tears.

"Ma —!"

The knife went clattering to the ground, the back door slammed and I was left alone. I tucked my hands under my armpits and eyed the blade from a distance as though it was still a danger to me. The world had gone mad and my Ma with it and I was very, very tired because I could see that no amount of embroidered handkerchiefs or wild flowers picked from the lane was going to put this right; that no matter how good I was, I would never be good enough. I leaned my cheek against the door and let the warmth of the wood enter me. I must have fallen asleep because I dreamt that I was standing on my stool by the sink and Ma was feeding my fingers through the mangle and they came out the other side in thick white folds like Mrs Parry's sheets. Then Delyth walked up the path home from Newport and shook me awake with a crisp comment about some people having to work for a living.

"Delyth?" I scrambled to my feet, surfacing from my dream to a life that was different from the one I'd known.

"Is that Dad's knife?" She stooped and picked it up. "You shouldn't play with things like that. You could hurt yourself," she observed, snapping the blade shut. "Where did you get it?"

"From Ma," I said. "She gave it to me," I held out my hand for it.

"You're a bit young for a knife."

"She said you can have his Bible. She said the penknife was for me," I answered defiantly. "There was a parcel in the post today."

My sister lost some of her teenage hauteur. "Oh." Her body drooped. She became a smaller size of herself. She handed me the penknife. "Is Ma…?"

The two of us stood staring up at the door without speaking.

"She's…" I hesitated. An account of what had happened was thundering inside me and yet, as circumspect as any grown-up, I spared Delyth the details. "Well, you know." I slipped Dad's penknife into my pocket and we knocked tentatively on the door although it was our home and we lived there. We waited for a second and then went inside for our tea.

I remembered making a universe for myself out of books, to please my Dad to begin with. *Get yourself an education, son.* I set my sights on the West Monmouth Grammar School as a point of honour and I'd got myself a scholarship before the penny dropped that there was no longer any way of pleasing him, no way of him knowing what I'd achieved; that I'd merely been treating the symptoms of my loss all the while. I learned to love reading, though, for the protection it gave against Ma and Delyth and for the legitimacy it conferred: "I'll just get to the end of the page," I'd say, barely surfacing from a realm I'd found where fathers and brothers avoided slaughter, where mothers were not sent half mad with grief, where living happily ever after seemed a proper ambition for a person to have. "I'll just finish this chapter." It turned out education was good for all sorts of things — I'd never have known about the French Revolution, about Stephenson's Rocket, about the elegance of Latin grammar — a system devised for creating order out of chaos if ever there was one, and I badly needed a sense of order. Without my time at West Monmouth Grammar, photosynthesis would have remained a mystery to me, ditto the circulation of the blood and the four moons of Jupiter named by Galileo after the lovers of Zeus. They say that knowledge is power, but to me it was insulation.

I should have realised I was a poor boy feasting at a rich man's table, but I was dazzled by all that learning, the irresistible poetry of information laid out before me. When the boys at school started discussing the merits of Oxford over Cambridge, going to university also seemed like a proper ambition for a person to have, for a short time, at least.

I was doing my homework up in my room, safe behind a barricade of textbooks, struggling to translate Appian's account of the second Punic war, longing for Hannibal to appear with his elephants, when Ma loomed over the crenulations waving a copy of the *Monmouth Guardian*. I hadn't seen her look so happy since the end of the war.

"See what I've found!" she cried, pressing the paper against the skirt of her apron as she thumbed through the pages. "Not there ... not there ... where the goodness was it? Oh, just look at that, will you?" she tutted at the newsprint coming off on her fingers, always clean and tidy, my Ma. "Here we are! What do you think?" She creased the page flat as though it were an ironed sheet ready for folding.

I stared at the list of classified advertisements without so much as an inkling of what was coming. "What is it, Ma?"

She read the advert aloud for me: "Wanted: Gardener's Lad. Eight to Sixteen Pounds a Year Depending on Age and Ability. Apply with References, Nanagalan."

"But —"

"A job at the big house!"

"But I —"

"Just like your father. Gardener's Lad at Nanagalan. That's how he started and he ended up as Head Gardener, so there's no limit really. Think what you could do with a job like that, Ifor."

I was fingering my pencil, tracing the letters embossed into the blue paint: HB. The Royal Sovereign Pencil Company Ltd. It's a wonderful thing, a pencil with a sharpened point: a remembrancer. I let mine rest against my upper lip for the faint smell of the cedar wood. "There's my studies…" I began, my gaze travelling along the line I'd been translating.

"You spend a lot of time with your nose in a book for a boy your age," Ma said with some asperity. There was a note in her voice, a tension, and I was conscious of the freight she brought with her: the expectation of what a son might do, crushed into dust on that July morning five years ago. *Lord Kitchener expresses his sympathy…*

"And there's my examinations…"

She sat down on my bed. "Examinations won't butter anybody's parsnips, will they?" she said quietly.

There was a silence between us. I sat staring at my pile of textbooks, my blotter, my pencil case, my exercise book, all the apparatus of the written word. Each one had a place and a meaning of its own for me.

"And besides, it would be so close to home…" she said.

I glanced round at her. I could see the first salting of age in her face; all the scouring of the last few years. Something in the curve of her shoulders, the leaning of her elbows on her knees with her hands hanging loosely down, made her seem resilient and diminished at the same time. I suppose she was both of those things. Stoic, and forlorn. For a moment, I wondered what the merits of Oxford over Cambridge really were. I thought about what my Dad said. It was the echo of an obligation, and here was my flesh and blood Ma who I loved until my heart hurt.

I laid my pencil on the table. "Do you think it would improve my chances," I said, "if I mentioned Dad in my application letter?"

She stood up and rested her hand on my shoulder and the two of us remained, staring down at my Latin textbook, touched with regret that she had been bound to ask and I had been bound to comply, until I put my arms around her waist and leaned my head against her apron, the loss of expectation a transaction between us.

I remembered setting off for my first day of working up at the big house.

"Better three hours too soon than a minute too late!" Ma had sayings for everything, it was her way of making the world seem known and safe and I was braced for more — "A good beginning makes a good ending," perhaps, but instead she gave me some sandwiches wrapped in a knotted handkerchief.

"Cheese and pickle," she held my hands holding the package as she spoke, "your Dad's favourite."

I nodded, then I looked down the lane, biting my lip, thinking of other departures. I couldn't shake off the feeling that we were relicts, Ma and I. There was something residual about us. She held me tightly for a moment and part of me wanted to bury myself in the kitchen warmth of her, but part of me couldn't get out of the door fast enough. I kissed her cheek and her letting go of me was more than just any old letting go and both of us knew it, and I practically ran along Front Street and down the road out of the village to stop myself from feeling sad.

I was out of breath when I hurtled into the green bowl of your valley and the first glimpse I had of Nanagalan stopped me in my tracks. The house was built in the borderlands in sight of Offa's Dyke, a dividing line keeping England and Wales at bay. They said in the village that it had been a nunnery once, built from good Welsh stone and simple faith sometime in the 1400s, and the windows were arched like hands held in prayer, contemplating the vineyard that unfolded down the hillside towards a copse of beech trees. The façade of the later, Georgian wing turned its pale shoulder away from the vines and gazed out at Dancing Green and the Herbar, then on to the nut tunnel and the wildflower meadow beyond, and I stood open-mouthed at the top of the drive, gazing down the length of the valley to the lopsided slope of Long Leap and on to Withy End and it could have been Eden on the first day.

I made my way round to the servants' entrance at the side of the house and knocked, then waited an age for somebody to answer, as the house towered above me and I shifted my weight from side to side, glancing back along the driveway. The approaching footsteps I could hear must have travelled several hundred yards to reach me. It was Mrs Brown who opened it, flushed from the kitchen range, bringing the heat of it with her.

"I'm —" I began. Her blouse was open at the neck, and I mean open, although she was the same age as Ma, maybe older even. She was tucking and patting at her hair, but she interrupted the small adjustments she was making to follow the line of my gaze and I thought I was going to die of the embarrassment as she fastened one button of her blouse, and then another, taking her time about it.

"I'm the gardener's new —" I gabbled, not knowing where to look.

"I know who you are," she said and she leaned forward and whipped the hat from my head. "Sam's told me," she added, "and you take your cap off when you're talking to your betters."

"Yes," I said. "Yes. Yes, of course," then, stupidly, "Sam?"

"Mr Samuelson." She raised her eyes, sardonic as you like, then handed me my cap. "He'll be at the press," she said. "That way. Down by there." She pointed in the direction of some out-buildings on the far side of the courtyard and scrutinised me as I turned to leave. "Tell him from me that three o'clock is alright, will you? Tell him, when lunch is over, if you will."

The press was in a wooden shed, hemmed with bricks around the bottom and small windows of occluded glass high up under the eaves. I put my cap back on so I could tug at the door to slide it open, then straight away snatched it off again. I stood in the vaporous gloom until I could make out the shape of the oak vat, and Samuelson mounted on a ladder propped against the side.

"Boy?" he said, without looking round and it struck me that he must have been the gardener's lad to my father back before the war. The shed was full of the scent of pips and stalks and the sweet contusion of the grapes, and full of ghosts as well.

He was a mighty man, mightier than the space in which he found himself, and I remembered watching with apprehension the workings of his arm as he tightened the press's wooden screw: muscle wrestling with sinew, with the kind of strength that cannot always be contained.

"Ifor Griffiths, sir, Mr Sam —"

"Well, boy," he swung round. His face had an edge of hunger unsatisfied, in spite of his stature. His cheeks were veined and ruddy; he wore a neckerchief and had jaw-length hair that Ma would have taken the clippers to. He was chewing on a matchstick. He didn't waste time taking stock of me. "Now that you're here, hand me up one of them picking bins," he jerked his head in the direction of a pile of crates, each one overflowing with bunches of red grapes. If I hefted one up to him that morning, I hefted a hundred, and in between I listened to the trickle of the juice.

"What happens next?" I asked at one point, to make conversation, "To the grapes?"

We've got a right one here, the expression on his face said. I watched the movement of the match as he chewed on it, but when I told him what Mrs Brown had said, that three o'clock was alright, when lunch was over, the stick was still for a moment in the corner of his mouth.

"We add yeast to the must," he grunted, "to get the fermentation going," and then he asked me: "Is there anything else you'll be wanting to know?" in a way which made it clear that the answer should be no.

Chapter Three

I remembered the first time I ever saw you.

Mr Samuelson told me to go and clean all the terracotta pots ready for pricking out later in the month and I was in the tool shed on my own. It was a chilly morning and I had the paraffin heater on. There was dust in the air from the sacks piled under the workbench. The windows were all steamed up and it made me feel that I was cut off from the world, and I wiped the pane clear and there you were, peering in. The condensation on the glass glittered around you. Your face was white with cold, blue tinged and there were drops of moisture in your curls, which clung in wisps like tendrils on the vines and I reached out my hand without thinking, as if I was in the vineyard thinning the leaves.

You tapped on the window. "Can I come in?" you mimed, and I remembered how delicate you seemed: the different golds of your hair; the ripe fruit of your mouth, raspberries and strawberries not mine for the tasting; the perplexing violet of your eyes. You were fifteen, same as me; home from boarding school, not like me.

My fingers were freezing and the latch was stiff and you looked impatient when I opened the door. You slipped into the shed, glancing behind you as though you wanted to be sure you could find your way back to where you'd come from. I started to remove my cap on a reflex, even though I was indoors and wasn't wearing one. I felt such a fool.

"Mother sent me." You held your hands in the shimmer above the paraffin stove. "She wants to do her inspection this afternoon."

"But it's a Wednesday," I blurted wildly. "The mistress always does her inspection on a Friday —"

You shrugged, and turned your hands over to warm the other sides and I was in awe of the smoothness of your skin. I shoved my fists into my pocket.

"Are you new?" You were studying the shelves, the tools hung on nails, the packets of seeds like index cards in their boxes. You were not looking at me.

"I've been here three months."

"I haven't seen you before..." You ran one finger along the workbench, then rubbed your finger with your thumb and the way you did it made me think that this was a mannerism you had learnt, something you thought you ought to do, in the circumstances.

"I don't go up to the big house much..."

"What's your name?"

"Ifor."

"Ifor." You tried it out for size. You were standing close to me and I was lost to your curving softness. I breathed in your scent — within the paraffin fumes I could smell flowers and I was concentrating, trying to work out which one, and I said without thinking, "What's yours?"

"Ella."

It was gardenia. "Ella," I said, inhaling again.

You withdrew your hands and tucked them under your arms. "You shouldn't really call me that, you know," you said, ducking your head as your cheeks turned pink from the warmth of the stove. You grimaced. "I'm meant to be Miss Ella, to you..."

Samuelson worked me like the devil throughout that autumn, tidying up the vegetable beds in the kitchen garden: crab grass, prickly lettuce, carpet weed, cocklebur, lamb's quarters, ragweed (it turned out that I was a bit of a maniac when it came to weeding), though the common purslane I would have left in place, I rather liked those waxy leaves and little yellow flowers, but rules are rules. My back hurt like billy-oh from all the bending, but if I straightened up for a moment or wiped my forehead on my sleeve, Mr Samuelson was out of the tool shed before you could say Jack Robinson, roaring, "Boy!" He took every opportunity to exercise his power. I'd made up my mind that he went up to the house, after lunch at about three o'clock, to have a drink with Mrs Brown, for I could smell alcohol on his breath of an afternoon. I mentioned it to Ma and she gave me one of her looks. "Ask no questions," she said tartly, "tell no lies."

On the day of my first ever staff Christmas party, the work done, I belted home. I was third in line for a wash in the leftover water at the bottom of the copper, the steam still clinging to the kitchen windows, Delyth squawking as she changed into her Sunday Best as instructed by our mother, and then rebelliously changing out of it again.

"They're no better than they ought to be, that family, and our pandering to them just makes them think that they are."

"We won't have any of your Bolshevik nonsense in this house, my girl, you mark my words," said Ma, who was rummaging inside the wooden chest that stood against the wall in the kitchen alcove. She lifted out a suit of navy wool and the smell of naphthalene turned the steam toxic. Poor moths, I thought, but I didn't say anything, because I knew the suit had belonged to my brother Glyn and maybe to Dad before him, and we no longer talked about our dead. At the sight of it,

Delyth left the room and came back wearing her Sunday dress once more.

"Do the buttons for me, will you, Ifor?" she said without looking at our mother.

At the last moment, Ma decided not to come. "There's the ironing," she said, staring at me in the navy suit, then she buried her face against my shoulder and I just stood there as she inhaled, my arms holding the air around her. I remembered opening a book from the library once and there was a pressed flower someone had left inside it and as I turned the page the petals went fluttering onto the floor as dry and colourless as paper, unlike anything you'd ever see growing in a garden. Sometimes I worried that this was happening to my memories of my brother and I used to tell them over to myself to preserve them: Glyn showing me how to make tea cigarettes and the two of us trying to smoke them up at the bus shelter; Glyn stealing cheese from the larder and me getting the blame; Glyn rubbing his hands together with the uncontainable physical glee of being alive — he sometimes did that; Glyn making an eye patch for me out of chewing gum when Delyth and I were playing pirates and Ma having to pick it out of my eyebrow with a pair of tweezers; Glyn crowing that no matter how much I tried I'd never catch up with him, he'd always be older. I touched the lapel of his suit, now handed down to me. He was wrong about that.

Delyth whistled 'The Red Flag' all the way to Nanagalan. She was a bit of a caution in those days, with her copy of *Das Kapital*, and those views of hers. I was inclined to think it was an act, a pose. People always noticed Delyth.

"Ring off, will you?" I said, as we trudged round to the servants' entrance near the kitchens. I didn't want them noticing her now, not when I had enough on my plate with the suit to contend with; it was two sizes too big for me and scratchy into the bargain. I thought of Ma and the snatch of a wave with which she'd sent us on our way. I wanted her to be waiting in the doorway for me whenever I chose to return, her large, chapped hands clasped across her apron. I wanted her still to be valiant; I wanted her to be as she was before the war.

"Ooh, get you —" my sister said, but she subsided into silence as we rang the bell and waited, although when Mrs Brown opened the door and led us through the corridors past the still room and the pantry, she started up a defiant little hum.

Tea was served in what had been the servants' dining hall, back in the glory days. I couldn't imagine having a house with whole rooms that you didn't need to use, when our cottage was splitting at the seams with so much stuff crammed in there was hardly space for the three of us as well. There was brown linoleum on the floor and brown paint that reached as far as the porcelain tiles which lined the walls. The shutters had been thrown open the week before for the annual airing and Mrs Brown had taken a desultory swipe at a few cobwebs with her feather duster. We had decked the hall after a fashion with holly from the gardens and on the long pine table in the centre of the room were arrangements of fir cones tied with red ribbon. My sister and I sat ourselves on one of the benches running up either side, taking the places of members of staff long gone, and for a moment I tried to picture our Dad having his dinner here, subdued mealtimes at which people spoke only when they were spoken to.

Half the village was gathered — most of us had connections with the big house through trade, or services provided, or as tenants. You and your mother served us tea as was the custom and, to begin with, you didn't even look me in the eye; you were nodding at my sister Delyth with the kind of smile that seemed to have been pencilled in place a little carelessly before you came down from your room. Your hands were trembling though, ever so slightly — perhaps it was the weight of the teapot — and some of the tea went in the saucer and both of us noticed and neither of us said a thing.

We ate cheese and pickle sandwiches with the crusts cut off — I couldn't imagine what Ma would say about such waste — followed by mince pies in fluted pastry and fruit cake covered in marzipan with drifts of sugar icing and people slipped what they couldn't finish into their jacket pockets, as their due. When it was time for us to go, we lined up by the door so that the mistress could shake our hands and gave us each our Christmas box. I got five bob, but that's not what I remembered most.

You were standing by your mother and you offered me your hand automatically and then you must have realised it was me, because you said "Oh!" before you could stop yourself, colouring slightly as you looked further down the line. Then you darted a glance in my directions and said, "Happy Christmas, Ifor."

I held out my hand for you to shake just as you withdrew yours. You fiddled with one of your earrings, tightening the clasp, then just as I shoved my own hand in my pocket you held out yours again, then straight away you tucked it behind your back. You stood on tiptoe for a moment, awkwardly, and the stain of your blush spread down your neck.

"Happy Christmas, Miss."

You turned your attention to one of the tenant farmers lining up behind me, but as your mother said my name and called me forward, you shot me a glance I wasn't meant to see, and the dark flare of your pupils softened before you looked away.

You used to pass me in the back of the motor car when I was on my way to work or going home, Brown in his uniform, his face set in tense lines as he negotiated the bends in the driveway that led up out of the valley. He was a nervous driver. When he first came to Nanagalan, the family still had a brougham, a gig and several horses. Now only the Master's hunter was left. Most evenings, I used to see Brown standing by the loose box, the old gelding's head resting on his shoulder and he was smoothing and smoothing the horse's neck, smoothing and smoothing, until I couldn't tell if it was an act of affection or obliteration, and what it was that he would want to wipe away. "You've got to stay ahead of the game," he used to say to me, with the air of someone struggling to keep up. "You're lost if you don't." The Daimler would make unsteady progress up the drive with you sitting in the back and I'd stand on the verge to let you pass and you'd be gazing straight ahead, but once you stared in my direction and I knew it was to make sure I had seen you; then the car seemed to move backwards a fraction before it moved forwards as Brown changed gear, and you made a show of surveying the valley towards Long Leap and I was left at the side of the road wondering if you were going on an errand to the village, or to the shops in Monmouth, or just out for a spin. I'd construct itineraries for you as I dug over the potatoes in the kitchen garden or cut the grass on Dancing Green. I'd imagine chance encounters.

That spring, as a few rays of convalescent sunshine streaked into the valley making the buds sticky and drawing the greenness up from the ground, I was working in the Herbar that my Dad designed, years before the war, mulching the borders and dividing the perennials. The birds, back from their travels, were deep in conversation all around me and I'd made a good start on the astilbe and was moving on to the phlox when I stood up for a stretch.

You must have been out for an early walk, for I could see you making your way back through the wildflower meadow. You were heavy-limbed, listless rather than tired, and I watched you pulling a frond of tall grass from its sheath then swiping the air with it, the thin blade such a weight in your hand, and, in that instant, I had a glimpse of what a burden privilege might be: the obligation to fill one's time, but the lack of necessity to do anything at all.

I thought of Ma, scarlet-faced over the copper at home doing the laundry for the big house and anyone in the village who could afford to pay, picking her way through other people's dirty washing, and I knew she wouldn't see it like that.

I began working my fingers into the clump of Phlox Paniculata, unthreading the roots, trying not to tear them as Samuelson had shown me, and a handful of earth went crumbling onto my boot. When I looked again, you were wandering through the nut tunnel, trailing the length of grass behind you, the canopy of branches forming a knotty frontier between us. You opened the wrought-iron gate in the waist-high wall and rather than follow the brick path to the front door, you hesitated. The sweep of heat that went through me!

I crouched down and shoved the phlox into the ground, dug another hole with my trowel and shoved more in and I'd got the peonies in the row behind within my sights, puce as a peony myself, when you looked up briefly at the high windows, then strolled towards me.

You laid the frond of grass across your palm, tracing of the seed heads with your finger. "What are you doing?" you asked me.

You were like a flower growing in my garden, slender-stemmed in your loose coat, your hat tilted sideways and I was so taken over, so awash, that I had no idea where to start with my answer.

"Are you doing anything?" You sounded quizzical.

"Just some gardening. Miss Ella."

"Yes…" you said dryly.

High above us, a blackbird loosed a few notes of song and I glanced up and around until I located him on the ridge of the house roof. You followed my gaze and we listened for a moment to the full-throated, complicated melody, silent ourselves.

I wondered if I was required to account for myself. "The flowers in the herbaceous border have to be divided at the start of the season, so that's what I'm doing." Then with a burst of confidence I added: "Next I'm going to put some compost on."

You nodded. You let the frond of grass fall to the ground and I wondered whether I should pick it up for you, but you were feeling in your pockets. You produced a silver cigarette case and a lighter that matched. They were monogrammed and to me that was a terrible sight: your initials, E.W. Privilege writ large.

"Do you smoke?"

I had done, on and off and not just tea cigarettes either. Sometimes I had one with half a pint on pay day. Nothing regular, though.

You took my silence for a no. "You should do." You slid a cigarette from your case and tapped it on the lid, then you put it between your lips. You waited. By the time I had twigged that you expected me to take the lighter and light it for you, you had done the job yourself.

"It's supposed to be awfully good for you," you said as you breathed in. "Some scientists in Paris have proved that it has antibacterial properties." I watched the smoke cloud from your mouth. "So it protects you against infections."

You smoked with the speed of the inexperienced: in, out, in, out. I thought of Samuelson with his drawling drag that seemed to go on forever, as he drained the nicotine right out of his fag.

"Do you like it here?"

I nodded, tongue-tied, and you gave me a smile so slight you can have had no idea of the transfiguring effect it had. I felt like running through the vines towards the Drowning Pool with my arms outstretched like aeroplane wings.

"Do you?" I asked politely, but you were careful not to answer. You were studying the nails of the hand that held your cigarette.

"Would you do something for me?"

I hoped my jaw didn't drop at that, although it might have done. "Yes," I said, thinking that I would do anything at all.

"Next time you're in the village, would you mind popping into Lewis's to get me a packet of Benson and Hedges? You can put it on account. Get a packet for yourself as well, if you like."

Gardener's lad. Errand boy. "Of course," I said. I stared at the serried ranks of the perennials, from the tiny bloodroot at the edges of the border to the lanky irises leaning against the wall, thinking that there was a hierarchy even in the planting. When I looked up again, you were walking back towards the house.

One hot evening when work was done, I was filling my pockets with windfall apples from the orchard, wandering through the vines in the direction of the Drowning Pool, the branches of the beeches yearning down towards the water. I settled myself into the roots of one of the trees that was sorrowing in the heat and opened my book. I was so deep in the poems that I never heard you approach.

"I didn't know you could read." I couldn't see where your voice was coming from and then suddenly you swooped past me, the rope swing riding the thermals, leaning back so that your toes pointed up to the sky.

At the time I could have thrown the book right at you, but that's not what I remembered. Your reflection flashed across the green water, I watched your dress trailing the surface, the hem wet and your underskirt showing. "I was a grammar-school boy," I said as stoutly as I could.

"Oh." You stopped working the swing. All I could hear was the ache of the rope, slowing. "Why are you here as the gardener's lad, then?" Your voice was cool; the only cool thing that summer's evening.

At a safe distance in the tree root, I watched you while I figured out how to answer. I watched you until I was hot all over. "My father was head gardener here, before the war," I began, thinking of my mother, not my father; of the obligations love places on a person. "If it was good enough for him, and he was a good man, then it's good enough for me," I said carefully.

"My father fought in the war." You bit your lip and looked away. "He was injured at Ypres."

"Is it true he's in the asylum?" I asked. "That's what they say in the village."

Your dragonfly eyes flickered blue. "It's a clinic," you whispered. "He's got neurasthenia." The swing was still. The trees loomed around us. You were looking down at the water, at the zithering insects. "Mother took me to see him once. Brown drove us there in the motor. We had to park away from the building because the sound of engines upsets the patients, so we walked the last hundred yards or so. He was waiting for us in the hallway, standing at the bottom of the stairs with one hand on the newel post. He was carrying a small box in his other hand." You rested your cheek against the rope. "Poor Papa."

The breath of a breeze ruffled the surface of the pool.

"He walked towards us and he looked almost like the pictures of him at home. 'Brown's outside with the motor,' Mother told him. 'We thought we'd take you for a ride. Bit of fresh air… Let me help you with that,' she reached to take the box from him and he went berserk. He clutched the box to his chest. Said it had been entrusted to him by the Colonel and that he would shoot anybody who tried to take it from him. They had to call a doctor who gave him an injection." You looked in my direction, but I couldn't meet your gaze. "He won't ever come back here. Not now."

I whirred the pages of my book between my fingers.

"Can you help me down from here?" you asked diffidently. "Only I don't think I can reach the bank…"

I waded out and, with my heart in my mouth, I lifted you from the swing. You were light as an armful of clippings and I could feel the shape of you in my arms. I was knee-high in the Drowning Pool, with the water streaming over the tops of my boots, full of wonder at your sapling limbs beneath your dress, the roundness of you. Grave with desire, I charted a safe course to the bank. "My father died in the war, at Messines," I said as I set you down, wanting you to know I understood.

You smoothed the folds of your clothes, though nothing was out of place. I lent you my copy of Edward Thomas to put things right between us and you never gave it back to me.

One morning in June, I was instructed by Samuelson to prune the wisteria that rippled like falling water over the summerhouse roof and the promise of heat lay in a haze over the valley as I took one of the ladders stored against the kitchen garden wall, strapped my tool belt around my waist and walked to the furthest corner of Dancing Green. A spinney of rowan trees and weeping birch screened the six-sided folly from the drive; it was both lookout and hiding place, with the white flowers of the wisteria picking out flecks as pale as bone in the flint walls and small arched windows echoing the ones in the main house. I leaned my ladder into the welter of frail pods, their cream veins turning brown, then I climbed the first few rungs, disturbing the thrum of insects, sending the bees scattering. I slipped the secateurs out of their sheath and set to work. I climbed higher, reaching up to where tendons of new growth were sliding under the roof tiles, listening to the click and snip of the blades as I worked, enjoying the sense of purpose in the sound, when the window below was flung open without warning and went slamming into the ladder, sending me flying onto the grass. As an afterthought the ladder came bouncing down beside me as I lay on the ground, winded, trying to catch my breath.

"Oh! I'm awfully sorry!" You came hurrying through the French doors and pitched yourself onto the lawn beside me. "Are you alright? I didn't realise you were there."

I scrambled into a sitting position, my mouth agape as I hacked away trying to get some air into my lungs. My chest was in spasm. I couldn't have answered you for the life of me.

"Are you sure you're alright?" You bent your head closer to inspect me. "Shall I go and get...?" You tailed off, sounding uncertain, then glanced back over your shoulder at the summerhouse. "I could get you some water..."

I wheezed something as best I could by way of reply.

You disappeared for a moment and, when you came back, you were holding a cracked china cup half full of water. "I'm awfully sorry," you said. "I had no idea you were there."

"Thanks," I managed, taking a sip. I breathed in and out, then in and out again. "That's better." I lifted the cup to my mouth for more.

"That's probably enough," you said intercepting it. "I'm meant to be doing some watercolours. Mama said I should. I brought this to clean the brushes with."

My eyes widened.

"Only it's a long way to go back for more. Don't worry," you added, "I haven't used it yet."

I handed you the cup and climbed to my feet, arching my back then bending forwards.

"Are you sure you're not hurt?"

"I'll be fine," I said in noble tones, then I arched my back again until the bones cracked.

"Perhaps you should sit down for a bit..."

It was too good an offer to resist. I followed you into the summerhouse. The small hexagonal room had a flagstone floor and a stone bench running right around the edge. There were blue Delft tiles on the walls showing ordinary people at work, like me: fishing, hoeing in the fields, weaving baskets. A small easel was set up in the centre, supporting a wooden board with a blank sheet of paper pinned to it. I perched on the edge of the bench, feeling the cool of the stone through my trousers.

You placed the cup of water on the floor beside the easel. "There," you said, sitting yourself a few feet from me. The open window swung on its hinge in the breeze and you stood up to secure it, flashing me a guilty look as you did so. You sat down slightly closer to me this time.

I made a study of the tiles directly opposite me; there was a blue galleon, its white sails billowing with wind on a blue, blue sea, and the blue shadow of a tiny gull cast against white clouds that billowed too.

"Well…" you said.

I bit my lip. "Do you paint, then?"

You glanced at the blank sheet of paper and pulled a face. "Not really. Mama thinks I should. She says it's one of the skills a young lady needs to acquire." You started patting your pockets. You were wearing some kind of linen smock over your normal clothes. "I don't think I've brought my cigarettes. Damn."

I blinked at your daring, at the language you used. "You've got the costume, though," I said, nodding at your smock.

You stared at me for a moment. "Don't you ever get lonely? When it's just you and Samuelson?"

I shrugged.

"Maybe I should paint you?" Before I could say anything, you stood up and went across to the easel. As you fiddled with the catch on a box of watercolours I felt the sear of panic run me through.

"I'm not very good," you said idly. The box opened and you took out a brush. "Would you mind?" I felt wild with unspoken excuses — but what about Mr Samuelson? What about the pruning? What about the ladder left lying on the grass? Look at the time, I'd better — I glanced towards the door, opened my mouth to speak, but said nothing. My clothes were laced with broken fronds of wisteria. There was grass stain on my shirt. I wasn't sure how I was going to endure your scrutiny. I sat a little straighter on the bench. "S'pose not."

You dipped your brush in the water, holding it against the rim of the cup to let the last drip drain away. "Can you look over my shoulder, just to the left? That's it, like that. Good. Stay still, now." I fixed my gaze beyond you, so that you were in my vision but out of focus. It's where I felt I existed with you, on the periphery. I was conscious of the time you took to choose a colour, listening for the whisper of the brush against the paper.

"Don't you…" I said, "ever get lonely?"

"All the time," you answered. "Dreadfully. Don't move," you said as my head swung round instinctively to look at you. I took up my position once again. I wasn't lonely in the sense you meant, what with Ma and Delyth and the lads in the village and all the work there was to do, though the feeling of being only half a family, the lesser half, was always with us. I had an intimation of what your absence might mean to me, if that counted as loneliness.

"You've got friends though."

"Yes, yes I have. Some." I was aware of you scanning my face and had to steel myself to keep staring over your shoulder. "Neighbours, mostly. Not the kind of friends you'd necessarily choose yourself," you said. I could hear your wrist move over the paper as you traced a line across the page. "You have nice eyes," you observed, your voice as soft as a sable brush mark. "Don't look round."

I could feel the blood flee from my brain and from my limbs and from my fingers' ends and settle in my heart. The Delft

49

tiles blurred and fused together. I kept staring to the left of you, just over your shoulder, although I was giddy with you. "There's no need for you…" I began.

"I don't necessarily have the life I'd choose for myself, come to that."

"…to be lonely."

You rested the brush on the easel. The summerhouse was full of a silence as noiseless as the flight of birds. I could feel the downdraught of what both of us had said, the slow fall of the spoken word.

"I'm no good at this," you said, dropping your head.

I wasn't sure if you were talking about the painting. "You're —" I didn't know what I was going to say. I thought if I started, something would come to me. I wanted to tell you that you were perfect in every way, that the thought of you being lonely filled me with terrible joy, that the thought of you filled me —

"Boy!" I was saved by Samuelson, his distant roar barrelling across Dancing Green. Both of us leapt to our feet, shooting stricken glances round the room: left, right, where to put ourselves, which way to go. Afterwards, I couldn't work out why both of us felt so guilty. I thought it was a promising sign, although I told myself it promised nothing, really. You rushed to the French doors and called out, "He's here. I knocked him off the ladder. I was just making sure — I won't keep him any longer. Ifor —" You stood to one side, shepherding me through the door. As I passed the easel, I couldn't help glancing at the piece of paper. There were faint lines of different shades of green, like a hayfield fading towards the horizon. I was full of the memory of your searching gaze upon me. You weren't painting me at all.

Chapter Four

I remembered the day the Duke of York was married to Lady Elizabeth Bowes-Lyon. What a to-do that was. We didn't have a half day holiday, which Ma said would have happened in the old days, but everyone who worked for the family and all the tenant farmers were invited up to the big house to drink a loyal toast to the happy couple.

There was a bit of an atmosphere when we arrived at Nanagalan and made our way to the kitchens: Brown and Samuelson had scant regard for one another even at the best of times. Brown had served in the infantry during the war, although he was too old for enlistment, but Samuelson took the exemption for agricultural workers and stayed at home for the duration, and the rot set in after that. I had a good deal of respect for Brown. He used to let me read the newspaper from the day before, when the family had finished with it: "Got to keep abreast of events, Ifor, or you'll be left behind." He was a worrier, always fretting about being on time, a stickler for rules and regulations, for saying the right thing, for being seen to do the right thing; he had the kind of anxiety that controls other stronger feelings. It would drive you mad if you had to live with it, until you reminded yourself that he was at the third battle of Ypres and on the Somme as well. The day of the Royal Wedding, he was wearing his chauffeur's uniform with his medals pinned to his chest and some of the substance seemed to have been put back into him.

Samuelson rolled up at the kitchen door and I don't believe that he had shaved, though he had his best trousers on and not his usual corduroys, with a clean shirt but no collar, just his old neckerchief tied skew whiff as usual. He was late. The rest of us were waiting, all chapel-pressed and respectable.

"What's a fellow have to do to get a cup of tea round here?" He lowered himself into a chair at the kitchen table without being asked, addressing himself to Mrs Brown in a way which seemed a little over-familiar, even to me. "Three o'clock, when lunch is over" appeared to hang unspoken in the air between them.

"This won't do, Samuelson," said her husband before she could answer. "This isn't good enough."

Samuelson's eyes flicked in his direction, taking in his cap with its patent leather brim parked on the table, his polished boots, his grey jodhpurs and jacket, with the medal ribbons the only dash of colour. His gaze flicked back to Mrs Brown. "What's a fellow have to do…?" he asked her in a voice that was soft and sly.

Mrs Brown opened the clasp of her handbag and then shut it again with a bashfulness she quelled as an afterthought, stealing a glance at her husband. He was livid: clenched and ready. He raised his hand and we all waited, then with terrible precision he ran his fingers through his thinning hair. For an instant the room relaxed as everybody dropped their guard, then like tracer fire, his arm up shot out, his fist a missile and I could see the trajectory arcing towards Mr Samuelson and, without thinking, I stepped forward.

"Mr Brown —?" I said like a juggins, as the blow caught me on the temple and sent me sprawling. I cracked my head on the table leg as I went down and strange blooms flowered brightly behind my eyes.

People were calling out my name: *Ifor! Ifor! Ifor! Ifor!* which confused me because I didn't know who to answer first and then I found I couldn't answer anyway. Someone threw a jug of water over me and hauled me up into a sitting position and I slumped one way and then another until I heard Ma's voiced raised above the others.

"You stupid, stupid boy," I'd never heard her so angry and I blinked and sat upright, about to protest, but she wasn't finished yet, not by a mile, "And as for the two of you! Grown men, are you? I can't think what possessed you. You should both of you know better." She read them their fortune good and proper, while Mrs Brown insinuated herself into the throng carrying a little pad of clean white sheeting. Ma plucked it from her hands without even looking and knelt beside me. "What time is it?" she asked, surveying me. She dabbed at my forehead and when she took the pad away it was red with blood. Her face whitened. The atmosphere between my Ma and me could sometimes feel … overloaded and all at once I needed some air.

"It's a little after half past four," Brown cleared his throat. "Must apologise. Didn't mean —" He was clasping the offending fist behind his back. "No harm done, eh?" he said uncertainly.

They sat me in a chair to bandage my head, Mrs Brown hovering with more sheeting and some safety pins. I was soaking wet, but it was too late to go home and change. I drank some water then stood up and took a few coltish steps, my knees a law unto themselves.

I had never been to the family's part of the house before; I had stomped my way around the kitchen a good few times but that was about it, so when Ma and Delyth helped me through the green baize door into the main entrance hall, my eyes were out on stalks.

There was a black and white marble floor the size of a cricket pitch and a central staircase which divided halfway up with one

53

flight curving away to the right and one to the left, both leading to a galleried hallway swagged with intricate plasterwork just like a wedding cake. There were family portraits and statues and a chandelier made with vast constellations of crystal. At the bottom of the stairs was a table holding a porcelain vase filled with white lilac that I had cut myself that morning and a photograph of the royal couple. There was a tray laid out with small glasses of sherry, about a mouthful each.

It was like being in church, the room full of restrained and respectful murmurations; I half expected the organ to strike up. Then you appeared on the landing, your mother leaning on your arm, looking as well-upholstered and as stiff and severe as Queen Mary herself. You were solicitous of her as you led her down the stairs and as you drew closer I could see there was a preoccupied look on the mistress's face, as though she wasn't here but somewhere else, and I remembered Ma remarking how sorry she felt for her, married yet not married, which coming from Ma, a widow, was quite a thing to say.

You handed round the sherry — the gentry making much of their humility, as Delyth observed under her breath — and when you came across to us I could see the shock on your face as you noticed my bandage, then the swift concealment of it as you looked down at the tray that you were carrying. You were wearing white gloves with seed pearls stitched along the back and your white dress with its embroidered loveliness skimmed your ankles and you could have been a bride yourself. My heart contracted when I thought that, and I held that minute glass of sherry miserably and you shot me a glance, curious and appraising, which only made it worse.

You cocked your head to one side. "In the wars again, Ifor?"

"Had an accident, Miss Ella."

"That looks nasty," you said, eyeing the makeshift bandage.

"It's nothing," I replied, untruthfully. My temple was throbbing and I felt slightly queasy. You opened your mouth to say something, but your mother raised her glass for the loyal toast.

"The happy couple," we chorused, all of us. "God bless the Duke and Duchess of York," and as we shuffled our way home, our duty done, it wasn't only Delyth who was sore at the inequity of life.

A few days after that, my temple still bruised like a rotten plum, work done, I made my way home to find that Ma didn't have my dinner on the table. I washed as usual, and waited, and she said nothing, though she made funny expectant faces from time to time, until I could bear it no longer.

"Ma —" I began, but I broke off because in the distance I could hear the unmistakably haphazard sound of the Daimler. I thought it might be you, on your way somewhere, so I hurried to the parlour window in time to see the car draw to a halt outside. Brown dismounted and came down our path to the front door. He was in full fig, medals and all.

"Answer it for me will you, Ifor?" said my mother.

I opened the door and Brown saluted, gesturing for me to climb into the motor. I looked back at Ma.

"Go on, off you go," she grinned.

I sat in the back of the car with a rug over my knees like royalty, while Brown perched rigidly up at the front negotiating the hazardous route between Morwithy and Newland, lurching round bends, slewing his way up hill and down again so that I was obliged to hold on to the armrest for dear life. We skidded into the village and came to rest beside the lych-gate into the churchyard — the Cathedral of the Forest. Brown took off his hat and fanned himself.

"The beast's got a mind of its own," he shouted at me through the glass partition. "At least with a horse you know where you are."

I was feeling as sick as a dog.

Brown opened the door for me, "Right, lad," he jerked his head in the direction of the pub opposite. "The Ostrich keeps the best pint of Brains for miles around." He was as animated as I have seen him. "Their steak and kidney pudding isn't so bad, either." He clapped me on the back. "This one's on me, because, well —" he glanced at my bruise. "Least said, soonest mended, eh?"

I made it into the pub and we settled ourselves into the inglenook, although it was a summer's evening and the grate was empty, and I managed to drink half of my half pint and to keep down the first few mouthfuls of the pud, but the kidneys got the better of me, so that without warning, knocking my stool over as I fled, I bolted out of the saloon and threw up into a flowerbed at the front.

"I'm awfully sorry, Mr Brown."

He was an extraordinarily kind man. He gave me his handkerchief so I could mop myself up, then fetched me a glass of water. We went back into the pub so he could finish his supper — they whisked mine away before I could do more damage — and afterwards he ordered an apple crumble with two spoons, in case I felt up to it. And it turned out that I did.

We walked round the village after, "To aid the digestion," Brown said with a wink, and we talked a bit about the Olympics in Paris and whether Eric Liddell would run the hundred metres, given that the trials were being held on the Sabbath.

"He's bound to," Brown said, fishing a tobacco pouch and pipe from his pocket. "Smoke?"

I shook my head.

"It'd be unpatriotic for him not to."

On the way home I sat up at the front with him, "For the fresh air," I said, winding the window down. As we crested the hill at Withy End and saw Nanagalan glimmering in the setting sun, he slowed the car and glanced in my direction. There was a sombre expression on his face.

"All those years," he said, "when I was away at the war…" he tailed off and we bumped along a hundred yards or so in silence. "Mrs Brown was on her own, you see," he said, his eyes creased up as if the light were bright, although the sun was almost gone. "A man does wonder."

"Mind where you're going, Mr Brown," I said, for I was young and there were certain things I didn't want to hear. Without warning, he swerved to avoid a pothole.

"The House of Lords wants to introduce a driving test," he said ruefully, when we were back on the straight and narrow. "That'll really put the kibosh on things, if they do."

Chapter Five

There was a brief period when we were in our late teens and hadn't yet kicked away the ladder leading back to childhood, when I never knew which Ella I'd be confronted with: Ella the girl, Ella the girl pretending to be a grown-up, or Ella the young woman. You confounded me every time. One moment you'd be contemplating me through the sophisticated haze of your cigarette smoke and the next you'd appear in the kitchen garden at the end of the working day carrying two old jars tied around the rim with string and a hunk of stale bread and announce that we were going fishing for minnows in the Drowning Pool.

"I've got cousins in Scotland," you said, when I gaped at you in surprise. "Distant ones," you added as you went speeding down the hillside. "They showed me how."

I went running after you. When we reached the gritty shoreline of the pool, I let you induct me into the innocent arts of fishing with a jam jar, although I'd been doing it myself for years with the boys from the village.

"It's easy. You tear off a piece of bread and you put it in the jar and you drop the jar in the water." You stood at the edge of the pool, suddenly uncertain. You hitched up the hem of your dress: it was green check, with a yoke and capped sleeves and you had on a pair of kid ankle boots. Frowning, you let it fall. You looked at me, but I was already delving into the undergrowth and I straightened up, brandishing a long forked stick.

"This'll do the job." I hooked your jar onto the end and handed it to you, then watched as you dunked your jar into the water.

"Sshh," you said conspiratorially. "You'll frighten the fishes."

I stood at a respectful distance from you, and solemnly we watched the bread swell and disintegrate in the tea-coloured water until it was nothing but cloudy particles, but no fish came. Disappointed, you tugged at the string. "They come for the bread in no time," you said, "in Scotland."

"Try over there," I jerked my head, "Where it's deeper."

You contemplated your dress again, then my jam jar lying between us in the leaf mould. "Why don't you try?"

I unlaced my boots and whipped off my socks before you could see that the heels were worn to threads, then rolled up my trousers and waded into the Drowning Pool. I let the string slip through my fingers and watched the jar slide beneath the surface and the scud of ripples as the glass neck disappeared.

We waited.

You crossed your arms and gazed in the direction of the rope swing, then you switched your attention to the boulders which lined the far side of the pool. You crossed your arms the other way. "Perhaps we should —" you began, but I put my finger to my lips.

"You'll frighten the fishes."

A smile stirred the corner of your mouth. After a second or two, you pressed your lips together. Above us, I could hear the throaty call of a collared dove. I watched some water boatman skating to and fro across the slick surface, conscious that your gaze was resting on me. When I turned my head around a fraction to see, you averted your eyes. I made an ostentatious study of the jam jar lying in wait beneath the water. I towed it a few inches in one direction, then the other, creating a lazy current and, in an instant, two tiddlers, tiger-striped and stealthy, flitted into the jar and before they could flit out again I scooped it high into the air, drips of water running down my arm.

"Let me see!" You stood on one foot, then the other, tugging off your boots, then with your dress hoiked up any old way you came scrambling through the shallows towards me. Our heads almost touching, in wonderment we watched the fish butt their way around the jar: small splinters of glass at acute angles, flashes of quartz and agate.

"They're blowing kisses at each other," I said slowly, tilting it this way and that for you to see the pop, pop, pop of their tiny mouths opening. "Fish kisses."

I shouldn't have said that. There was a line between us drawn by you that I could never see. "We could make a fire and cook them for our tea," you said, after an embarrassed pause.

"Too small for that..." I said quickly, eyeing the little creatures, their hectic spirals.

Tiring of the game, you stretched, making your shoulders rise and fall so that your dress untucked itself from under your arm and slid into the water.

"I've done it now," you exclaimed. The material billowed round you, the green cloth folding and unfolding itself, spreading, sinking. "Well, I can't get much wetter, can I?"

You started to run as best you could through the water, dragging the weight of your dress in your wake, exuberant and unguarded.

"Can't catch me," you called and you threw your head back, laughing. "You can't catch me..."

Oh, but I could.

Quick as a fish, I was bounding after you, splashing wildly, the gales of your laughter urging me faster. I could have caught you sooner, as your dress twisted and twined around you slowing you down, but I didn't want to spend all my happiness in one go so I made it last and let you run until I had no option: I caught one trailing arm and you spun around so fast that I reeled you in without quite meaning to and there you were, a minnow in a jar shimmering in my grip. I let you go at once, as if I were pouring you back into the Drowning Pool and we stood there, thigh-high in the water, panting.

While I carried you back to the shore in my arms, I thought back to the day you found me reading and I think you must have remembered it, too. The laughter and the breath went out of us and the silence which followed recalled us to ourselves. You looked down at your soaking clothes.

"Oh well," you said, wistfully. You started to wade towards dry land and I hesitated before I followed you. Your mother gated you for spoiling your dress and I didn't see you for a whole fortnight.

Soon after that, I bought my bicycle. Proper old bone-shaker it was, I got it second hand from a knife grinder living in Wyesham who was selling up and retiring. He wanted me to take his whetstone too, but it had been a struggle to save up enough for the bike itself.

The brakes squeaked and the chain rattled and the cracked leather saddle was designed with medieval torture in mind, but that first ride home through Monmouth then along the lanes to Morwithy took my breath away. I could feel the thrill of perfect alignment: how the lean and list of my body made the bike turn then straighten as if by magic. I swooped round corners and thundered up hills, then came soaring down the drive into the valley singing hymns at the top of my voice, with my hair standing up on end and the antiseptic sting of the wind against my cheeks and my chest bursting with alleluias.

Later that day when work was done, before I set off up the hill to home, I rode it round the courtyard at infinitesimal speed, seeing how slowly I could go without falling off, seeing how many circuits I would have to make before your curiosity got the better of you and you came to see what I was up to. Round I went, and round, and round, wobbling away, clicking the pedals so the chain moved one link at a time and the handlebars threatened to jack knife. I knew you were watching me from some window or other. I could just tell.

You appeared eventually with a trug over your arm. As you set off in the direction of the wildflower meadow, I went shooting after you, sketching a flashy curve across the flagstones and then skidding to a halt in front of you, so that you had to stop.

"Got a new bike, miss."

"I can see," you said, not looking. Dust from my skid still hung in the air.

"It's a beauty, isn't it?"

You slid the trug from one arm to the other.

"It's a Beeston Humber, an ancient one, but all the same..."

"Yes, it's very nice, Ifor. I can see," you said, but you did look at it, for a moment, and then you looked away. "I was going to pick some blackberries, as it happens."

"There's a rare crop on the road to the village..." I glanced up the drive, waiting to see if you would take the bait.

"Hmm." You were eyeing my bike. I caught you red-handed! You were giving it the once over because you couldn't help yourself. You ducked your head, then the better part of you observed, "Actually, it's top notch, Ifor. It really is."

Though nothing was said, we set off together, you walking sideways to watch me wheel and loop around you. I must have cycled several miles up that drive, doing figures of eight, doubling back, spinning in ever tighter circles. I let go of the handlebars and went no handed, my arms spread wide with the gladness of being.

"I wish I was a boy," you said enviously.

I swung back round. "Girls can ride bikes too."

"Not all girls."

I came to a halt beside you, my tyres spraying chippings in all directions. "Don't you know how to ride a bike, miss?" I asked incredulously.

You didn't reply, but I could tell from the defensive set of your shoulders what the answer was.

"Blimey," I said. "My Dad taught me when I was knee-high to a grasshopper."

"I don't think Papa…" you tailed off.

"It isn't difficult, you know. I could show you how," I ventured.

You shrugged and resumed walking up the drive.

"It's the next best thing to flying…" I said persuasively, dismounting and wheeling my bike beside you.

You smiled at that. You had a way of looking sad and amused at the same time, a complicated mix of detachment and enjoyment that I could never quite unravel. You didn't say anything though, and we trudged up the drive together as far as the lane.

"You were right about the blackberries," you said. The hedgerows were glossy with them, the brambles barbed like green-thorned wire, the berries slick with juice.

I wasn't especially interested in gathering fruit. "It's a nice flat stretch along here," I said casually. "And there's nobody around to see."

You were reaching up into the hedge, starting to pick.

"Of course, if you're scared…"

You dumped the trug on the grass verge and the blackberries rolled together fretfully at the bottom of it. "I am not scared," you exclaimed. "It's not that."

"What, then?"

You looked as prickly as a bramble yourself. "It's just —"

"Anyone can do it," I said, daring you to prove me wrong.

"Alright then. Show me how, if you're so good at it."

"I am good at it, Miss Ella," I said softly.

Still a little disgruntled, you swung your leg over the saddle and found a way of sitting so that most of the material of your skirt was folded underneath you. Your weight and the weight of the bicycle were resting against me. I put one hand on the handlebars within touching distance of your own.

"I'm going to have to —" I felt tinged with heat as I regarded the saddle, your behind resting on it — "hold you like this," I said in a rush, latching on to the metal springs coiled beneath the leather. A fold of your skirt, overhanging, skimmed my fist. I swallowed. "Then we'll just go a little way, ever so slowly…"

I walked beside you, wheeling the bike, your body leaning into me, so that suddenly I found I didn't want you to make too much progress. I didn't want you to go off without me. I'd have been happy to wheel you along the lanes until dusk came breathing down around us and we could no longer see the sheen of the road ahead. Your hair smelled freshly washed, my nostrils full of the scent of expensive soap. You were so unblemished.

After a hundred yards or so, you straightened up. "Let's go a bit faster, shall we?"

You grinned and all the awkwardness between us evaporated as I broke into a run and we went bowling along side by side.

As we rounded a bend in the lane, I took my hand off the handlebar and you shot me a look of alarm.

"Keep pedalling!" I cried, gripping the stem of the saddle. "I've still got you. I won't let go."

You were pounding the pedals so hard that one of your feet skidded clear, making the bike lurch.

"Ifor!" you squealed, but I had you, I had you safe.

"Keep going," I yelled.

You found your footing again and off we went, faster, faster, so that I was panting to keep up with you, couldn't keep up with you. You were launched.

"Look at me!" you crowed, your eyes full of the harvest light of that early autumn afternoon. "Look at me going! Look at me!"

"Careful!" I called, watching you flee the harbour of my arms.

"Look —" you sang, then in a panic, "How do I make it stop? What do I —?"

"Stop pedalling," I shouted, "Stop pedalling!"

"But I'll wobble if I do that," you cried, illustrating the point. "What do I —? Help! Ifor —! Help!"

It was a graceful fall, as falls go, or the slow inevitability of it made it seem so. You landed in a heap in the middle of the lane, the Beeston Humber skewed at an awkward angle next to you, its front wheel spinning tickety-tick.

"Are you alright?"

I suspect you wouldn't have told me even if you weren't.

"Turn around, don't look," you said, shaken but still in one piece, apparently.

I turned my back and waited. I could hear the rustle of your skirt and I wondered if your knees were grazed and pictured you examining the skin, all scraped and sore. I felt a wring of tenderness at the thought of you being hurt.

"Do you need a handkerchief?" I called.

"I've got one." A minute passed, then I heard you scrambling to your feet.

"Can I turn around now?"

You were closer to me than I had realised. There was oil on your clothes, which were horribly rumpled, and dirt on your hands from the road. Your hair was undoing itself, a hank of it hanging down over your shoulder.

"Miss Ella!"

You bowed your head and I had an uneasy premonition that you might be about to burst into tears, but instead you said in a muted voice, "I wish it wasn't like this…"

That stopped me in my tracks.

"I … I don't know how to be," you whispered. "When it's just you and me..."

"Well, I think you're —"

"Or perhaps I just don't know how to be, with you, or anyone."

"Just right," I gulped.

You gave me a searching look, as if you wanted to believe my stammered protestation.

"It's just that we're…" I said, floundering. I couldn't finish. "You know." I hauled the bike up and gripping the front wheel between my knees, I straightened the handlebars. "Next time I'll teach you the other way of stopping," I said, to give myself cover, "if you like."

"Mama has told me I mustn't play with village boys," you replied and for once I found I could read your expression. I was unexpectedly fluent in your shame and your regret.

"But we're not playing, miss … are we?" I said judiciously. "I've been teaching you to ride a bicycle, that's all."

I could see you considering my words until you were — almost — satisfied. You nodded, still testing the weight of them. "Yes," you said, in the end. "I suppose you were. That's all you were doing. Teaching me." You took a step in my direction and your leg buckled.

"You are hurt!"

"It's nothing; I must have twisted my ankle when I fell." You limped a few paces further. "I'll be fine in a minute."

"Here, let me —" Neither of us knew quite what I was suggesting. You brushed one hand against the other, studying a few faint abrasions beneath the dirt on your palm, the blood risen to the surface of your skin. I looked the length of the lane. "It's a long way back, miss. You could sit on my bike, if you want. I could wheel you."

"I'm not sure I could…" Dubiously, you flexed your foot. You glanced at me. "I'll be fine."

"You could just sit on the crossbar."

You gave me that same searching look you had before, as though there was more at stake than I could know. "Alright," you said. "Just to the top of the drive."

You hobbled over and warily you perched yourself sideways on the crossbar.

"That's just the job." You leaned your weight against me by degrees, and by degrees I put my arm around you to reach the far handlebar. "Rest your bad foot on the pedal, that's right," I said hoarsely. "We'll have you home in a jiffy."

I wheeled you with agonised concentration along the lane, steering a course between the ridges and the potholes, my cargo the more precious for being salvage.

67

"Ifor —?" you said, turning so you could see me, making the bike sway.

I gripped the handlebars more tightly. You were so close, if you had blinked I would have felt your lashes move.

"What, miss?"

"Nothing." Dimly I understood that saying my name proved your ownership of me, if it needed proving. My own small act of possession, holding you on my bike and almost in my arms as well, filled me with a kind of sad elation.

At the top of the drive, you slipped down from the crossbar, flinching as your foot touched the ground.

"Will you be alright?"

You nodded, bending a little stiffly to reach your trug, abandoned by the wayside. "It's probably best if I go on ahead," you said, watching the handful of berries roll from one end of the basket to the other. You picked one out, black and flagrantly ripe and held it between your fingers. For a strained, uncertain moment you looked as though you might slip it into my mouth. "That's for you," you said, dropping it into my palm.

I took it and bit into it, fruit not really mine for the tasting. It made me bold, though. I leaned over and with pilgrim fingers which shook a little, I swept the fallen hank of hair from your shoulder and tucked it into place with the tortoiseshell comb which had worked loose. "There you are," I said. "The Mistress will be none the wiser, now."

Chapter Six

I was watering the rhododendrons on Dancing Green in the late spring of the following year, making the spray from the hose play with the sunlight, passing the time by creating flashing prisms of colour, when I saw Mrs Brown heading towards me across the lawn.

"Will you pick some cherries for me, Ifor?" She was a handsome woman in spite of her age — she must have been within spitting distance of fifty — only, the fact that she knew it somehow demanded acknowledgement from other people too. "If I don't make my Brandy Cherries soon, they won't be steeped in time for Christmas, see?" She watched me training the water into the impenetrable darkness beneath the rhododendrons, where the roots writhed blackly. "I'd do it myself…"

"Oh, we can't have that, Mrs Brown," I said, tickled by the thought of her wobbling about at the top of a ladder.

"You're so tall now…" When her voice went all breathy, you could hear the Welsh in it. She'd been a girl from the valleys, once upon a time. "It's a fine lad you're growing into, Ifor Griffiths," she murmured, so quiet I could barely hear her above the noise of the hose. "You'll break a few hearts before you're through."

I shrugged. This was a kind of grown-up sport I wasn't used to, like being teased at school when you don't know how to take it. "How many cherries, Mrs Brown?"

"As many as you can pick, young man. I might even make a pie." She smiled, allowing her gaze to travel the length of me, from the toes of my boots to my fingertips. "Bring them up to the kitchen for me, when lunch is over. Shall we say three o'clock?"

Three o'clock came and I set off with a basket of cherries in each hand. The back door was ajar, so I walked in without knocking, just calling out, "Hello?"

I hesitated, thinking of the kitchen at home, Ma, a ghostly presence looming out of the steam — a wraith of the wash. I took a few steps, fearful of intruding, then collected myself and strode the rest of the way, poking my head into the kitchen. "Hello —?"

With the range on full blast, the room was baking hot, even though the windows were thrown up to the limit of their sashes. Mrs Brown had her sleeves pushed back and beneath her apron her blouse was undone I don't know how many buttons. She was kneading something in an enormous bowl; a dusting of flour hung in the air, the atoms of it radiating out as if charged with energy.

"Ifor!"

"I've brought the cherries, Mrs Brown," I said, hovering at the entrance.

"Put them over by there, will you?" She wiped her sleeve across her forehead, leaving a streak of flour. I wondered if I should mention it. I set the baskets down where she indicated.

"You've got a —" I gestured. "On your —"

She put the bowl to one side, covering it with a cloth. "I'll leave that to prove." She brushed her sleeve across her forehead once again.

I shook my head. "No … it's not … it's —"

There was a lengthy pause.

"You do it."

I made a start towards her, then I stopped. "It's just on … where the…"

70

"I won't bite."

"No," I said, "I should think not," and then I laughed and it sounded loud in the silence which followed. In the end there was nothing for it: I fairly sprinted over to her, smudged the flour away with my thumb and sprinted back. "If that's everything…"

"Are you fond of gingerbread nuts?"

I hesitated, "I like ginger cake." I glanced along the corridor towards the back door, with the vaguest sense of trespass. I knew that I should go, but a part of me was curious to stay. Mrs Brown reached for her reading glasses and consulted her recipe book and the sight of her in her spectacles was oddly reassuring. She began to read the recipe aloud, savouring the instructions as if she could taste them in her mouth.

"You take one pound of treacle and a quarter of a pound of coarse…" she lingered over the word, giving it due consideration, "…brown sugar. Then it's two ounces of ground ginger, an ounce of candied orange peel, an ounce of candied angelica, and an ounce of candied lemon peel." I was watching her read, all that sing-song Welsh coming out, the relish of each individual syllable. I liked the way she said "candied". I found myself mouthing it with her.

"These should be chopped into very small pieces, but not," she glanced at me, "…bruised."

I swallowed. Worse still, I blushed.

"I'm going to start by heating the treacle and the sugar together with a little melted butter…"

It was the warmth in the kitchen.

"And when I've mixed in all the ingredients…"

It was the ferment of the baking.

"…I'm going to break an egg."

With a smile that left her lips half-parted, she leaned over to select an egg from a bowl in the middle of the table, and the indolence of her reach afforded me a glimpse of this and that, and the candied scent of her caught me unawares, so that for a dreadful moment I found myself racked with impure imaginings, though she's the same age as my Ma. Only for a moment, because then I thought of you, and I thought of Mr Brown and our trip to Newland, and then I thought hats off to Samuelson.

And I fled.

I came home from work one day to find my sister Delyth, back from the factory where she'd been assembling circuit breakers since the war, all hot under the collar. She was in militant mood. "Have you got yesterday's newspaper, Ifor?" she asked before I was over the threshold.

I handed it to her, gave Ma the half dozen misshapen potatoes the kitchen had rejected and flopped down at the table.

"Tea?" said Ma.

Delyth had this habit of reading things under her breath so you could hear the clicking of the consonants, but not what she was saying and it used to drive me mad. She was ticking away like a clock, taking little sips of outraged air.

"It's not right," she said. "It's just not right."

I was watching Ma pouring boiling water onto tea leaves that we used this morning and I was sore inside that she should have to live like this and sorer still that somehow, although I was doing the job she wished me to, I was falling short in my responsibilities. A proper son would have made sure there was fresh tea when she wanted it. She felt my gaze and shrugged.

"Did you know," Delyth leaned both elbows on the newspaper; she brought her face, full of accusations, up close to mine, "that since the war, miners' pay has gone down from six pounds a week to three pounds eighteen shillings?"

"No, Delyth, I didn't know that," I answered, eyeing the grey tea Ma was bearing in my direction.

"Well, you know now," she said grimly. "The pit owners want to reduce pay even further, on account of Germany giving their coal to France for free because of the war; it's always because of the war." She sounded aggrieved, as though she had been cheated of something. "The Miners' Federation of Great Britain is drawing a line, though. Not a penny off the pay, not a minute on the day. It says it there, in the paper. I'll stand by that."

"It won't affect many people in Morwithy, will it?" I sipped my tea dubiously. "Ianto Pryce's family, maybe, but mostly we're farming folk."

"Ifor," my sister upbraided me, "it'll affect us all, every man Jack of us. They'll squeeze us till the pips squeak, then they'll go on squeezing after that."

"Keep your hair on!"

"You've been working up at Nanagalan for too long. You've turned native," she snapped.

That stung me. "Look —"

"Now, now," said our mother. "Lay the table, will you, there's a boy."

Delyth's words stayed with me. I thought of the hours I worked in God's fresh air with the weather in my face and the light streaming into the valley. I couldn't begin to picture the black of the coal face, a darkness so intense that it blinded the ponies who toiled in it. I thought what would happen to our precarious household if our income was docked by a quarter:

thin soup a little thinner, meat and two veg reduced to just two veg. And the twice-brewed tea? How far could we make that go?

The day that eight hundred thousand men were locked out of the mines because they wouldn't accept new terms, a general strike was called. Delyth downed tools straight away and refused to go to work.

"You're not going up to the house," she said in disbelief, when I came down in my working clothes.

"Someone's got to," I said, hunting for some cheese on the cold shelf, so I could make a sandwich for my lunch. "We've got to eat," I added pointedly, when all I could find was a small piece of Double Gloucester pared back to the rind.

"You're a scab."

The words were so quiet I wasn't certain that I'd heard them. I turned to face her, to be sure. "What?"

She gave me a look of scalding contempt. She didn't need to repeat herself. I wrapped the sandwich in my handkerchief, making brisk folds in the material and pressing them flat meticulously. "You go your way," I said when I could fold the thing no more, "and I'll go mine."

Samuelson skived off, never one to miss a chance, though his only notion of solidarity was to himself, so I went down to the vineyard to finish off the tying in I'd been busy with the day before, removing the side shoots on the vines and training the principals between the wires so the sun could get at them. I liked the rhythm of it: the snipping and the reaching and the twisting. I worked for an hour or two, making my way along the slanting hillside, up one row and down another, interrupting the bees, humming myself.

At the top of the slope the front door slammed and you came running through the Herbar out onto Dancing Green, another young lady at your side and I could hear the two of you laughing. You had a couple of racquets and some tennis balls and you began knocking them about and I kept my head down and made my way along another row, listening to the thwack and twang as you returned the balls to each other. From time to time I glanced in your direction, following the swallow flight of your run as you darted hither and thither, your hair like a banner in the breeze.

I heard the miss-hit, the dull groan of the racquet, before I saw the ball soar down the hillside towards me.

"Ifor," you called, laughing. You didn't need to ask. I found the ball in the lumpy grass between the vines a few rows down and made my way up the hillside, tossing it and catching it, tossing it and catching it, until I reached you and I placed it in your palm.

"Thanks," you said carelessly in front of your friend, who looked at me, then looked at you and simpered.

I nodded, turned on my heel and headed back down to my work. A few minutes later, the ball sailed in my direction again. It landed several feet away.

"Ifor…?"

I snipped away at the vine in front of me.

"Our ball." Your voice had a trill in it that I didn't recognise. "Do you mind…?"

I tucked the shoot between the wires, and then lay my secateurs on the ground with a tense deliberation of which you might have taken heed. I found the ball and, with a steely swing, I threw it back up the hill. Your friend giggled as you caught it and I couldn't decide if it was me that you were showing off to her, or your power over me, which was a different matter.

I picked up my secateurs and moved on to the next vine, trimming away more curtly than before. Within minutes, there was an eruption of laughter as the ball came flying through the air at me once again.

"Ifor…?"

More laughter which, poorly suppressed, fed upon itself. I didn't want to hear it. I clipped at the vine until it was almost shorn.

The two of you were helpless with it.

"Ifor…? Will you get our ball?"

I thought about the eight hundred thousand men locked out of their workplace for asking for a living wage, and the degradation of that, and my own small humiliation seemed, in that instant, to be of a kind. I bent down and placed my secateurs on the ground with all the slow defiance I could muster. When I straightened up, I folded my arms across my chest and shook my head.

Your laughter slowed to a trickle and then stopped. "Ifor…?"

I didn't answer. I clasped my arms more tightly as though to emphasise the position I had taken, while you fiddled with the strings of your racquet. You turned the leather-bound handle over in your hand.

"Make him get it," your friend said, less coy now. "Go on, he's your servant. He should do what he's told."

You cleared your throat, not looking at me. "Fetch the ball, will you, Ifor?"

I stood stock-still, the anger glinting off me, staring up at you. I would not be a dog to fetch and carry, not for anyone.

"This is the most frightful bore," I heard you say and you came traipsing down the hill towards me, tripping on a tuft of the rough grass which only made you crosser, so that by the time you reached me, the incident had become more than it was meant to be.

"When I ask you to do something…"

I wouldn't upset you for the world, not for the world, but I had no option other than to stand my ground. "I'm nobody's servant," I said. "I garden here, and I tend your vines. But not this afternoon. This afternoon I'm out on strike."

"Don't be ridiculous." I could see the unease in your face as you wondered how far you should push this. "Just get me the ball."

I shrugged. "I can't."

"You mean you won't."

"Alright, I won't."

"That's that, then."

"You can sack me if you want to," I said as wretched as I have ever been, and there was nothing left for me to do, but to turn on my heel and walk away, leaving my secateurs lying discarded on the ground.

I walked back to Morwithy, a terrible incantation of regret going round and round in my head: what have I done, what have I done, what have I done? Ma was pegging out some sheets in the yard when I got home, a gathering breeze twining them round her in a damp cotton embrace.

"Ifor?" she called, but I wasn't about to do her bidding either. The shame of what I had done made me feel too complicated for my own skin.

"Yes, Ma," I stood at the back door, slumping against the jamb.

"Watch out, or the wind will change and you'll be stuck with that face forever."

I didn't answer. I chewed at some skin inside my mouth. She busied herself pegging out a row of pillowcases with lace around the edge of them.

"You're home early," she said, her voice a mite too casual.

I stared with hostility at that lace. "Yes." I had a ludicrous picture of myself setting off for work tomorrow, with no work to go to, because I couldn't bring myself to tell her. Could I pretend the day after? And the day after that? And what would I do when pay day came? "Samuelson was off with the strikers. There wasn't much for me to do."

"He's a fool, that man," Ma said curtly.

"Where's Delyth?" I asked, thinking that Samuelson wasn't half the idiot that I had been.

"It would appear that she's a fool as well," she swiped the washing basket and the peg bag off the ground. "She went off with a placard she had made. I didn't ask." My mother sighed and the heaviness of the sound singed my conscience till I felt burned up round the edges with it, sick at what I'd done.

"Oh Ma, I'm so —"

"You can lose your reputation in this village overnight and then it's a life's work to get it back again." The basket was made of sea grass which was unravelling at one edge. She started worrying away at it with her thumbnail, splitting the loose stalk. "People are very swift to judge round here. They might be your neighbours, but…" She took a breath, then buttoned it up somewhere inside her. "I don't know what your father would say. He'd be very —"

"Ma, I've —"

"— disappointed."

The silence was broken by the clicking sound of the latch and Delyth breezed her way through the yard and into the kitchen. "I'm starving," she ranged around from cupboard to cupboard. "I've had the most thrilling time — there were about twenty of us."

"Thank you, Delyth," Ma crisply closed the cupboard doors. "Your tea will be at half past five, the usual time, and not a minute sooner."

"Ifor?" My sister deigned to notice me. "Your boss was out with us," she said with emphasis. "For a short while, anyway. He's got principles, at least. Oh," she started, recalling something. "Are these yours? I found them on the doorstep. You must have dropped them."

She handed me my secateurs.

I went to work the next day in trepidation. Samuelson was looking green around the gills and I waited for him to ask me why on earth I had bothered turning up, but he made himself comfortable on a pile of sacks in the fermentation shed and waved me away as if I were the chief cause of his evident headache. His rough rawness rose from him like civet. "What are you staring at?" he asked, opening one bloodshot eye. "Finish off the tying in, boy."

I didn't need telling twice.

I made my way to the vineyard, the late spring singing like a hymn around me. At the top of the slope the knuckled walls of the old part of the house gleamed white as bones in the sunlight. Brown once told me that the nuns made wine here back in the fourteenth century. They supplied the bishops of Gloucester, Hereford and Worcester. He said that Nanagalan meant women, singing, in Old English and if you were a lad green in the green world like I was, when the wind stirred the leaves on the vines and whispered through the arches of the beech trees soaring round the Drowning Pool, you could almost believe it was ancient voices you could hear, raised in plainsong.

I pulled my secateurs out of my pocket and weighed the meaning of their return in my hand. I was full of all the things that it might signify. I set to work at double quick time to make up for what I had not completed the day before, steaming my way along the rows all morning.

Perhaps it was the heat unfurling round me, or the smallness of my lunch, but after a while I began to imagine that I could hear music. I stopped to listen. It wasn't a ghostly Gregorian chant, but fragments of something fraught and feverish. I snipped at a side shoot, then another, but all the while these ragged phrases tugged at me, my head full of the jangle of them until I couldn't help myself.

I climbed the hillside then skirted round Esther's Garden to the front of the house. The music was coming from one of the downstairs rooms and I stood there, not quite comprehending the jittery, jaunty heart break of it. The record slowed, slurring the notes until someone, I knew it must be you, wound the gramophone again. I inched closer, at an oblique angle to the window, hovering, until I saw you.

You were dancing the Charleston on your own, your eyes closed, your arms jerking, your feet snapping, caught endlessly in the private compulsion of the beat. The sight was somehow pitiful to see. On and on you danced, with your head thrown back, imprisoned by the music, until I thought you might do yourself an injury.

The record slowed and you unwound yourself for long enough to crank it up again, then off you went with your solitary dancing and I stood watching you, a lonely dervish, whirling round and round and round. When the record slowed again, you kept on spinning, a little out of kilter, your orbit suddenly uncertain. You opened your eyes and stretched out your arms to steady yourself. And then you saw me.

I don't know which of us was the most mortified. You were giddy still, your chest working, your pink face gone pale. You took a few skittering steps and on a reflex I held out my hand to support you, though I was outdoors and beyond your reach. I let my arm fall to my side. You moved closer to the window, casting your net, drawing me in. I was caught in the slow tide of the look you gave me, walking forward until I was so close I could see the cirrus featherings of your breath upon the glass.

You ran a single finger down the pane, tracing the outline of my neck and then my collarbone with one stroke, all the while considering me. I raised my hand and put it to the window to capture yours and you traced that too, the tip of your finger searching and intent. Through the glass you pressed your palm to mine and the two of us stood, like that.

In a distant room, the telephone began to ring. You took your hand away, curling it closed and holding it to your lip, hesitating, before you turned, taking your bearings, then headed back to your own world, and the brief sketch of me you'd started was erased.

Chapter Seven

I remembered the first ever cricket match I played in, on an irretrievably golden afternoon in the summer of that year. Brown told me that before the war, there were enough staff at Nanagalan for the house to form an eleven of its own, but with the names of so many fine batsmen carved in stone on the village memorial, it was all we could do to muster a single team from the whole of Morwithy.

That year we played Llancloudy, the pitch laid out on Dancing Green, Samuelson's contribution to roll it assiduously day after day. He was touchy about the lawns, territorial; his hypothesis that if you came up trumps with the things that people noticed, the rest could go hang. He never played in any of the matches, he lurked at the back of the marquee, a pint of cider in his hand, a cigarette in his mouth and another tucked behind his ear for later. There was something fugitive about him.

Brown broached the subject of the match when I went to pick up the newspaper from him on my way home from work. The coach house and the stable block, which formed one side of the courtyard, had been converted into a garage for the Daimler, a workshop and two cottages, one for the Browns and one for Mr Samuelson. There were some loose boxes as well and I fished a couple of carrot tops out of my pocket and fed them to the master's hunter, his muzzle whickering for more until he had the button of my jacket in his teeth and I was caught up in a proper tug of war when Brown appeared. He freed me with the assistance of a lump of sugar.

The workshop was his private kingdom. All the doings for the motor were up one end: a mechanical ramp for lifting it, wrenches and pumps, cans of oil and tubs of grease, valves, filters and plugs for which I could never quite muster an understanding, although I did try, in order to please him.

His snug was up the other end. Sectioned off with a rough timber partition, Brown had imported a few sparse creature comforts: a varicose old armchair whose springs formed unpleasant contours no matter where you placed your weight, a threadbare rug, the same paraffin stove that Samuelson and I had in our shed, an Aladdin, its glass shade holding captive a sliver of blue flame which, with some strange, superstitious sense of continuity, he never allowed to go out. He had nailed some wooden wine crates to the partition to make a rudimentary set of shelves, which were lined with scrapbooks and manuals, a collection of different types of tobacco tin (one or two of them older than me) and a row of stubby yellow books.

"Wisden," he said, following my gaze. "I've got every single edition they've ever printed, starting in 1864. Do you play?"

The first cup of tea I drank there, a whiskery, bristly brew made on a tiny primus stove, was my rite of passage into manhood. There was a whiff of the dugout about the place, its makeshift appropriations a male redoubt without the flanking defences of domesticity.

"Play?" I asked.

"Cricket," he said, stirring his tea, tapping his spoon on his mug, then handing it to me so that I could do the same. "Your father was a very fine wicketkeeper, in his day."

"Was he?" A sudden glimpse of my Dad, unanticipated, always hit me, throwing an unsparing light over all that I didn't know about him. I couldn't picture him playing cricket; I could barely summon the sound of his voice, though a brief image of the way he could twist an apple in half with his bare hands flashed into my mind and I recalled him teaching me how to make fountains with a clench of my fist in the water butt in our yard, wet-sleeved, my chin on a level with the rim. "A wicketkeeper?" I remembered him not sitting in his chair in the parlour, after he went to war. I remembered his absence, as much as anything about him.

"A very fine one."

"No," I said, "I don't know how to play."

"We'll soon put that right. There's six weeks until the match. Plenty of time."

Every day after that, when work was done, Brown took me up to the wildflower meadow where we wouldn't be disturbed and bowled at me, ball after ball after ball: bouncers, beamers and indippers; inswingers swiftly followed by outswingers; leg cutters, off cutters, slow balls, yorkers and just to fool me, the odd full toss. He spared me nothing an in my turn, I failed to catch most of them.

"Let's have another go at this," he'd say, thundering through the long grass towards me, launching the ball so that when it went spinning to the left, I was at the limit of my reach in the opposite direction, and when it bounced to the right I was lunging forwards. I rolled and dived and flung myself after the blasted thing until I was black and blue all over. "You'll learn," he'd say imperturbably, rotating his shoulder, preparing to bowl at me again. "There's plenty of time."

The weeks rattled past and Brown explained the rules to me, then tested me on them during breaks which were becoming shorter and shorter, our tea growing cold while he talked at me. Then it was up to the meadow for more catching practice, more question and answer sessions, more bowling and rolling, more hurling and curling. When I mentioned batting, he brushed my question to one side.

"We've got batsmen," he said. "It's a wicketkeeper that we need. First team practice on Saturday, Ifor. You watch the others. Best way to learn. The sound of leather on willow," he sighed. "Life doesn't get much better than that."

Our team was full of elderly men and lads like me: the oldest was Gwlym Jones the Ancient, then there was the watchmaker Dick the Tick, Tom Ten Bricks Pritchard, not known for his speed as a builder — ten bricks a day was his limit — Iwan the Milk, Parry the Paint and Ianto Pryce. Not a single one of us could be said to be in his prime. Tom started calling me Green Fingers Griffiths and it stuck. He also showed me how to hold the bat, where to put my feet, how to lean into the ball, though he was noncommittal about my progress.

"You'll probably do," he said, scratching his jaw, then he added as an afterthought, "you might put in a bit of practice after work, though. If you've the time."

The night before the match when I dropped by to pick up the paper, a heaviness had settled on Brown. He was at the business end of the workshop, still in his overalls, when I stuck my head around the door. He looked up when I came in, then wiped his hands on an oily rag.

"Nervous, are you?" I said, all eager for the pre-match pep talk.

He shrugged. He was slow to put the kettle on the primus stove.

"What's the matter?"

He let the tea sift from the spoon into the pot. "It gets you down a bit," he said, staring at the small accumulation of leaves at the bottom. "Politics and suchlike. That's what."

"Politics?" I repeated, wondering if he'd got wind of something Delyth had been up to. My sister, the activist.

"World affairs," he said, pouring the boiling water into the teapot and sliding a gnarled old knitted tea cosy over the top of it, the wool stained with tannin. "You think they won't affect you, but look what happened last time."

"Last time?"

"I don't like the cut of that fellow's jib." He jerked his head in the direction of yesterday's newspaper, lying open on the worktop. I peered at a grainy picture of a man with black hair geometrically slicked across his forehead and a repressed little black moustache.

"German fascist." Brown said with distaste. "Adolf Hitler."

I shook my head. "Never heard of him."

"Out of prison on parole after an attempted putsch. Nasty piece of work. Head of the National Socialist Party. Not socialists as you or I would recognise them, mind you. Very right wing, Ifor. Very right wing. Calls himself Fuhrer — that's leader to the likes of you and me." He subsided into his armchair, making the springs heave. "You pour the tea there, will you?"

He nursed the mug when I handed it to him. "Never trust a Hun," he said quietly. "That's one thing I have learned." He sat there, brooding, out in no man's land beyond the wire, on the recce in a landscape known to him and alien to me, sniffing the cordite in the air. "The war to end all wars," he said, picking at some skin fraying round his thumbnail, worrying it back to the quick. "That's what they promised us," he licked his thumb, the pinprick of red blood. "We'll see what Mr Hitler has to say about that."

Ma went berserk with all the washing and enlisted Delyth too: the men's flannels, the women's summer dresses, the tablecloths and napkins — the borax and the corn starch were rife in our kitchen, the irons in constant rotation heating on the range and my sister in a state of collapse over the mangle, but walking onto Dancing Green that Saturday, the marquee up and the bunting flying and the sunlight shining linen white on all their hard work, was a sight to behold.

Llancloudy won the toss and put us in to bat. Tom Ten Bricks opened for us and he was a hungry man, absolutely ravenous for runs and I couldn't take my eyes off him. I made such a study of the man, the artistry of the angular shapes his body made as he swung and struck, each movement so calculated, so precise. He scored a four in the first over and I jumped several feet in the air from purest joy and we were off.

I was hatching all kinds of bargains in my head — let him make fifty, let him make fifty — then Gwylm Jones was bowled out for eleven and Dick the Tick came in and made a useful twenty until the butcher from Llancloudy, I didn't know his name, he was a big bloke, caught him at short leg and it was Parry the Paint's turn.

My ears were full of the sound of gloved hands clapping and the clink of ice in lemonade. I glanced around, at the gardens in my care, at the big house on the far side of the lawn, at Brown analysing Llancloudy's tactics with his elbow resting on his arm and his chin cupped, and I wondered if I would have the courage to fight to defend it all, the village and the valley and our way of life, as he had done, and Dad, and Glyn; whether I would be able to rise to the occasion if I were ever called upon to do so.

When my turn came, we were eighty-three for seven: Tom Ten Bricks out for thirty-eight, Iwan the Milk out for nine and now it was up to me and Ianto Pryce. I walked to the crease with the bat under my arm, as I had seen the others do. I knew exactly where you were sitting, at a table in the centre of the marquee with your mother and the vicar and some other toffs I didn't know and I glanced in your direction as I positioned my bat just like Tom and shifted my weight, and squinted into the light, as he had done. Out of the corner of my eye I saw you set your cup back in its saucer and lean forward.

The bowler came for me with his hooves pawing the ground and much spittle flying, at least that's how it felt, and loosened the ball from his meaty grip and it went scything through the air towards me and if you hadn't been there I might have ducked. I stood firm though, and swung the bat as Tom had shown me and heard the sweet, astonishing sound of leather on willow and felt the shock of the impact shoot through my fingers, making them sting.

The ball looped uncontrollably high into the air and Ianto charged in my direction, so off I bolted, thinking that Brown was right, life doesn't get much better than this. The ball began to descend gracefully through the streaming light, and I was racing with my bat outstretched to claim my run, when with a casual cupping of his hand one of Llancloudy's fielders caught it and I was out. For a duck.

Polite applause is one thing, but laughter...

"What a hit! What a hit! Just get it over the boundary next time," Brown hurried over and slapped me on the back as I walked off the field. I couldn't look in your direction. I handed the bat to Iwan and part of me wanted to keep on walking, right away from Nanagalan, but the lads were clustering round me, grinning.

"Move over Jack Hobbs, Green Fingers Griffiths is coming through," said Tom Ten Bricks and they all joined in after that, with their banter and their jokes, until I began to see that this was another rite of passage, and found the balm in that.

We were all out for a hundred and forty, no thanks to me.

All those evenings in the wildflower meadow with Brown bowling at me fit to bust seemed to pay off in the end, though. I took my place behind the wicket with my pulse in full flight round my body, ticking in my throat and my belly, even in the pads of my thumbs. As I crouched down waiting for the first ball, reminding myself to breathe out as well as breathing in, I was conscious of the other blokes around me — Tom and Parry within earshot at short leg, comfortingly close, Jones and Dick further out towards the boundary — and that sense of being a part of a team kindled inside me, so that anything seemed possible.

When Brown bowled the first over it was as if we were out in the meadow, just him and me, flattening the cowslips and the dandelions with our efforts, the batsmen an afterthought getting in the way. They scored two runs. After we had changed ends, Brown came at me again and I could hear the wrenching noise he made as he let loose the ball; I could see the spin on it, the wily curve which lured the Llancloudy man way beyond the crease and before I knew what I was doing, I was up, taking it and breaking the wicket and there was a whooping sound which might have come from me, or Tom, or Brown, or Ma, or any one of us and the patter of applause echoed like my pulse in every part of me and I had never felt more alive in all my life.

I got five men out that day. Five men. The last off an atrocious throw from Gwilym Jones who, frail but enthusiastic, lobbed the ball through almost a hundred and eighty degrees towards the marquee rather than in my direction. I threw myself after it, my eyes fixed on the stitching, the red leather beyond the furthest reach of my fingers. I almost achieved lift off, I ran so fast. I caught the blighter then hit the wickets with a direct throw and we beat Llancloudy by nineteen runs.

A small table was placed at the edge of the pitch and the two teams lined up, forming a triumphal arch with their bats held aloft and the spectators were garrulous with chatter as Brown marched up — and he did march, his arms impeccably in line with the seams of his trousers — for the presentation. Your mother handed him the cup and the vicar hovered in attendance seizing the opportunity to pass it to her.

"And now," the mistress said in her hot house voice, all cultivated vowels, "I will call upon my daughter to make the award for the Man of the Match."

You stepped forward and with the slow dispersal of conversation, the garden filled with the tiny sounds that make a silence — footsteps falling on close-mown grass, the creak of a branch, the swish of a cat's tail at the perimeter of the lawn. There was a medallion on the table, a tinny little thing, its brass too bright, and you picked it up and twined the ribbon round your fingers. I glanced along the line at my teammates and then at our opponents, wondering who the lucky man would be.

And then you said my name. Ifor Griffiths. I was watching the progress of the ribbon and it was as if I didn't hear you, I was so lost in the gaudy red and gold. Iwan the Milk, who was standing next to me, jabbed me in the ribs.

"That's you, lad."

I came to, and ducked under the archway made of bats, oblivious to the catcalls and the whistles and the stamping. I couldn't look at you. I turned my gaze upon your mother instead.

"Congratulations, Ifor," you said and as you gave me the medallion and shook my hand, I was close enough to see the stealthy flight of colour cross your features. "It's for your batting skills," you added with the twitch of a smile, "obviously," and then, on impulse, when all of us were unprepared, you stood on tiptoe and kissed me on the cheek.

As I turned round, swallowing, casting a wild glance at my teammates, I saw Tom and Parry nudging one another, making sardonic little clicks with their teeth. I felt more full of shame than elation to be the butt of other people's ribaldry, but when I checked to see if you had noticed I caught sight of your mother standing as stiff as a ramrod, frowning. That air of distraction, of wishing that she was in, if not another place, then certainly another time, was gone. She fixed her corvine eye upon me, her dark sheen ruffled, and hawk-like she jutted out her chin.

As I returned to my place in the line I touched my skin where you had kissed me, to see if your mouth had left a mark.

Chapter Eight

The first time Delyth brought her fiancé Ted to meet us, the tight fist of winter had gripped the village, and from the start, he was a difficult man to like, not just because I was her brother and had a vested interest in her happiness. He was a literal fellow, too full of explication to have any room for humour, too condescending in his righteousness, with his pale, belligerent eyes and his mastiff's build, all shoulders and no neck, so I couldn't help feeling some antipathy.

They'd been courting since the end of the war and my sister regarded him as if he were God's Own, seated on the edge of the sofa in our front parlour, the anti-macassars washed in his honour and a fire blazing in the swept hearth, and I wanted to lean across and give her a good shake to bring her to her senses, but she was so fizzing with nerves she would have popped if I had done so.

Ma was muted, the inside of her lip caught between her teeth in a way that made me think there was a good deal she wasn't saying. She seemed distracted, as though she were awaiting the arrival of someone else with a kind of sad expectancy. "Where did you say you met?" she asked, surfacing, back in the conversation, ready to atone for any absence noticed.

"I told you, Ma," said Delyth, still looking at Ted, "at the miners' fundraising social in Mynydd Maen."

"Mynydd Maen?" said Ma. "Ah yes, you said. I remember." She nodded. "Mynydd Maen..." she repeated. "More tea, Ted?"

While we drank our tea and ate our bakestone cakes, Ted embarked on a detailed account of the organisation and aims of the miners' social club, having convinced himself that we liked the sound of his voice as much as he did. On and on he went about workers' rights and though I'm not opposed, far from it, I did find myself retreating into my own thoughts from time to time. I was struck by how we misconceive what makes us happy, wondering what life Delyth imagined for herself, what she would be left with when she no longer took Ted at his own value, the complex bargain which must be struck between compromise and self-deception. Then I fell to thinking about my own happiness and I could only picture you. A prospect with no future, I thought, looking at my sister and wondering if both of us were done for.

In the end, (it seemed to take hours and hours and a whole new pot of tea — fresh leaves, I noticed) Ted put the world most thoroughly to rights for us and judged it time to head off on his bike to Monmouth station. Delyth saw him off the premises and I remembered the icy blast of air as they left the house. Ma and I exchanged a look. She opened her mouth to say something, but thought better of it. Circumspectly, she began stacking the best china onto a tray. After a few minutes Delyth came gliding back into the parlour, her feet several inches off the ground.

"You do like him, don't you?" was the first thing she said. "He's so deep. He's such a thinker. I never dreamed —" she broke off and her odd, blunt face was as soft as I have ever seen it. "I never dreamed I'd be so lucky," she breathed. She held out her hands for me to take, offering me all her joyful expectation, but I put an arm around her and hugged her instead.

"I hope you'll be happy," I said, choosing my words, but all the while I was thinking that she'd get her heart's desire, which would be her curse, and I wouldn't, and that would be mine.

I remembered, oh, how I remembered hearing about the accident at the pit in Cwm; the Marine colliery was far enough from Morwithy for none of our families to be involved, but it still felt personal, the shock of the loss: fifty-two men. That's a whole generation in a small village. All those cold spaces in half-empty beds, those places at table not taken, those clothes still holding the shape of the departed, hanging unworn in the cupboard. With so many men gone from the valleys because of the war, we couldn't afford to be losing any more. Gas and coal dust, that's what caused it, the explosion. Fifty-two men. Even Ted was reduced to silence.

We all went to the memorial service, of course we did, held on a merciless March morning, the chapel full of people thin with grief. I stood next to a man with a hacking cough, a proper a pair of miner's lungs he had on him and looking back, that was probably where I caught the influenza.

The onset was ferocious: one moment I was cleaning the green furze from the flagstones in Esther's Garden, one of my favourite spots at Nanagalan; it was tucked into the lee of the house and laid out in the Italian manner, with a small pool and an ornamental fountain, and stone seats lined up against the wall beneath pleached trees. Whenever I thought of Nanagalan I thought of Esther's Garden: the bristling velvet brown of the bulrushes fringing the pool, the pale limestone, the little cupid gurgling into his bowl, the golden light that shed itself over everything until the long shadows of evening fell.

The flu nearly did for me. One moment I was working in Esther's Garden with a stiff brush and the hose, scrubbing at the algae and then sluicing it away, my trousers sodden, the marrow of my bones turned to iron with the cold, then I had the touch of a headache, and before Samuelson could shout out, "Boy!" I was flat on my back in bed under two eiderdowns, my teeth chattering, and Ma hunched beside me bathing my forehead with wet flannels.

She never left my side, sitting at the bottom of my bed, keeping vigil. At first I was vaguely irritated. I kept rolling into the dip her weight created and I believed her presence made me hotter, but then the fever got a grip of me and I set off into the sweltering darkness of the inside of my head, in a state too restless to be sleep, but even across the ocean of my illness I sensed her nearness. I'd fling myself awake, drenched and shuddering, startled to see the wisp of her, white-faced, close by. She stroked my forehead, her chapped hand catching my dry skin and I drifted off with my eyes closed, miles and miles I went, my only link with the mainland the pressure of her fingers soothing me.

The doctor came and I remembered thinking I must be dying, for how would we afford the expense of his visit otherwise? His glacial fingers tapped against my chest and he listened with his stethoscope. "There's quite a rattle down there," he said, not telling Ma the half of it. "Both lungs. The best thing you can do is get a kettle boiling next to him. The steam will help to clear it." He unclipped his stethoscope and folded it up and put it in his bag. "He's still quite young," he observed and I couldn't work out if that was a good thing or not, and to be honest, I was past caring.

Ma took to spooning sips of water into my mouth because I didn't have the strength to swallow. The heat was tropical, moisture running down the walls as the kettle steamed on a primus stove beside me, but I was still in spasms with the cold. Ma wiped her own forehead with the flannel and our eyes met as she folded it into a tidy pad and everything we needed to say was in that look: I can't hold on / You mustn't leave me / I'm doing my best / Hold on / What if I can't hold on?

95

She leaned over and took me by my shoulders, "Ifor," she said, and I remembered that tone of voice from when I was a child, the unarguable command of it and in that instant I could have believed that I was all that mattered in the world to her. My eyes slurred shut.

When I came to, I knew I was hallucinating because there you were, I could see you plain as day, wrapped in a coat with a fur collar, carrying a box of Cadbury's Milk Tray with your gloves on. Ma was hovering, her hands hesitant in mid-air, caught between taking you by the arm to lead you away, although she would hardly have dared to touch you, or pulling up the quilt and generally setting the room to rights.

"Is he awake?" I thought I heard you say.

The Ma of my overwrought imagination was in an agony of distraction. "Maybe. Yes. He comes and goes. Best not stand so close, miss, ma'am."

"He's so thin."

"Yes."

"I hardly recognised him."

"I know. Shouldn't you be —?"

"A thousand people died of it last week. It said in the paper."

The spectre of my mother didn't answer that.

"That's why I came. He won't —?"

She didn't answer that either.

"— will he?"

Ma slid her hands in the pocket of her apron, then realising she was wearing it, she whipped it off and folded it, then stood there holding it, not knowing quite where to put it.

My eyelids fell shut and you went fleeing from my dream.

The fever broke, almost breaking me with it, and I was left with the cough to contend with: the machine gun hack, hack, hack of it at me day and night. Ma hauled me upright and held a bowl for me and I was halfway to heaving up my lungs when, out of the corner of my eye, I saw a purple box sitting on the windowsill.

"Chocolates," Ma said, following my gaze. "From the big house." She didn't say your name.

The first day I was well enough to come downstairs, Ma boiled an egg for me and there was chicken broth for tea.

"What about the money?" I wheezed. "For the doctor. For all of this."

"You need to get your strength back. Money's not important. Money's the last thing..." She took my hand and traced the veins too raised, too blue. "I don't know what I'd have done —" She broke off and made much of clearing her throat. "We've had lots of help, in any case," she said, changing a subject that wasn't quite broached. "Delyth has mucked in with the laundry. Ted sent ten bob over. People rally round."

"Will you have the Milk Tray, Ma?"

She didn't want them. I could tell as soon as I made the offer that the chocolates were an awkward gift. She turned my hand palm up and searched the length of the lines on it. "Give them to your sister," she said.

The spring came and went without me. It was a month before I was back on light duties. Samuelson didn't look at all pleased to see me, keeping himself at a distance as though I were still contagious, his aggrieved little gestures — a sigh here, the martyred droop of a shoulder there — making it plain what a burden my absence had been.

I was sitting in the tool shed filling out an order for the seed merchant; it was undemanding work and my boss was uncharacteristically coy about his handwriting. The table, a rickety, bowed old thing green with damp, wobbled as I wrote. I had the door open and the muffler which Ma held out to me as I left that morning to protect my chest sat in a heap beside me on the bench. Every now and then, I raised my head and inhaled the mineral scent of air fresh from the valley, savouring the healing traces of all the different elements: loam and leaf and spring water and lingering winter wood smoke.

I was engrossed in the catalogue, cross-checking my order against last year's invoice — I'd begun a rudimentary filing system gleaned from the thick clot of screwed-up papers Samuelson stuffed in one of the drawers. He had been digging over some of the beds in the kitchen garden ready for planting out, with much sighing and drooping of shoulder, for the work was too demanding for me to tackle yet. He had left his spade stuck into the earth — it must have been three o'clock, or thereabouts — and I glanced up to see if the magpie which I had noticed earlier had returned to its perch on the handle. Instead of its thieving, glinty blackness, I saw you coming towards the shed, with the same fretful compulsion I had seen on your face that day when you were dancing.

"Ifor," you said with a start. "No, don't get up," for I had half risen from my seat, and then after a pause that lasted several moments, "May I come in?" You slipped inside the door. Briefly, you leaned against the jamb. "I heard that you were on the mend." Your gaze fell upon my muffler on the bench. Irresolutely you picked it up, kneading the thick yarn between your fingers and I realised too late that it was a prelude to sitting down beside me. You wound the muffler around your neck. "Does it suit me?" you asked with a woeful smile.

"Yes," I nodded, glancing at the rough navy wool against your skin.

"It smells of you," you said and your voice sounded sad, which made me feel intolerably anxious. I was on the whetted knife edge of wanting everything about you. I nodded more slowly, once, twice, thinking that I ought to stand up and make my way towards the door, to a place of safety. Sitting side by side the way we were, our thighs almost touching, we created a seam of private warmth between us. I couldn't move.

"You came to see me," I said in the end, "when I was ill."

You were staring at the floor. "It's what we do," you answered. "When our people are sick. You know — Lady Bountiful."

The magpie alighted on the spade outside. I watched it settle its feathers, the lethal action of its beak tempered for grooming. "Look at him," I whispered. "He's a beauty."

Under your breath, as though you had thought about it long and hard, you said my name. I kept my eyes fixed on the magpie, black and white and blue in all its wickedness.

"What I said just now … that wasn't … it wasn't why I came…" you stammered, "I came because I heard that you were dying."

I didn't move. I didn't stir. I thought I'd frighten you off.

"I came because I couldn't —" You hesitated as if your mouth were dry, "…not."

We moved to the beat of the same wing, turning to face each other, drawing closer, drawing closer until I could feel the rough navy wool at your neck graze against my beard. I was mesmerised by the texture of your skin, the line of your jaw, the contour of your cheek, all the twisting mysteries of your hair.

Perhaps I could have kissed you; perhaps I could. I don't know, now. Maybe each of us was waiting for the other. We stayed like that in tense proximity, almost touching. After a minute you lowered your head and you unwound the muffler as though the effort was exhausting. With both hands you held it over your nose and mouth, breathing in, and above the navy wool your eyes were narrowed blue. You set the muffler on the table and stood up, then walked to the door, where you remained for a moment with your back to me, resting against the frame. The magpie flew upwards in alarm, its wings clattering, and you straightened up and without looking round you set off for the house.

Your mother bundled you off to Scotland for the summer after that and you didn't find time to say goodbye, and I spent long days making up excuses for you to soothe myself. The bank holiday that August was the wettest one since 1879, which summed up just about everything. Samuelson had me cleaning out the glass houses ready for the winter planting and the rain sluiced down the windowpanes unceasingly and I felt utterly submerged.

All afternoon the colours of the garden leached together, the greys and browns and greens stippled in the downpour and I kept hard at it, scrubbing the terracotta tiles on the floor, wiping down the slate-topped work benches, sorting out the pots and trays.

Around teatime the weather lifted, a few raindrops falling from time to time as an afterthought, scattering over the glass like broken beads. I had taken to running to recover my fitness and I made up my mind to run the long way home around the perimeter of the estate. I set off through the beech wood down to the Drowning Pool, the rope swing hanging still above the water, my life defined by absences, and was halfway up the hill the other side when the rain came scumbling down all over again.

Within minutes I was drenched, my shirt sticking grittily to my skin and my boots waterlogged. I took shelter under a tree, but there was no sign of it letting up, so on an impulse, wet through, I decided to run up through the vineyard and take cover in the fermentation shed. I sprinted past the rows of vines laden with dripping fruit and skidded to a halt outside the shed. Panting, I hesitated, my lungs raw with the exertion. I slid the huge door open, stepped inside and pulled it closed behind me.

A bruised beam of light filtered through the windows high beneath the eaves. I leaned against the wall to recover myself, taking my bearings in the half darkness. Rainwater was trickling from my hairline and I shook my head, sending the drops flying. I wiped my forehead on my wet sleeve then searched for my handkerchief, but couldn't find it. The breath was quieter in my chest, but as it subsided, I started to hear other breathings. I peered deeper into the interior, my eyes adjusting to the pewter gloom. Nothing. Then, in the quietness, I heard the shudder of a pent up exhalation.

I made my way around the great oak vat and there I saw them: Samuelson and Mrs Brown, coupling on a pile of sacks. He was reared up over her, she had her legs gripped around his waist, and her skirts flung back so far I could glimpse her stocking tops. She twisted her head round and saw me, but she was already far beyond herself, hurrying and hurrying, her face stretched wide and her teeth bared.

I leapt back as if I'd been scalded, stumbling over the ladder propped against the vat, as Samuelson roared himself inside her. I got myself out of the shed I don't know how, out into the rain, and all I could think of was Brown sitting in the dugout with his mug of tea, and what the Bible said about adultery, and three o'clock, when lunch is over. What would I say when I went to get the paper? How would I look him in the face? I couldn't stop thinking about it. I had witnessed enough living in a rural valley — the dogs in the village, the sheep tupping — to have a rough idea, but I never pictured anything quite like that. The abandonment of it. The disregard for everything.

I walked back through the vineyard with the wind gone from my sails, past the shuttered house and along the driveway up the hill away from Nanagalan, oblivious to the falling rain. I couldn't rid myself of the sight of Mrs Brown's mouth, so distorted; it went round and round inside my head. I couldn't forget what I had seen of the thrust and snarl of love.

That summer seemed the longest summer of my short life, although I knew nothing of long summers then: the summer of rectitude, of saying nothing and thinking everything and how polite we all were to one another, Brown and Mrs Brown and I; how considerate, how treacherous.

Samuelson was a law unto himself: with the family away, he did the minimum, so that moss grew in the lawns and the vines stooped with unpicked fruit and I fought on every front to keep things tidy for when you came home. I couldn't picture what Scotland would be like and got a book out of the library and then, feeling abject, I took it back unopened. I read Walter Scott instead, *Ivanhoe* and *Waverley* and to my running I added a programme of self-improvement — I took an evening class in social history to give myself a chance of besting Ted and busied myself with doing jobs at home for Ma — the steam from the kettle when I was ill had lifted the paper in the bedroom so I redecorated for her. I bought a box of old maps second hand from the thrift shop and pasted them over the walls and lay in bed imagining all the journeys I might make, but in spite of all that, in spite of it all, I was eaten up with thoughts of you, a consumption of the heart, when the whole point was not to think: not to fall sicker, but to recover.

Most of the cricket team came up to help with the grape harvest, except for Gwilym Jones, whose back was bad. Late summer eased into autumn with a perverse alchemy that turned gold to bronze and I made a bonfire on the cinder patch in the corner of the kitchen garden, not far from the well in case of unforeseen eventualities.

I wheeled over barrowloads of clippings and prunings, the dry stalks of the runner beans, cabbage stubs, old roots; all the leavings. After the wet weather it took a while to light and I had to borrow some paraffin from Brown. There was as much steam as smoke, the salt smell dissolved to almost nothing in the air and I had to search for the scent of it.

I leaned against the stone wall of the well, listening to the distant workings of the water far below and the gunshots sounds of the fire as branches cracked and seeds exploded. The wind shifted and the smoke reshaped itself and I saw you in the shimmer of it. I screwed up my eyes to be sure. You hurried towards the tool shed and peered inside, then turned and scanned the walled enclosure and my heart performed the trick that it had learned: contracting and expanding at the same time, so that I was full of you and empty too. Happy and sad, bitter and sweet, the contradictions obvious and complicated. You saw me, and you came towards me and I searched your face for signs of the stifled joy that I was feeling and saw an embarrassment that I didn't know how to read.

"Hello," you said.

"Hello." I examined the corduroy covering my knees in minute detail, scratching the nap in one direction and then the other with my thumbnail.

"I'm back."

"Yes."

"From Scotland. We've been staying in the Highlands. Near Inverness. My father has relations…"

"Yes." I couldn't look at you. I traced the brittle lace of some lichen clinging to the mortar of the well: green and silver, gold and green.

"I was looking for Samuelson," you said, "actually."

"He's somewhere," I shrugged, thinking of the fermentation shed, the pile of sacks, although in fact Samuelson had been working like a demon for the last week or so, getting everything ready, making up for lost time. "Would you like me to find him?" I stood up.

"No — don't go —" you spoke in a rush that you might have thought revealed too much, for you added, "I can find him myself. It's not urgent. Mother wants to know about the vendange, that's all…"

Cautiously, I allowed my gaze to switch to you, to the neckline of your dress, a thickly woven cream material that I guessed was silk. I could see the stitching, tight and straight. "How was Scotland?"

"Oh, you know…"

I kept my thoughts to myself about that, because of course I didn't know.

"We stopped in Birmingham on the way home. Mother took me to the Rep. To see a play. It has a very good reputation, the Birmingham Rep. She said it was a part of my education."

"What did you see?"

"I thought my education was just about over and done with, but it seems not," you said, biting your lip. "Something called *Bird in Hand*." You came and perched on the well beside me and fished out your cigarettes and this time I lit one for you.

"Was it good?" I handed you back your lighter. "The play?"

"It was all about class, Ifor," you said. "I think she particularly wanted me to see it."

A piece of wood in the bonfire split open sending out a fusillade of sparks. A fleck landed on your sleeve and you started brushing at it.

"Boy meets girl," you said. "Rich boy meets poor girl — not like —" You broke off and gave a small, evasive sigh. "'I know that she won't be happy if she gets tangled up with a man out of her own station.' One of the characters said that — her father, I think. The message came over, loud and clear." You drew on your cigarette and then exhaled, in your own, swift way, glancing at me through the filmy, smoke-edged air. "If only you were —" you said, but you ducked your head and didn't finish.

I reached for the fork to stoke the fire, making the flames flinch then leap with a bitter sense of the lack in myself, a lack I had learned at my mother's knee. "All I want is for you to be happy."

You contemplated your fingernails. "Do you think I'll be happy in Switzerland?"

"Switzerland?" I said, at once alert.

"My mother's sending me to finishing school. It's what we do, apparently. In Lausanne."

I mouthed some kind of a reply and there was a stumbling silence and then I looked at you and your eyes were liquid bright, brim-full. "I'm sorry," you whispered, "I do — I would have —" you said, your voice so small, so folded up and tucked away inside you that I could hardly hear it, "feelings, if…" I stared at my boots while my heart performed the trick that it had learnt. "Lausanne," I echoed and then I nodded. I could feel a terrible charring inside me. "A finishing for both of us," I said.

PART TWO

Chapter Nine

Western France, June 1940

All at once the momentum of my jump seemed to spend itself and I started to rise, struggling to scale the black wall of water. My boots were so heavy I thought there must be dying men gripping them, dragging me down deeper in order to save themselves. They were laced so tightly I couldn't kick them off. I kicked and kicked and kicked; I started tearing my uniform instead, ripping the buttons off my jacket, clawing the jacket off my back.

I surfaced, inhaled a wild gasp of diesel, and went under again. On the cusp of life I was, right on the cusp. I knew it was now or never. I kicked; I pounded the water with my boots made of lead and came up again, throwing my head back to breathe, gulping and gulping the greasy air. Through a smear of oil, I could see the sea all silver around me: thousands of tiny fish like litter, everywhere. I thought it was the fuel that had killed them, but then I heard the knife blade sound of bullets hitting the water. The Jerry planes were back, gunning the dying. We were dead men anyway and they were firing at us with their machine guns. What kind of world is this, I thought; what kind of world?

One little lapse like that and death will get you. In a second I was back under the water again, but as I spiralled lazily, spread like a leaf, drifting down and down, so tempted to let go, some words from the Bible, dinned into me at Sunday School when I was a little lad seeped into my head: "I will bring thee again into this land…" If ever I needed some chapel comfort, it was now. "I am with thee, and will keep thee in all places whither thou goest. I will not leave thee."

I breached the surface once again with someone's boot in my face and I was knocked backwards. I steadied myself in the black soup. The bloke was floating with his head off at an angle; dead. He was wearing a lifejacket. Loads of men jumped and their rigid cork lifejackets broke their necks when they hit the water. I knew I'd never get it off him, my fingers were rope-burnt and raw, so I clambered up as best I could and half straddled him. His eyes were open with the surprise of it all and I put my skinless hand across his face to stop him staring at me.

The *Lancastria* was almost gone, the steel petals of her propeller in silhouette against the sky. On the wedge of her hull were maybe a thousand people. I was still so close that I could see a fellow pat his pockets for his cigarettes and lighter and settle for one last smoke.

A woman took off her life belt and threw it to a young lad in the final stages of drowning, his arms scissoring the waves each time he went under. Someone else started singing 'Roll out the Barrel' — you could tell from the ripeness of his voice that he was a Taff and soon other men were caught by the thread of his song.

The ship was sliding further into the water. I could feel the suck of the sea pulling her deeper. I knew I wouldn't survive being swallowed again. I began to paddle the raft of the dead man beneath me. I didn't look back.

I must have been in the water for three hours; it might have been more. The slick of oil was burning in places and through the smoke I could see a lifeboat going round and round in circles, crazily, because the men were too stunned to row in time. A lone voice was singing, "There'll Always Be an

England", a fine tenor voice, he had. Above us the seagulls were keening in the desolate sky. There was so much wreckage that the ship didn't take down with her — chairs, boxes, a ladder, planks of wood of every shape and size, a broken piece of banister, all of it jostling for space with endless bodies in the huge sea. People were dying every minute. A few yards from me was a table; I thought I'd paddle my way across to it, but one of the Tommies said in all politeness that there was only room for the wounded to hold on.

All I could think of was getting myself home to Nanagalan so I could put right the wrong between us. It was the only thing that mattered. It was what saved me from drowning.

Chapter Ten

The day that Jenny and I were married, I allowed myself to believe that she would have the healing of me: she'd be my refuge, my forgetting. It was a piercing April morning, cold and bright, with cherry blossom splashed against a clear sky. The clarity of the light threw everything — the chapel, our two families, Jenny in her homespun dress — into sharp relief, and I saw it all with horrible lucidity.

Your finishing took three whole years, Ella. Two years at the school itself, and then all the European travel with your mother after that. You came back once, flitting home to see your father who was still living out his days in the asylum, fighting a war of attrition between the present and the past more remorseless than any conflict in the trenches. You came to back Nanagalan, you emptied your suitcases and packed them for the coming season, saw friends, wrote letters — I know because Brown passed them on to me to post; once, you turned to wave at me as I was working in the Herbar — he was driving you into Monmouth in the motor and your head craned round as the car lurched past and you lifted your hand, then half retracted it, converting the gesture into an adjustment of your hair. You were wearing grey gloves that buttoned at the wrist and your face was lost in the reflections on the window. You were becoming a blur to me in any case: if I tried to picture you I couldn't, but if I didn't try, occasionally I saw you at the periphery of my vision as if you were on your way somewhere: the flick of your skirt, the sense of onward motion, sometimes it was not much more than the intuition of colour in the air.

Being without you was familiar territory; I thought I'd got the measure of it long ago. Yet I missed being able to tell you things: when a tidal wave filled the moat at the Tower of London, I wanted you to know; I wanted to hear what you thought about Amy Johnson flying all the way to Australia; when *The Times* started publishing a crossword, I wanted to do it with you instead of with Brown; I was sick of hearing Ted's views when the number of jobless hit two million and the government cut unemployment benefit — I wanted to know what you thought, sitting on the deck of your cruise ship, or on your hotel balcony, or in your cocktail bar; I wanted to hear your justification; I wanted you to see the hunger marchers; I wanted to hear how you would vote now that women had been granted suffrage; I wanted to give you a copy of the *Oxford English Dictionary* which took forty-nine years to complete, full of all the words and words and words I'd never say to you; I wanted not to be bitter; I wanted you, Ella, it was how I lived my life.

I met her at the Booklovers' Library run by Boots the Chemists; she was an assistant there and she noticed I was reading Walter Scott. She asked if I had come across Hugh Walpole and when I said no, she suggested that I try *Farthing Hall*. She went and found it for me.

"I think you'll like it," she said, stamping the date in the front of it then handing it to me, and I was struck by the fact that she had formed an opinion about my tastes. I glanced at her with a tic of curiosity, but she was already serving someone else.

After that, she put me on to Galsworthy and I raced to the library late in the afternoon, straight from work, to return the book before it was overdue. I borrowed the second volume of *The Forsyte Saga* and was the last to leave and as she was locking up she asked me if I ever read any verse. "Try Masefield," she said and the thought of talking to someone who liked poetry made me set aside the weight that I was carrying for a moment and I felt a small sweep of relief pass through me: the claustral tightness in my chest — the clench of missing you — felt looser.

I berated myself afterwards. You were my every point of reference, my distant star. I felt that I deserved every day of your absence. I didn't return to the library for several weeks and I had to pay a thrupenny fine.

When I did go back, she had put the collected works of Rupert Brooke on the reserve shelf for me, "But perhaps you're fed up with anything to do with the war?"

I shook my head and then I nodded and the smile she gave me was a kind of balm and I was sore and susceptible.

"Did you…? Did you lose a loved one?"

"We lost my father and my elder brother."

"Then Brooke is the best medicine," she said.

I looked at her for the first time, properly: her knot of dark hair; the way her short-sightedness tightened the muscles around her eyes, making her seem interested and intent; the deprecating tilt of her head. There was a reserve about her, a diffidence which summoned something inside me. "Did you?"

She scrutinised the spine of the book, running her thumb along it as though testing the quality of the binding. "My cousin."

A queue was forming behind me. "Would you like to have a cup of tea?" I said, thinking the law of cure dictates that pain heals pain, "After work, perhaps? One day this week? Or not?"

She appeared to be uncertain, as though she wanted to, but wasn't sure. She opened the book and stamped it. "Read the one about the busy heart," she said, and gave a shy nod. "Yes please," she added, "I think I would."

We went to the Kardomah Café and talked about the books we liked and whether Jane Austen or Charlotte Brontë was the better writer, although she thought that George Eliot trounced them both and I've always been a Hardy man. I found talking to her easy. There was no freight, no undertow; just chat. The coffee machine blared in the background and the windows steamed up and she made patterns in the sugar with her teaspoon and the ordinariness of it was sweet and unexpected.

We went for a walk on Sunday across the hills surrounding Nanagalan, skirting the edge of the estate.

"Wet strong plough lands, scarred for certain grain," she observed, her hands on her hips as we paused to catch our breath, gazing down at the corrugations of the field below. It was from the poem that she recommended.

"The Busy Heart?" I said, so she would know that I had read it.

The two of us stood there, the path of Offa's Dyke discernible, fingertips of wind combing the meadows as cloud shadows played different greens against each other. It was a moment of shared solitude, new to me; I only knew the kind of loneliness you couldn't share.

"Have you ever had a girlfriend?" she asked, putting up a hand to shade her eyes, still looking at the view.

In love with you for as long as I could remember, I didn't know how to answer. "Not really," I said in the end, recoiling inside, my words a painful truth and the better part of a lie, "I've — no." Then, in a scrupulous attempt at honesty, I added, "I've never kissed anybody."

"I walked out with someone for a while," she said and her hand dropped to her side, and I wondered what other hand had held it and, briefly, how it would feel to take it, to slip her fingers between mine. "His father was laid off after the crash and the family moved away to find more work."

"Then we're both of us walking wounded," I said, turning to look at the route ahead, where the path snaked off into an alley of brambles and alder.

"Well, you're not," she pointed out. "And I'm not, really. It was a long time ago."

I smiled: a smile of several syllables — defensive, awkward, solicitous, and I remembered another line from that poem. "I have need to busy my heart with quietude," I said haltingly and it was she who slipped her hand into mine and we walked on like that, the two of us, our grip hesitant and unpractised.

She courted me with books and I read to be obliterated, plunging myself into any narrative other than my own which so confounded me. When I wasn't reading, I let the stories take root inside my head, so when I was out in the gardens, picking apples in the orchard, cleaning the press, digging over, pricking out, I was living other people's lives and it helped me, in some small measure, not to think of you. But in the cold sting of a winter's morning leaning on my spade, or in the evaporating heat of a summer's afternoon when I stopped to wipe my face, you seemed so close to me I could have reached out and caught you by the sleeve to stop you leaving once again.

Ma found out from Mrs Parry, who spotted us holding hands together in Monmouth on Jenny's half day.

"What's this I hear?" she said. "About to you and a certain young lady?"

It was a Sunday morning and we were walking along Front Street on our way to chapel. I blushed to the roots of my hair. "We're just," I began, "I mean, we're only —"

I had never seen my old Ma being arch before. "Will you be bringing her home to meet me?" she asked with a sideways glance.

"Of course, I was going to," I stammered, and a train of events that I hadn't begun to consider was set in motion.

I did take Jenny home to meet her: tea and bake stone cakes taken in the parlour and when I returned from walking her home, my mother darted out from the kitchen before I could make it to my room.

"Is she the one, then?" she asked. I made a study of her tremulous face, seeing all the small erosions of the life she had lived worked into it, the weathering of the steam from the laundry and the weathering of loss, too.

My gaze flickered. I remembered you sitting beside me on the wall of the well before you went away, all salty with the smoke from the bonfire. I remembered you telling me that you would have feelings for me if … "I — haven't asked her."

"You will though, won't you?"

"Ma, what if —?" I began. What if things were different? What if you were here? What if I, if I…?

"Well?"

Love, in the conditional tense.

"She'll be the making of you, Ifor. All that learning — you like that kind of thing, don't you? And she's a local girl, what's more."

I knew the fact that Ted lived in Mynydd Maen more than twenty miles away preyed upon her; it was as good as abroad as far as she was concerned. He and Delyth were still saving to get married: the longest engagement in the history of the world and Ma was dreading the day. I glanced at her again, and the loss of Glyn's promise hung in the air between us. She seemed to swell with the waiting, her breath held. I bowed my head.

Events took on a momentum of their own, after that: the chapel and the April morning and the cherry blossom splashed against the sky. I proposed to Jenny and in the moment that I asked, I loved her. I loved her gravity, her integrity, her simplicity; I loved the fact that she loved me without any ifs. We were married without any fuss, though anything she set her heart on I would have given her. Perhaps she knew my largesse had a taint to it. I was attentive, I was kindly, and I tried to anticipate her wants and needs.

There were times when I felt her eyes upon me, her earnest and myopic gaze, and once she asked me straight, "This is what you want, isn't it, Ifor? All of this?"

We were at Ma's, where we would be living after the wedding. Jenny spent most of her free time there already. I looked blankly round the parlour. "This," she said, clasping her hands and then, when I was slow to respond. "Us."

"It's what I need," I said, taking care to speak the truths I could to her and she stood there, rubbing at her palm as though the texture of her own skin was of absorbing interest.

"As long as it is," she whispered and with a horrible awareness of what it feels like to be second best I reached out and held her, burying my face in her black hair.

She and her mother made her dress, a sensible cream wool shift with a coat to match which would do for later on as well. I gathered the flowers for her bouquet myself: narcissi, white tulips, ranunculus and some tiny, early lily of the valley I found beneath a hedgerow on the edge of Dancing Green. Delyth tied them up with a piece of lace into the prettiest bunch that a girl could wish for. Mrs Brown made our wedding cake, her lips pursed knowingly, and Samuelson gave us a bottle of Nanagalan Blanc de Blanc 1930 to drink the toast at our wedding breakfast.

The night before, Brown took me out for a drink at the Fleece in Morwithy. A few lads were playing shove ha'penny at the far end of the bar and somebody's lurcher was stretched out by the fire, keeping watch. We found a table by the window and Brown squeezed into his seat, carrying two pints of cider and some pork scratchings.

"It's not too late to change your mind," he said without beating about the bush, setting the glass down on the mat in front of me. "If your heart's not in it." He took a swig of cider and smoothed the ends of his moustache with his finger and thumb, then added with feeling, "I'm saying this as a married man myself."

I didn't know how to answer him. He was opening the packet of pork scratchings, shaking them out for us to share, his face set with the unbreachable stoicism that the older generation had made its own. He looked over at me, his gaze probing and I suddenly understood that he knew more about my secret life than I thought I knew of his and I was mortified to think that I had contrived to keep from him knowledge of Mrs Brown and Samuelson, never mind the rest of it, when there was nothing that he hadn't seen or guessed or suffered. I was a green lad indeed, with my heart waving about on my sleeve for all to see. I could feel myself turning a painful shade of red.

A bead of condensation trickled down my glass. At the far end of the bar somebody whacked a halfpenny right off the board and it spun in circles on the flagstones until it came to rest. There was a scrabble to retrieve it. The lurcher yawned and worked its jaw.

"Have one of these," said Brown, more kindly, nudging the packet of pork scratchings in my direction. I helped myself to one, politely; it had a single orange bristle protruding through the rind.

"I'll break my teeth on this," I said, starting to chew. "I'll be at the dentist's tomorrow, not the chapel."

Brown sipped his drink. "You might think," he said, "that hearts and loaves are one and the same, with a half being better than none at all."

I swallowed. I picked up my glass, slippery with condensation and some of the cider splashed on to the table. I was about to wipe it with my sleeve, but he rummaged in his pocket and produced a handkerchief.

"But you'd be wrong. Half a heart isn't enough for anyone to live on, not properly, not in the long run." He regarded me steadily and I stopped dabbing at the table and gave the handkerchief back to him. He stowed it away in his pocket. "I know what I'm talking about."

"I'm very fond of Jenny," I began, but he shook his head vigorously as though I ought to know better.

"Fond doesn't begin to cover all those promises you're about to make: for better, for worse, in sickness and in health. It doesn't come close." He drank several gulps from his glass and wiped his mouth. "Fond isn't worth the paper that it's written on, if you want my opinion."

"I love her, in my own way, and I'll be a good husband," I said. "I've made up my mind. I will."

"Ifor —" he exclaimed. "If you were my boy, I'd —" He tailed off and fell to looking out of the window with its blackened metal frame and its thickened glass and its bleary view of the street beyond, his eyes hooded and remote. "If you were my boy..." he said again, more benevolently this time; wistfully, almost. He reached across the table and held his hand out to me gruffly and I laid mine in his for a second or two.

"You be sure that you are a good husband," he said, giving my hand a shake. We picked up our glasses with faint embarrassment, then drank our cider and nothing more was said.

I remembered the photographs more than the day itself; the proof that I had married Jenny there in black and white. The images seemed to overlay my memory, reducing our wedding to a series of snapshots: the confetti captured as it fluttered through the air, Jenny flinging her flowers towards Delyth so that she would be the next to marry, the way our families flanked us in the formal pictures, not just witnesses but reinforcements.

I was vehement in the taking of my vows and Jenny's eyes were round with hope and I could feel her sensible presence soften beside me as I said them. I knew that I could honour her and I wanted to believe that all the rest would follow. I made my heart hard to any thought of you: you were not present. That was my relief and all my sadness too.

I remembered how I loved her on our wedding night, in bewilderment and release; and how I held her afterwards, filled with anguish. When she turned to me the following night, her face uplifted and her eyes closed, I placed my mouth against her parted lips and neither of us moved.

"I'm sorry," I said, "I'm a bit tired, if that's all right. After yesterday. The excitement…"

The following Saturday night we lay side by side, not quite certain how to reach across and touch each other. "I do love you, Ifor," my wife whispered. "You know that, don't you?"

I took a stabbing little breath, bracing myself to answer her, but the words wouldn't come. I leaned up on one elbow, trying to discern her features, the night dark and diplomatic around us. I wanted to be gentle. I was conscious of all the harm that I could do to her. "You're the best girl," I answered and I rested my head on her shoulder. "And I'm a lucky man." The cotton of her nightdress creased against my skin and she held me in her arms, uncomprehendingly.

In my bones I knew that if we didn't have relations the following weekend, then we probably never would again: the journey back would be beyond us. Saturday night was bath night and the four of us took turns in the zinc tub in front of the range: Ma first, then Jenny, then Delyth, then me. After my bath, wrapped in a towel, I climbed the stairs. I was still glowing from my scrubbing in the tub as I closed our bedroom door behind me. A single candle stood lighted on the chest of drawers, scattering indolent, gauzy shadows across the room. Jenny was sitting on the bed in her dressing gown, brushing her hair with meticulous strokes, counting the numbers defensively under her breath, "Eighty-four, eighty-five…"

"Let me do that," I said, reaching to take the brush from her.

"You're meant to do a hundred, morning and night."

"I'll do two hundred, if you want."

She darted a glance at me, as if she wasn't sure that she had heard me right. "Though it's probably some old wives' tale…"

I started brushing, her thick hair black as an oil slick spilling through my fingers.

"Eighty-seven … eighty-eight … eighty-…" her counting tailed off, but I kept brushing.

"It's the first thing I noticed about you, your hair," I skeined the soft rope through my fingers until I had made a coil of it, a little hesitantly. "What's a young wives' tale, then?" I asked.

She tipped her head back; in the half-light shed by the candle I studied her inverted features, the topography upset and strange. I kissed her chin, upside-down, and waited.

"A young wives' tale," she whispered, sliding her arms around my neck, "involves a man and a woman, and a warm night, and a dark room, and a soft bed." She released me, standing up and twisting round to face me and we stood for a moment, alert to each other, primed yet unmoving. "And a dressing gown that slips open, just like this; and a towel which falls…" We were guarded in our nakedness, our innocence pretty much intact in spite of our wedding night. "Touch me," she whispered. Cautiously, I ran my finger down her forearm and she circled my wrist and drew me close. "Kiss me."

I felt a terrible sorrow for Jenny; and guilt, as well. My thing was limp with it. I hadn't thought that it would be like this. I hadn't thought — that was the truth of it, because I had no experience to frame the complication of it all. I wrapped my arms around my tentative, supplicating wife, who shouldn't have to ask for love. She sought my mouth and desperate for the scent of gardenia, I closed my eyes.

I kissed her lips, but it was you I tasted, Ella: my tongue travelled the slow escarpment of your throat, following the swell and curve of you, of you, of you. I lowered you onto the bed and lay beside you, coursing the length of you: nape, nipple, spine, hip. I covered you with my longing. Your thighs, your bush, my cock: the annihilating tangle of you and me.

Afterwards, the candle extinguished, I lay stretched out on my back staring up at the ceiling, moonlight mapping the cracks in the plaster. For a long time I studied the fine, illuminated fault lines, conscious of Jenny lying beside me, her black hair in straggling disorder over the pillow. All that brushing, I thought, all that brushing. I listened to the sound of her breathing, its intimate tempo so private, so vulnerable. I shifted my head so I could see her. Her face had lost its intentness, her myopia hidden behind closed lids, her skin a drowsy, new-born pink.

I couldn't sleep, for the shock and the shame at what I'd done. This wasn't how it was meant to be. It was my first, hard lesson in infidelity, and I was unsure whom I had betrayed the most: you, or Jenny, or myself.

Chapter Eleven

I remembered the day Brown told me the family was returning. "For good," he said, and I could hear the reproof in his voice, the almost indiscernible note of accusation. "It's official."

Germany had just walked out of the World Disarmament Conference and Jenny had brought back from work a copy of the bestseller that everyone was talking about, *Brave New World* and all at once the world seemed neither brave nor new. I swallowed.

"Just so you know," said Brown.

I didn't go straight home after work. I made my way up to Long Leap, the ground loamy with fallen leaves beneath my feet and autumn streamers strung out from tree to tree as though to welcome you. I found a cool lip of granite to sit down on and stayed there, staring back along the valley the way that I had come, not seeing the winding path or the downward flight of the slope. The darkness settled around me and the cold from the rock I was sitting on entered my bones and I could just pick out the pale outline of Nanagalan and the gardens, all expectant, and I kept my vigil.

I trimmed the creeper on the old wing of the house for three days in a row and you didn't seek me out. I asked Samuelson if I could give Dancing Green its final cut of the year, a task he normally reserved for himself because it provided easy evidence of work done while requiring less effort than say, digging, which was my job. He shrugged and rolled his eyes, though he always wanted me out from under his feet.

I razored perfect stripes into the lawn and lost myself in the green rhythm of the back and forth, until I looked up and saw you standing by the morning room window. Your hair was cut short, something I hadn't prepared myself for, and you looked straight through me so that I knew that you knew. Your hair was cut short and I couldn't quite believe that you'd come home.

Your mother brought oranges and grapefruits back from Spain, your final port of call apparently, and gave one to every family on the estate as a Christmas box. Our orange still had leaves on it and it was wrapped in tissue stamped with a coloured picture of a tree in a landscape which could have come from a Bible story.

"You have it," Ma offered, handing the fruit, rare and beautiful, to Jenny. "It'll be good for you," she said meaningfully, impatient for signs of a baby, a new little Griffiths to dandle: a tiny Glyn, preferably; or an Angharad, perhaps. She smoothed the tissue with her elbow until it was flat, and then put it by to keep. "That'll come in handy, sometime," she said. "Everything does," while Jenny watched her, levelly.

It was a staff Christmas party with a difference that year. The King was to make his first broadcast to the nation at three o'clock on Christmas afternoon, a time convenient for the far corners of the Empire. Ted came over for dinner and we stuffed ourselves on roast chicken and a plum pudding with all the trimmings; Ma did us proud. Delyth was civil to Jenny, putting the resentment she felt at her married status to one side for the occasion: Jenny had everything my sister wanted — a respectable job and a husband, though she wouldn't have envied her that, if she had known. They took an artificial interest in each other's doings while Ma looked on with anxious encouragement and Ted and I talked politics.

We walked from the village to Nanagalan, the vicar and one of the tenant farmers falling into step beside us. Ted was sounding off about the fact that a tiny percentage of the population owned a vast proportion of the country's wealth, most of it unearned and in the end the vicar quickened his pace so that he arrived several minutes before us. I wasn't listening. I was concentrating with all my might on the feel of Jenny's hand in mine, holding it as a reminder: I will be a good husband, holding it like a talisman.

It was the custom for the family to wait upon their tenants and employees and you were standing on the threshold to welcome us, with a cool poise I didn't recognise. You had … deportment, with your pale yellow dress of continental jacquard silk and your endless string of pearls, your bobbed hair, your neck which, now that I saw it, took my breath away. Ma and Delyth and Ted, who was still talking about class warfare, went in first and I stood stock still on the path, looking back at the plants in the Herbar crimped and folded up for winter, as though I had forgotten something, as though I might just have to leave, because —

"Hello, Ifor."

I turned to face you and you held out your hand with a spontaneous politeness that someone had taught you, not the quizzical impulsiveness I used to know. I took it as though it would burn me and shook it, conscious of every slant and tilt and shadow in your face. You smelled of gardenia, still, and the scent of it cut me to the quick.

You turned to Jenny without a flicker, "And this must be … Mrs Ifor," you said with your head on one side, the blue blade of your gaze unsheathed.

125

"Jenny," I said, seeking her hand and holding it, "Jenny Griffiths, my —" I held her hand for dear life, while you waited for me to say it and I couldn't.

You pointed languidly across the hall. "Tea will be served in the drawing room."

We perched on upholstered antique chairs and grappled with bone china so thin it let the light through, us rude mechanicals making conversation with each other as though we were strangers meeting for the first time: What did you get for Christmas? An apron? That's nice. What do you think the King will have to say? Your mother served us mince pies not much bigger than my thumbnail and Jenny eyed hers disdainfully.

"I'm on Ted's side," she said in a low voice.

"They're not so bad, when you get —" I broke off.

"To know them?"

I didn't answer. At a signal from your mother, you crossed to the table radiogram and switched it on.

"That'll be a Marconi 42," Brown said confidently. "It shares a chassis with the HMV 501." Samuelson was picking mincemeat from his teeth.

The vicar rose to his feet and cottoning on, we all stood too.

"It wouldn't be respectful for the likes of us to be sitting while the King is talking," Ma said approvingly, folding her hands in readiness.

Then, out of the ether, as if by magic, "I speak now from my home and from my heart to you all; to men and women so cut off by the snows, the desert or the sea, that only voices out of the air can reach them…"

"Rudyard Kipling wrote the words for him," Jenny murmured. "They're not his own." I glanced down at her and gave her a smile, a proper one. I wanted to be tender with her. I wanted it to be alright. I looked the length of the room. I often thought of you standing in doorways, staying and going all at once, and there you were, leaning against the frame, while hanging above your head was a bunch of mistletoe tied with a Christmas ribbon.

Men and women, I thought. So cut off...

I remembered the first snow that winter, the valley revealing itself differently, as if it had rolled over in the night exposing the whiteness of its underside. I fetched a spade to clear a path through the Herbar to the front door and I shovelled a few yards then I glanced up and for a moment I was so enchanted by the shapeliness of the landscape, the drifts forming in soft curves, that I couldn't help myself, the boy in me took a hold and I threw my spade to one side without thinking and fell backwards into the snow.

Barbs of ice penetrated between the neck of my coat and my skin and I shuddered with the wonder of it: the torn veil of my breath against the blue sky. I started laughing and I couldn't stop, swooping my arms and legs up and down, making angels' wings so that I didn't hear your footsteps until you were almost on top of me.

"Miss Ella —" I stopped mid-swoop and the narrow ridge of snow that I'd been carving toppled down onto me and you laughed too, and you leaned over without thinking, with your hand outstretched to haul me to my feet, before your laughter died. You tucked your hand into your pocket. You were wearing jodhpurs and boots and a short fur jacket with an enormous collar pulled up right over your ears and there were flakes of snow like gypsophila in your hair. Distracted, I watched a single petal of it melt, then came to, and began to clamber to my feet.

"I was clearing the path —"

"On your back? Very novel."

"It's difficult to resist, miss. Don't you think?"

You turned to regard the cleft of the valley, widening to meet the scattering of clouds on the distant hills. "You're covered in snow," you said, glancing at me and you flicked at my shoulder, hesitating a moment, then brushing again with a longer, more proprietorial sweep. I thought of the thinness of your leather glove, the protection it afforded.

"Will you walk with me?"

"What about the path?" I said, eyeing the spade.

"You can clear the way for me," you said. "I'll go mad if I have to stay cooped up in the house all day."

I nodded, and neither of us moved. "Where do you want to go? To the village?"

You shook your head.

"Or —?"

"Not the village, no."

"You'll get cold, standing here like this…"

"Why don't we walk to Withy End?"

"That's miles —" I looked at the spade and the obliterated path again, feeling uneasy.

"I'll settle it with Samuelson," you said carelessly.

I hunched into my coat. I could feel the chill in the material from where I had been lying down. "Alright then." We stood facing one another, measuring what we saw against what we remembered.

"You haven't changed," you said.

"Oh, but I have —"

"Not really. Not like me…"

"You've had your hair cut."

You gave a funny, rueful smile, tugging at a strand of it, twining it round. "Yes," you said. "Yes, I have."

"My feet are blocks of ice," I said, after a beat or two. "Shall we get going?"

We set off, half-wading, half-climbing through the submerged nut tunnel, which had icicles hanging from its twisted branches. I went first, tamping down the snow for you and you followed in my footsteps until we reached the unmarked passage through the wildflower meadow. You stopped and looked back at the house and gave a little shiver.

"Are you cold?" I said, fearing you were tired already, or that you'd changed your mind.

"No. Keep going."

On we went until we reached a row of silver birches on the fringes of the tree line. We were panting with the effort and I paused beneath the nearest one to catch my breath. "How have you changed?" I asked, staring at the peeling lesions in the whitened bark.

"I think silver birches are my favourite tree," you said, leaning against the trunk of one a few feet further off. You stripped off your gloves and slipped your cigarette case and lighter from a pocket in your jacket. "Do you want one?"

I shook my head, but I took one and put it in my mouth and lit it for you. "There," I said, handing it to you, wondering if you still smoked with the same ferocious speed.

You stood there, one foot against the tree, your knee bent, drawing on your cigarette. A dusting of snow fell from a high twig as you exhaled, mingling with the smoke. "Someone I was … fond of … got married," you said lightly, "while I was away." You smiled one of your learnt smiles with its finishing school veneer. "I think perhaps that changed … something."

My pulse was hammering and I stared intently at the lipstick traces on the cork tip of your cigarette until I was the master of myself. I thought of what Brown said, about fond not being worth the paper it was written on. Not this fond, though. I'm lost, I thought. I'm lost, and I turned to you, ready to —

"She seems very nice, your wife," you said, taking a last drag and throwing your cigarette into the snow. There was a sharp hiss and then silence as it was extinguished, a silence that extended around us, accumulating into drifts.

"She's a gentle soul," I said, in the end.

"Yes…" It was a single word, but it covered all that we had spoken and had not spoken. It was a pitiful word. A bitter little word.

We stood looking at one another, taut with stilled momentum. I would have given anything to have taken you in my arms. Steeling myself, I ducked my head, glancing out from beneath the trees to the top of the ridge. "Weather's drawing in," I said quietly.

"It is, isn't it?" You didn't move. You took a breath to say something else and then thought better of it. Instead, you put one of your gloves back on and then the other, slipping the leather into place a finger at a time and it burned me to be watching you. "If I'd known that you would…" you said in a whisper so soft I wasn't sure I'd heard you right.

"Ella —?"

You lifted you face to look at me and you held my gaze and you held it and held it. Then in that same thin breath of a voice you said sadly, "It's Miss Ella, to you," so that I knew you were reminding me of the paraffin stove and the dust in the air from the sacking and the first sight we had of one another, and of the way it must be.

The thaw set in some time after that, coming home one evening when work was done, heeling my way out of my boots by the back door and washing my hands and face and neck under the tap in the kitchen, and then towelling myself dry.

"Where's Jenny?" I asked Ma, who was sitting by the kitchen table darning in the drone of yellow light shed by the gas lamp in the bracket overhead. I was still smarting from the cold water and gave my head and shoulders an extra rub.

Ma placed the mending in her lap. It was an old jumper of Ted's, gone through at the elbows. She took her time tucking the needle into the wool for safe keeping. "Upstairs," she said, pulling the sleeve tight, then angling it this way and that to inspect her work. "It's almost too far gone to rescue," she sighed. "I don't think this darn's going to hold. It might need patching."

"Ma?" I was halfway to hanging the towel back on the hook under the sink. I hesitated and then straightened up, still holding it. I folded it in half, then in half again. "What do you do when someone's…" I said, not quite knowing where to start. "I don't think Jenny's very…" I sat down in the chair opposite her, tired after a hard day. I was still holding the towel and I set it down so that the hem lay with the grain of the wood, giving myself time to think, "The thing is, I'm not sure I know how to make her happy." I glanced at her. She was still examining the darning, tilting it so that the needle caught the light. For a moment I watched the flash and glint of it. "I don't seem to be able to."

She regarded me with an unvarnished look, critical and astute, "Well, perhaps it's time you had a home of your own," she paused. "And a family of your own —"

"We're saving. As soon as we've —"

"That's what women want, most of them. It's only natural."

That wasn't the whole story, I knew. "I'm worried that she's … disappointed," I began, wary of my own disclosure, as if saying something might make it so. "That this isn't what she —"

"There's always the expectation. And then there's the reality. It takes a bit of time to make sense of how they fit together."

"I think I'm not what she —" I blurted the words out, as near to a confession as I could manage, when what I should have said was, "She's not what I —"

Ma cast the darning to one side, then rose from the table, picked up the towel and hung it on the hook, as though to have it out of place upset her sense of order. "It's early days," she said.

"Yes," I echoed, "It's early days."

Sitting down again, she retrieved Ted's jumper, then slid the needle out of the wool and resumed her mending. "These things have to be worked at," she remarked. "They don't happen by themselves."

"What was it like, with you — and Dad?"

She didn't look up from her work, not for a moment. "I always knew he wanted to be with me, more than anyone else."

Her face didn't soften into sentimental reflection, but the set of it shifted slightly. She worked her needle through the yarn and pulled it tight, worked it through and pulled it tight, so that for a second I could see the on-going acceptance of loss, the continuum of grief in action.

"We always talked. We spent what time we could together. He was my —" she was running out of wool, she tied it off and snipped it with her sewing scissors. "He was my first thing in the morning and my last thing at night." She gave the smallest shrug, hesitating before she placed the scissors in her sewing basket. "There," she said. She reached across and kneaded my upper arm with distracted affection, as though testing the fibre of me. "Talk to her. Spend some time with her. Take her out. Have some fun."

I thought for a bit, casting around for something to suggest. "I could take her to the pictures. Do you think she'd like that? Next week, maybe?"

"Ask her, not me," said Ma, shaking her head as though I hadn't understood a single thing that she'd been saying to me. I nodded and headed for the stairs.

On the landing I hesitated. The bedroom door was closed and so I tapped on it, feeling uncomfortably like a visitor in my own home. I hovered and when she didn't answer, I opened it and slipped inside. Jenny was sitting in the rocking chair in the corner of the room with her arms wrapped around her in a kind of solitary embrace. There was a book lying on her knee.

"Jenny?"

She turned her face a degree away from me, staring through the undrawn curtains at the encroaching night. I sat on the corner of the bed. After a moment, I rested my hand on her dress and she tensed, so I lifted some of the weight of it to be gentle, but I didn't move it away.

"Jenny?"

I looked from one wall of the room to another, at the maps I'd pasted up there, following a single road as it looped from hill to wood, wondering where she and I would find ourselves. I glanced down at the book discarded on her lap.

"Hugh Walpole?" I said, picking it up. "That's where it all began, with you and me. Hugh Walpole..." I turned it over. It was called *Wintersmoon*.

"Read it," Jenny said in a stifled voice. "I'd recommend you read the opening paragraph."

I crouched forward to be closer to her and wanting to be conciliatory, I turned to the first page.

"A fortnight ago you asked me to marry you. You said you weren't in love with me but that you liked and respected me, that you thought we would get on well together."

I closed the book very, very carefully.

"That's us," she said, and she began rocking to and fro in the chair, soothing herself, soothing herself. "That's you and me, isn't it?"

I stared at the cover: it was made of woven cloth and had a paper label.

"Don't tell me that you like and respect me. Please don't do that."

I knelt beside her. "Until I met you I was always..." I hesitated for a long, long moment, "The one who wasn't..." Like a penitent I bowed my head. "Nobody has ever loved me like you do," I said, haltingly. "And that's a fact."

"Oh, Ifor." She wiped her face on her sleeve although there was no sign that she was crying. She looked small and crestfallen.

Cautiously, I rested my forehead against hers and we leaned together with lowered eyes. "I mean to care for you and make a good life for us and to be a proper husband."

"You once said that you were walking wounded," she whispered. "I didn't think much of it, at the time." I put my arms around her, the jumble of her elbows between us. She picked at a button on my shirt. "Who wounded you?" she asked.

"Oh, Jenny," I said, the two of us rocking imperceptibly for comfort, trying to find a common heartbeat. "It was a nothing, a stupid dream — nothing. Nobody wounded me." She buried her head in my shoulder and I stroked her hair. "I wounded myself."

"Will we be alright, do you think? You and me?"

I cupped her face in my hands and read the sorrow there as if it were a poem she had found for me, the way she used to do when we were courting; all the verses of her sad uncertainty. "We must love each other," I said and I kissed her mouth. "Then everything will be fine."

After that, I remember standing in the queue outside the New Picture House in Monmouth eating cod and chips wrapped in newspaper. Jenny and I had one portion between us and took turns holding it to warm our hands and Jenny said her mother disapproved of eating in the street and I said mine did too and it became a small transgression for us to share. There was fat and newsprint on our fingers and both of us breathed the same steamy, greasy air. Jenny said she rather wished she'd had a pickled egg as well and I offered to go back and get her one if she kept my place, but she caught me by the coat.

"Ifor —?" She was wearing my old navy scarf and a knitted blue cloche hat on her head and peeping out between the two, her face had an affirmative, look at us enjoying ourselves expression, drawing attention to the fact, using it in evidence.

"I'll get you an egg, if you want," I said.

She shook her head.

"You finish the chips then…" The queue advanced a few paces and I put my arm around her to shepherd her forward and she curled against me.

"We'll share them…" She found the fattest chip left and held it up to my mouth and as I was taking it between my teeth I heard the familiar, intermittent sound of the Daimler, Brown declutching to change gear as he pointed it in the general direction of the kerb. It came to a halt a few feet from us and he bustled round to open the door, holding it for you as you stepped out onto the pavement.

I bit into the chip, then chewed and swallowed it. You swept by in evening dress, some kind of velvet cape not designed with warmth in mind, held in place by a brooch in the shape of a jaguar picked out in diamonds. It looked like a jaguar, but with inexplicable agitation I wondered if it might be a leopard, or some other big cat and I was so intent on resolving the matter to my own satisfaction that I didn't notice the gentleman stepping out behind you until he slid his arm around your waist to guide you past the head of the queue and into the cinema. There was black braid down the side of his trousers and his patent leather shoes had a celestial gleam. I couldn't take in anything else. I closed my eyes, remembering your slightness as I carried you in my arms across the Drowning Pool. I felt skinned alive by what I'd seen.

"What's wrong with queuing, like everyone else?" muttered Jenny.

I blinked. We reached the kiosk at the entrance and I bought our tickets: there were only balcony seats left and I got two in the front row, with only a dim idea of what I was doing or where I was. My head was full of the hurt that you and I had inflicted on one another.

"Ifor?" Jenny tugged at my sleeve.

"I'm just going to the gents," I said. "There's your ticket. I'll see you inside." I reached the foyer wall and leant against it, feeling slightly sick as the patterned carpet shelved away beneath my feet. The people pressing into the auditorium were a series of broken images with no sequence or continuity, a blur of faces, hats, coats, a handbag, a silver-topped cane. I kept seeing the man's arm slide around you and all I wanted to do was to elbow my way through the throng and plough along the rows until I found you. I wanted to rescue you.

I waited, leaning against the wall until my breathing slowed and the moment passed. I could hear the crackle and hum of the audience whispering and unwrapping their chocolates, then the crash of cymbals as the music started. I ran up the stairs to the balcony two at a time and made my way to my seat as the lights were dimmed.

The film was some Noel Coward frippery called *Bitter Sweet*. I watched the opening scene in a stupor, staring at the pleats of cigarette smoke rising in folds above the stalls. At one point Jenny leaned over and murmured in my ear, "Hugh Williams is very handsome," meaning to get a rise from me, but I was scouring the darkness below to see if I could find where you were sitting.

I recollected myself. "I thought the other chap would be more your type," I whispered back and then I spotted you, your outline silvery in the light from the projector. I'd know the shape of you anywhere, even with the cusp of your cheek turned away as it was then. I watched you watching the screen, taking in your small responses: shifting your weight against the armrest then settling further back into your seat, the rueful play of your features as you listened to the song the heroine was singing — something about the world having gone awry. Your face was expressive even in repose, I wanted to interpret every nuance, to be your diviner, your willow witcher.

I'd have taken any kind of proximity, whatever the collateral cost, so I sat in a vigilant, dream-like state, suspended between what I could see of you, what I imagined and all that I remembered. When your companion, whose broad back and sandy, thinning hair I had dismissed as an irrelevance after the shock of the first sighting, inveigled his arm around your shoulders you stiffened, but you didn't pull away, and I glimpsed the incline of your nape in the treacherous shadows, knowing that I was a traitor myself.

Chapter Twelve

I remembered the heat of the summer before the fire struck, how the migrainous sunshine cracked the earth and shrivelled the plants, so that everything seemed to cling: people, places, clothing. The cottage felt far too small for us, though Delyth had set a date for her wedding at last, and each exhalation that we made seemed to add to the sum total of the warmth so that we hardly dared to breathe.

Day after day I worked in the vineyard, carrying a cylinder of copper sulphate solution in a harness loaded onto my back, spraying the grapes to protect against downy mildew, the old house like a mirage shimmering at the top of the slope and the sky above an undeflectable blue. The valley no longer seem to be full of living things, I kept finding small desiccated creatures in the flower borders and under the scanty shade of the brassicas in the vegetable garden: mostly dormice, but once I came across the dried-out punctuation mark of an adder.

We were all of us turned to tinder in the exterminating heat, which sent fissures shooting through people's composure that opened up without warning into ravines of irritation. A whole roster of arguments took place: Ma had a go at Delyth for leaving the tap on or some such nonsense and Delyth had a go at Ma for nagging and sometimes in the evening when I went to Brown's dugout to pick up the paper I could hear Mrs Brown and him tearing each other to shreds, blistering rows they had, and I walked straight past, wondering what was waiting for me at home.

Brown was mightily impressed by hearing the King at Christmas and he set his heart on having his own wireless, although it cost him a good part of his savings. He wouldn't tell me how much exactly, he came over all evasive, but he said it was more than fifteen pounds. Fifteen pounds! Perhaps that's what the rows with Mrs Brown were about.

He went all the way to Cardiff to fetch it and when he got it home he set it up in pride of place bang in the middle of the shelving made from wooden wine crates — his collection of tobacco tins was consigned to a cardboard box on a high ledge to make a space. I went round after work to see it.

"Known as the Dartmoor Special," Brown said. "It's a Murphy A3." Before he got properly into his stride I asked if he would turn it on for me, but he wasn't going to be that easily distracted, "Look at that grille silk now, will you?"

I looked, obligingly.

"Grey — see? Your Ekco wireless uses copper coloured silk, but not your Murphy. More pleasing to the eye, the grey — wouldn't you say?"

I would. I did.

"R. D. Russell design," he said, modestly. He scratched his head as though he couldn't possibly take any credit for the excellence of his choice. "They've recently brought out the Murphy A3A. They've moved the tuning window slightly on the newer model, but I'm rather taken with this one, I must admit."

"Can we have a listen, Mr Brown?"

He turned it on and twisted the dial with such attentiveness you'd have thought he was cracking a safe. The sound came and went amongst the bristling static until, unmistakably, we heard a woman singing. I thought for a moment of the nuns at Nanagalan intoning their plainsong in the olden days and in a way this voice was just as eerie. The song she sang was husky with smoke, a late night song full of whisky and regret and Brown and I were open-mouthed at the wonder of it.

"Elizabeth Welch," he said in awe when it was over, blinking as though coming from darkness into light. The next song she sang was 'Love for Sale' and the two of us sat there nursing our cups of tea imagining ourselves in some Harlem speakeasy. "A bit racy, that one is…" he said after, clearing his throat, concerned for my innocence, my married innocence.

It was a rare evening, sitting rapt in the dugout listening to the strange, spellbinding acoustic of the Murphy A3 and it stuck in my memory because so much of what we heard on the wireless after that was bad news. It seemed that there were other conflagrations breaking out before our fire started. We heard reports that in Germany the Nazis had started burning books only months after Herr Hitler became Chancellor. A book is a terrible thing to burn, all that civilising knowledge destroyed on a whim, and the Jews began fleeing from the encroaching flames like the poor field creatures I kept finding as I worked in the gardens.

I was doing the final spraying about two weeks before the harvest was due and a bumper crop it was, on account of the weather. I saw a young lad working his way down the hillside towards me, a proper dandy in a linen suit with a silk cravat and a handkerchief that matched and I braced myself for the fact that he was probably another of your suitors — there had been one or two, of late — fearing that if I hardened my heart too often it would stay hard, that already, for too much of the time, it felt like a calcified fist in my chest, when I realised that it wasn't a young lad at all: it was you.

"It's my Marlene Dietrich look," you said, dismissively, then you took a little swipe at me because you could. "Nicholas says he likes me in trousers."

I stood there thinking that I wouldn't play a game of parry and thrust where the only aim was to draw blood, I wouldn't play a round of Lucky Nicholas with you. "Looks good," I said. "Takes a bit of getting used to, mind. Thought you were a bloke…"

"How is Mrs Ifor?" you asked sardonically, but I answered your gaze and held it, until your pupils widened and all I could see was the darkness at their centre, none of the oceanic blueness which I loved, and I wondered if your heart was becoming as calcified as mine. "Actually," you glanced away, wanting to ask the question but not to hear the answer, "I came to find you because we've had a call from the fire brigade in Whitecross Street. There's a forest fire on the Crown Estate near Monmouth —"

"I know," I said. "They were talking about it in the village yesterday. Bound to happen. We've had temperatures of ninety degrees or more for weeks now."

"Yes," you said. "Well." You slid your hands into your pockets and for a moment all your sophistication disappeared and dressed up in your strange attire, you looked as young as a girl fresh from school. "They've advised us to dig some fire breaks." You turned and gestured to the wooded slope beyond the Drowning Pool, our ruined cathedral made of beech trees open to the sky. "Along the top. Over there."

I nodded. "How big do they want these fire breaks to be?"

"As wide as you can manage, I suppose?" you said. "Only, Ifor —?"

Our eyes met again and I was disarmed without any warning, doubled up with wanting you. I shifted the weight of the cylinder on my back. Sometimes the desire I felt for you rose like violence from a part of me I didn't much admire, outstripping politeness and respect and all of my good

142

intentions. I gripped the straps of the harness for something to hold, hating everything about the situation we were in, wondering if it was the not-having that made the wanting so unquenchable and whether we should just give in, forget what people would say, forget Jenny and your mother, lose ourselves…

As if sensing the contagion that had a hold of me, you glanced along the row of vines, then at the ground, then at the slope beyond the Drowning Pool; you looked everywhere but at me.

"Don't spend too long on it, will you?" You fiddled with the end of your cravat and the tension was as tight as wire, humming between us. "With the harvest so close I'm sure you've got better things to do with your time," you said and I saw you realise that you had no idea what I did with my time and that the thought was a brief affliction to you, sharp and swift as a paper cut.

"Yes, Miss Ella," I said and then added, because I couldn't help myself, "Who's Nicholas, then?"

You didn't answer, although you considered my question for a moment with the ghost of a smile. "Let me know if you need extra help from the village." You began to walk back up the hill and I unclenched my hands, examining the welts which the strap of the harness had made in the hard skin of my palms, until you were out of sight.

We dug a flat, wide trench through the woodland on the brow of the hill, Brown and I, while Samuelson gave us the benefit of his close supervision. He raked the leaves and twigs into occasional piles and at around three o'clock he sauntered off in search of a tarpaulin to put them in, whistling the while, and Brown didn't alter the pace of his digging by one jot, he kept at it with stoic persistence, just the set of his mouth a little tighter, that was all. An hour later Samuelson came back without the tarpaulin and lugubriously regarded his piles of leaves. With a sigh, he rolled a cigarette, lit it, and then dropped the match on the ground. Brown shouted then, he fairly bellowed at him.

"Samuelson! You stupid — blighter!"

"Keep yer hair on —" Samuelson growled, stamping on the match.

"Can anyone smell — burning?" I interrupted, sniffing the air and Samuelson looked at me witheringly and waved his cigarette under my nose.

"No — not that," I said brushing him away and sniffing again. It was unmistakable: the briny smell of wood alight in the open air.

The first wisp of smoke was like mist rising above the escarpment beyond the Drowning Pool, a vaporous breath lost against the blueness of the sky, and in the course of one long day the mist darkened into something swollen and grey. Too late, we realised we should harvest the grapes and Brown drove to Morwithy to round up anyone who was able to come and help us. Ianto Pryce, Tom Ten Bricks and kindly Gwilym Jones the Ancient came bowling back with him in the Daimler looking as pleased as punch at the ride and before long all of us were busy with the picking bins.

I ran to find Delyth, and Ma came too, and halfway through the morning Mrs Brown hurried down the hill with her sleeves still rolled up and flour smudged into her blouse. "I've made the family sandwiches for lunch. It won't kill them, just this once," and she set to work with a will, speeding up and down the rows of vines stripping the fruit.

The skin on the grapes was taut, the flesh unyielding, but a poor vintage would be better than no vintage at all. It was backbreaking work, the stooping and the reaching, then the carrying of the overflowing crates to the fermentation shed, all of it done in heat which came over us like an ailment robbing us of our strength. I paused for breath at one point and raised my eyes to the plume now rising over the hill from the next valley. There were smuts peppering the air and the feathery remains of one came spiralling down onto my outstretched hand. After that, I started tearing the bunches from the vines, ripping the shoots and tendrils that I had tended so carefully all the summer through.

Mrs Brown had made sandwiches for the workers as well, but none of us stopped to eat. As word got round, more people began trickling down from the village. I caught sight of Jenny carrying several crates full of grapes and Dick the Tick, still in his green apron with his watch mender's torch strapped to his forehead, closed his shop and joined us, bringing Parry the Paint along with him too. I could taste the smoke, resinous and caustic, in my mouth and the heat chafed my skin red raw, but we couldn't stop the race against fire and wind and time.

I looked up at the house, at Nanagalan under siege, the surface tension of its tall windows as glassy as still water. Framed in one of them I could see you and your mother watching in horror as the first flame sidled over the brow of the hill, flicking through the undergrowth, roiling round trunks and lapping at the lowest branches. There were live sparks in the air now, not perished cinders, and as Samuelson gave the order for all the men to leave off picking and form a human chain up through the woods, we heard the bell of the fire engine clanging out the alarm as it came rocketing down the drive towards us.

Captain Thomas was as cool as ice and twice as welcome —
I'll never forget the sight of his huge, slow-moving frame
dismounting from the cab. He led from the front with a kind
of ponderous certainty, suggesting rather than ordering — why
don't you, and it might be an idea to — so that soon his men
had set up a pump in the Drowning Pool and we could begin
to believe that things were under control.

The hose they brought was as thick as a man's wrist and the
water they couldn't pump through it we manhandled in
buckets along our chain to fill the shallow trench that we had
dug the day before. The women left off picking too,
clambering up the slope and forming a line parallel to ours,
passing down the empty buckets to be refilled. With our
woodland turned into a pyre, a black pall hung above us so that
we could hardly tell day from night.

We kept the buckets coming, slopping water everywhere in
our haste and once, when I was temporarily empty handed, I
glanced with impatience down along the line, and there I saw
you: you had seized a pair of filthy overalls from Brown's
workshop and pulled them on although they were far too big
for you, and you were standing in an enormous pair of
wellingtons knee deep in the Drowning Pool taking the empty
buckets, filling them up and passing them on. We flung them
up the line, spilling water, the bark exploding from the
branches high above, scattering shrapnel over us.

Then all at once, I noticed Brown standing white-faced
further down the slope with his eyes pinned open. He
appeared stricken. He was stumbling around in short, jerky
trajectories, every route seemly barred to him; he had his hands
pressed against his ears to block out the barrage, as though
there was shellfire sounding in his head. I wanted to hurry over
to him, but the buckets kept coming and before I could reach

him Gwilym Jones the Ancient left the line and put an arm around him, and the two of them inched their way down through the chaos together. The pump was working flat out with Captain Thomas at the forefront manning the hose, the arc of spray high and hopeless, and without turning or ceasing, he gestured for us to retreat as well.

We went herding into the Drowning Pool like frightened animals, the valley floor a bright savannah all around us and we formed a new line horizontally, soaking the ground with as much water as we could. The flames reached a hundred feet into the air. I craned my neck to see the conflagration, stalled by the towering beauty of it. The heat was enough to flay the skin from your face and I put up my hand to shield myself and some drops of water spattered on to it. Captain Thomas was spraying indefatigably and at first I thought it was a wetting from the hose.

I swung round. Above the house the sky was filled with billows of smoke, but further over in the direction of the village there were different shades of grey shelving into one another, not smoke, oh my God not smoke, but storm clouds: it was rain that I could feel, sweet, absolving drops of rain.

Our deliverance sent us all a little crazy, manic we were, sloshing our buckets everywhere: up at the trees, over the ground, over each other and those of us who didn't have buckets scooped armfuls of water and hurled them all around, and all the while Captain Thomas and his men kept the pump in operation and the hose trained on the fire. The first bolt of lightning ignited, silver against gold, then we heard a cannonade of thunder as the heavens opened, loosing the rain down onto us.

We worked through most of that long night until the rim of the valley was luminous with the approach of dawn. There was no colour left in anything at all and we hardly knew if we were ghosts or survivors walking through the wasteland back towards the house. Jenny found me, somehow, she had been working through the night as well, and all of us trooped into the kitchens lightheaded with exhaustion, except you. Out of the corner of my eye I saw you detach yourself and make your way, forlorn and drooping in Brown's overalls, around to the front door.

Mrs Brown ransacked the kitchen cupboards. There must have been thirty of us crammed around the table and she conjured up thick slices of bread and dripping, tranches of cheese, cold meats, potted shrimps and slabs of bara brith followed by pint pots of tea to finish with. I could have put my head down on the table and slept right there. Captain Thomas levered himself up from the bench and shook the hand of every one of us, thanking us each in turn and after his brigade had taken their leave, the men from the village, Tom, Ianto, Parry, Dick and all the other helpers began to troop in ones and twos towards the door. Jenny was sitting next to me, listing limply, and I put my arm around her shoulder.

"Time to go, old girl…"

We were halfway to our feet when the green baize door was tugged open and you appeared on the threshold, a grimy waif streaked with ash standing unsteadily in your trailing overalls. "Can somebody help me —?" Your eyes had that same shell-shocked look I'd seen on Brown's face as Gwilym Jones the Ancient led him down the hill away from the inferno. "Upstairs —" you stammered, as if you had no idea where such a place might be.

"Show me," I said, jumping to my feet at once, but it was I who led you through the hall of your great house and up your sweeping staircase which divided into separate galleries and you followed in my wake with a docile bewilderment that frightened me almost as much as the fire had done. One of the bedroom doors was open and at the sight of it you burst into tears. I held my breath and looked inside. Your mother lay splayed on the rug in front of the central window, a chair that she had clutched at to save herself toppled over onto her; she was as dead as the valley with the fire burnt out.

I was standing in the rain the day after, the ferny air filled with sulphur, surveying the smouldering remains of the beech wood and the wreckage round the Drowning Pool. The first few rows of vines were scorched black and would have to be cut down to soil level, perhaps we'd lose them altogether, but the trees — our wind snaring, echo sounding, sighing, threshing beech trees! I couldn't take it in. It was like the aftermath of a massacre, the charred skeletons of our dead waiting to be buried.

I was standing there thinking that we'd have to do more than digging in some winter clover to replenish the soil after this, when Samuelson came shambling down the hill towards me, his hands shoved into his pockets and a ferocious scowl on his face. I stared down at the ground. A worm trickled out from the clod my boot was resting on. A nervous refugee, it dangled and coiled in empty space and I cupped my palm to catch it when it dropped, then tossed it into a fold of softer earth. He was huffing and puffing when he reached me, and he fished a pouch of tobacco from his trouser pocket and rolled himself a cigarette.

"The young mistress wants you up at the house," he grunted.

I glanced up the hill at Nanagalan wreathed in the rain and smoke and steam that squalled down the valley, watching as the wind shifted and the house was revealed and then concealed, revealed and concealed, wondering if I would catch a glimpse of you.

Samuelson crooked his body to one side so that he could light his cigarette out of the draught. His veiny face, skin chapped red with a five o'clock shadow bristling through, hardened as he smoked.

"Did she say what she wanted me for?"

He shrugged, contemptuous as ever. "You're the privileged one, though, boy. She's seen the vicar and that fellow from Hammond and Burgess, the family's solicitors, and now she's asking to see you." He glanced sideways at me, a dead-eyed, calculating stare.

"Better go," I said, hesitating. There were questions in that sideways look I didn't want to answer.

He picked a flake of tobacco off his tongue and spat. I left him swaying on the balls of his feet, staring beyond the hillside with his lips ruched up, lost in bitter speculation.

Mrs Brown was dressed from head to toe in mourning, with a jet brooch pinned to her collar, and I wondered what exactly she was grieving for. Piously she told me I'd find you in the little yellow sitting room on the first floor.

"It was Mother's favourite room," you explained when I knocked and entered, as though this was a fresh cause for grief. Your voice was split and raw and there were unspilled tears in your eyes. You were sitting hunched in a chair as if you couldn't get warm, crumpled and distracted, pulling a handkerchief taut between your fingers. The wet material was translucent and I could see the pink of your skin through it.

I reached into my pocket, ready to hand you mine, which was a bit grass-stained, but at least it was dry. I couldn't do it. I didn't know how to give it to you, with your mother gone and everything changed overnight. I cleared my throat and looked around the lofty room instead. The panelling was picked out in cream, and I was thinking that it could have been yellow once — the little yellow sitting room — and I was wondering if there was a blue one and a red one and a green one as well, and whether sitting rooms came in different sizes: large and small, and wishing so badly that you had come to see me in the tool shed or one of the greenhouses, instead of making me come to you.

"It was a heart attack," you said. "What am I going to say to my poor Papa?" You covered your mouth with both hands, "I don't feel very ... capable..." The tears brimmed in your eyes and you stared upwards at the ceiling, so that they wouldn't fall, "Not at the moment..."

I almost went across to you, thinking I might touch your shoulder or hold your hand, or just stand that little bit closer so that you would know — Oh Lord — what you must know, what you must surely know: that I would do anything for you, but you pinched the bridge of your nose, concentrating intently, then you marshalled a smile, a slightly broken one, "I'm perfectly alright, really." You swallowed and then you nodded to convince yourself.

And all the while I stood clutching my dry handkerchief in my pocket, unable to offer you anything, not even that.

"I gave Samuelson the sack this morning," you said. "He's never been any good. I don't know why Mama kept him on for so long. I was wondering if you would take on the responsibilities of Head Gardener for me...?"

On the day of your mother's funeral her death seemed to stand for the death of so much else. All of us were conscious that one door had closed, slammed shut, more like, but it was hard to see where another one might open, though it wasn't for the want of looking.

The smell of burning wouldn't leave our valley: the graphite scent of it was present everywhere, rising up from the hare bells and the musk mallows that clung on, wide-eyed with alarm, in the wildflower meadow. It was in our hair, the folds of our clothing, the seams of our pockets; it seeped from the curtains when we drew them in the evening, it was in our bed linen, our mattresses. It covered us like a shroud.

I made my first purchase as head gardener: a petrol-powered chainsaw. I had to go all the way to Gloucester to fetch it. I would have taken Jenny, but she couldn't get the time off work. I spent the day before your mother's burial out on the hillside facing my own bereavement, ankle deep in ash which foamed like surf, the black trunks of the trees broken lances, defeated cohorts of them. For the whole of that afternoon the chainsaw roared as I lopped off the lowest remaining branches, but it wasn't a job for one man —we'd need ropes and ladders and a cohort of our own.

As I was working, I spotted Brown standing at the top of the slope as straight as a lance himself, his hands hanging by his sides in an attitude of unwavering patience. I called to him and although he appeared to be keeping watch, he didn't seem to notice me. When I looked his way again some twenty minutes later he was rooted to the spot, and then it dawned on me that he wasn't watching, he was waiting, but what he was waiting for, I couldn't tell.

The morning of the internment we were in our best clothes, which rendered us unfamiliar to one another and I was struck by how conventions separate us rather than bringing us together. People talk about observing a period of mourning rather than enduring it and we stood in the courtyard at the side of the big house in isolated clusters, observing each other.

I assumed we were waiting for Samuelson to scuff his way around the corner and then I remembered that he didn't work at Nanagalan any longer. I glanced around our little groupings.

"Is Mr Brown collecting the young mistress…?"

Mrs Brown, depleted by other losses, was staring into nothingness with a listening expression on her face, although I didn't think it was the Daimler she was straining to hear.

"What?" she said, startled.

"Mr Brown —? Is he…"

"Search me," she answered. "Mr Brown's a law unto himself."

Some of your relatives had come down from Scotland and there were two or three cars parked in front of the house waiting for your motor to take its place at the head of the cortege. A few people milled round, entitled and discreetly impatient, glancing up the drive in the direction of the village and fingering their watches. Brown wasn't at the cottage and he wasn't in his dugout and the Daimler was still standing in the garage. I was out of breath from searching and hot in our Glyn's suit. The rain was coming on again. Out of the corner of my eye I saw an orchestration of umbrellas going up. Maybe it was thinking of the downpour, then the fire, but I remembered the solitary figure he cut at the top of the slope while I was working and I raced in the direction of the vineyard.

The sight of him, a lone sentry in his uniform and cap, standing in the same spot, was the first intimation I had that something in the core of him was wrong, something irrevocable and deep.

"Mr Brown —?"

He turned to face me and regarded me as though from an immeasurable distance. "Ifor?" he said with some misgivings, as though this were the last place on earth he expected to see me.

"It's the mistress's funeral," I began. "This morning. Now, in fact…"

With the rain dripping from the brim of his hat he resumed his impassive contemplation of the destruction of the beech wood, as if there was nothing in the world that he could do about the funeral or anything else.

"They need the motor…"

He sighed, bowing his head. I took him by the elbow.

"Come on, Mr Brown."

Although he was stone cold sober, he turned with a drunkard's precision which made me see how careful of himself he needed to be. We made tentative progress past Esther's Garden and into the courtyard: everything was done with slow caution. I hoped the sight of the Daimler gleaming in the garage might bring him back to himself, but I was disappointed.

"Right," I said. "Here we are."

He stood there in a quandary he seemed unable to resolve.

"Mr Brown?"

There was a flurry in the corner of the courtyard and I turned my head and saw you hurrying in our direction, driving the rain before you with your umbrella.

"Ifor," you called. "What's going on? We're going to be late."

"It's alright, Miss Ella," I called back as meaningfully as I could. "We'll be round in a jiffy."

"We're going to be late," you said, hesitating, peering uncertainly at Brown.

"Just give us a moment," I said.

You glanced over at your guests and then at Brown and you nodded. You retraced your steps, looking back at us over your shoulder.

"Let's get out of the rain," I said gently, leading him into the garage. We stopped beside the door on the driver's side. "It's only as far as the village," I said. "Just to the church. That's all."

I didn't want to treat him like a child, but the church was booked and the guests were waiting and I needed to get him into the motor. With infinite sadness he ran his hand across the paintwork almost as if it were the flank of the master's hunter, then he leaned against the door, pressing his forehead against the glass of the window so that his cap fell off. He remained in that position without moving.

Disturbed, I stooped and picked his cap off the garage floor.

"I can't do it anymore," he said, his voice shaking and I stared at him, appalled.

The Brown I knew seemed to have temporarily mislaid himself. I gripped him by the shoulder and straightened him up, dismayed to see my good companion so undone. I didn't care about the funeral. I could see quite plainly that if he didn't drive the motor now, he would never, ever drive it again and then all would be lost.

"You can do it. It's only from Nanagalan to Morwithy." I held onto him with one hand and opened the door with the other. "Two miles, that's all." He regarded me helplessly, as if he would have come to my assistance if only he could. "You can do it. I know you can."

He allowed me to lower him into the seat. Once there, he put his hands upon the steering wheel, though I sensed he was doing it merely to oblige me.

"That's right," I said, placing his cap back on his head. "Hold on now." I took the crank out of its housing beneath the bonnet as I had seen him do so many times and ran round to the front of the car, where I cranked the engine vigorously until it started and then I jumped into the passenger seat beside him.

Brown was staring through the windscreen, his eyes narrowed with the effort of looking so far into the distance, way beyond the courtyard and the Herbar, way beyond Long Leap.

"Let's make a move, shall we?" I suggested with more optimism than I felt.

The thrum of the engine filled the garage. Bleakly, he regarded the steering wheel, tracing the cloudy grain of the walnut from one strut to another. He was sat beside me, but he wasn't there, he was holed up in some redoubt cut off from the line. Rousing himself, he turned to face me; his jaw was working and I saw him clench the muscle hard. He nodded grimly and his hand was trembling as he let out the clutch and we began to inch forward out of the garage and across the courtyard.

The rain was streaming all around us. Painfully, we rounded the corner and came to a halt beside the front door. Everybody sprang into action, shaking their umbrellas and closing them, stepping into their cars. I jumped out and opened the rear door for you, with the smallest shake of my head.

"Don't —" I said. "Don't say anything."

We drove in silence all the way to Morwithy, never moving out of first gear, grinding up the hill to the village with Brown hunched forward over the dashboard, staring straight ahead. When we stopped at the church he slumped back in his seat, then he wiped one hand across his face and closed his eyes.

I remembered the first ever weekly meeting that I had with you. You commandeered the downstairs parlour with views over the copper beech on Dancing Green, facing north so that the light seemed business-like. You set up a gate-leg table on a Persian carpet in the centre of the room. There was a partner's desk under the window and next to it a filing cabinet with a lock. On the opposite wall were two one-inch ordnance survey maps pinned up side by side showing the bounds of all your land, too big for a single sheet. You started calling it the Estate Office and I was tempted to smile, but I think I underestimated you.

I stood there waiting for you that first week, staring at the maps, taken aback by how many of the cottages in Morwithy you owned, including ours. Ma was always going on about setting enough money aside to pay the rent, but it never occurred to me she was paying it to you. As I stood there I became conscious of my boots on the carpet and stepped fastidiously on to the polished floorboards instead, then after a beat I stepped back onto the carpet: "Start how you mean to go on, Ifor," Ma said to me, one of her sayings at the ready, as she waved me off that morning.

I studied the map, examining the contours around Withy End which tightened like a noose as they ascended, and I took some small delight at the thought of coming to see you in your office each Thursday, a limited tenancy which allowed me an hour or two every week, of every month, of every year for as long as I dared to contemplate, in this place, with you. It was a room that offered little, with its austere maroon décor and its polished oak furniture dark with the patina of mourning, but to me on that day of our first meeting, it seemed to promise everything.

I shifted my attention to a large oil painting that showed a brace of inert pheasants, some grapes and oranges and a long clay pipe lying on a sideboard. I studied the faint cracks in the varnish and thought *Still Life* was a strange name for a picture so redolent of death and dying and that Juan Bautista de Espinosa had somehow missed the point, whoever he may be.

"It's ugly, isn't it?" you said, closing the door behind you. "I ought to get rid of it, really."

"Well…" I began, beyond my depth in the field of art appreciation, conscious that you had shut the door and that we were on our own together, in the kind of privacy that was untasted and untested between us.

You were saying something about hanging the picture in one of the bedrooms, "Though it would be unkind to inflict it on some poor guest…" but you tailed off as I ventured a glance in your direction. You looked thinner, dressed in black, your hair slicked close to your head and held in place by a tortoiseshell slide, so that even its golden colour was dulled. "Won't you sit?" you asked, waiting for me to help you into your chair first, which I did, happily, but I couldn't help marvelling that great wealth didn't confer strength upon the privileged; it seemed to make them weaker than the rest of us, it made them oddly dependent.

We sat opposite one another; you leaned your elbow on the table and cupped your chin in your hand, covering your mouth. For a moment we regarded each other in silence, as though working out how we had arrived at this point and now that we were here, what we should do.

"I'm going to need a lad to assist me," I began, for the sake of something to say.

"A gardener's boy? Of course. Do you have anyone in mind?" you answered, and we were safely launched on our way.

"I'll need some extra hands for clearing the hillside, too. Can't do it on my own," I added. "I thought I'd advertise. For the lad. If that's all right with you. Then I can take my pick of all the old men and boys in the county."

"The lost generation," you said with a sigh. I knew what you meant; it was a fact that all of us still lived with after so many years: the war had taken the best of us and the rest of us had to make do.

On the table in front of you was a notepad and pencil. You picked the pencil up and fiddled with it for a moment, then you wrote the date at the top of the page and put it down again. "Well," you said. There was a catch in your voice. Your mother had been dead for less than a fortnight and the grief appeared to come at you like slanting rain from a clear sky. You stared at the sheet of paper, trying to steady yourself.

"Are you alright, Miss Ella?"

This was a question that made your lip tremble until you folded it tight. It was a question you didn't care to answer.

"Miss Ella…?"

I slid my arm across the table, my fingers closed across my palm as though I had captured something small and alive inside. I opened my hand and offered it to you and keeping your head bowed, without looking at me, you took it and held it for a minute. I could have done anything: pressed your fingers to my mouth, touched my lips to the inside of your wrist, or knelt beside you and rested my head in obeisance in your lap.

For sixty seconds we sat in silence, holding hands. You traced the tip of one of your nails across my skin, and then you

159

let me go. I felt the kindle and spark of intimacy still between us and without thinking I reached to capture your hand again, but you lowered your eyes, shaking your head imperceptibly.

"Should we talk … about the replanting of the beech wood?" you said in the end, staring out at Dancing Green, the partial light from the north shining down on you.

"I've been thinking about that," I answered, the static in the air making me prickle all over, "It's the chance to plant a proper arboretum. I was wondering…"

You turned your head and regarded me and it put me completely off my stroke, your gaze saying one thing and your words and actions something else. I swallowed.

"I was wondering if you might discuss it with your father? If you might visit him at the … clinic? He may have some advice to give. No one knows the estate as well as him…" It was the only way I could think of to people your world for you, to make you feel less alone.

"I think he's gone beyond…" you tailed off. "Unless, perhaps, if you came with me…?" you murmured, artlessly studying the sheet of paper with the date of our meeting written at the top. "You might be able to get some sense out of him. I'm not sure that I can."

Afterwards, I told my conscience that all we did was to hold hands for the length of a single minute. I told my heart that it was something more.

Chapter Thirteen

I remembered the day we moved into our new home, Jenny and I. The job of head gardener came with one of the tied cottages in the courtyard at the side of Nanagalan, where our neighbours consisted of you and Mr and Mrs Brown. Samuelson vacated the property leaving behind him sediments we didn't try to identify: limescale, nicotine and tannin were the least of our worries; the privy in the little yard out at the back defied description and I cleaned it myself; I didn't want Jenny to have to face it, I didn't want our life together to start on that particular note. There were two bedrooms upstairs divided by a partition made of faded blond wood, the front one overlooking the courtyard with its clock which chimed, we discovered, on the quarter all through the night, so we moved our things into the back room with views across the kitchen garden and the fields beyond, swerving off down the valley as far as the eye could see.

We spent a week cleaning out the grease and grime and scum. Ma, her eyes watering with distaste, removed the curtains and returned them three days later cleaned, starched and pressed and an entirely different colour: primrose yellow instead of tobacco brown. Jenny washed down the paintwork and I put a coat of fresh distemper on the walls and we kept the windows open all day long, filling the house with November mist, the first damp breath of winter's icy exhalation.

Once the chimneys were swept, we lit fires in all the grates and when Jenny went to pack two suitcases with all our things from home, I put a milk bottle full of frail lisianthus twined about with ivy on every windowsill, to show her — as I made a small adjustment to the arrangement in the front room, tucking a frond of ivy behind the modest little flowers, I wasn't sure what I wanted to show her: that I meant things to be right between us, that I loved her as well as I could.

I hurried back to Morwithy. Iwan the Milk had brought his cart to help with our removal. He had a weather-beaten, seafarer's face from all those mornings in the cold and he stood holding his pony's head while we loaded our possessions: the suitcases, the blanket box full of our linen, three tea chests containing an assortment of cast-off crockery and the two rag rugs that Ma had made us as a house-warming present.

Delyth was busy at one of her meetings, a convenience I suspect, because she didn't want to see us leaving, even though she and Ted were getting married in only a few months' time — it was weeks before she came to visit and then she only stayed for twenty minutes. So Ma stood on the doorstep on her own. She had both hands in the pocket of her apron, and I could see the clench of them under the material, her face a mask of neutrality that was a work of art, carefully constructed and maintained.

Jenny kissed her formally on one cheek. "There'll always be a welcome for you, at the cottage," she said, her words hinting at the shifting status between the two of them, although my valiant old mother didn't falter, but hugged her impulsively. "And a welcome for you here as well, my dear. Whenever you want it."

Ma opened her arms to me and I was conscious that, as a grown man, I no longer had need of the refuge, that other havens now took precedent, but I craved it all the same. I didn't quite fit the mould of her embrace, but she clasped me

162

to her with her large, reddened hands as she had when I was small, "My boy…"

I understood what she was saying and held her to me, "It's only two miles, Ma." I breathed in the smell of her, the fresh air scent of washing brought in straight from the line, of folded sheets, of carbolic. Whatever else, she'd done her best to make my existence simple for me — that was the protection she'd afforded me — and it felt anything but simple now, at the point of my departure.

"Be a kind man," she said quietly, "If ever there's a choice."

I nodded and full of the unassuageable love I'd had for her since I was hip high, I stooped and kissed the top of her head, "Right, Ma…"

"Go on, off you go," she said, holding me at arm's length. "And remember," she added, "Don't —" Catching herself at the mothering she broke off, biting her lip, then with a slight shudder from the cold, she gave that snatch of a wave I knew so well and released me into my own life.

Jenny and I sat at the back of the milk cart with our legs dangling over the end, listening to the whistle of breath drawn through missing teeth as Iwan the Milk kept up a soft but impenetrable dialogue with his pony: a whole philosophy was expounded between them in a series of chirrups and snorts as we bumped along Front Street and then wound our way down through the valley to Nanagalan, past the big house and under the clock tower into the courtyard, and home.

Iwan stayed sitting up at the front staring at the façade of the building with a look of faint mistrust on his face, while I jumped down and unloaded our stuff. It didn't take long — we didn't have that much. I handed him two bob which he pocketed in spite of himself, and Jenny and I stood side by side watching as the pony and trap did a circuit of the courtyard

163

and then disappeared beneath the stone arch. I could feel the old sensation of being left behind.

We turned to face each other, my wife and I, strangers in a foreign land, newly disembarked. I found the key in my pocket and inserted it into the lock, then turned it, conscious of Jenny's eyes upon me. There was no mediation between us any more, just the two of us and what we could make of ourselves, together. I pushed the door open and stood aside with a wary smile of deference, for her to enter first.

"Aren't you going to carry me over the threshold?"

I wiped my hands on my trousers, "Of course."

I scooped her up and gripping her workaday frame — no sapling body, light as an armful of clippings — I carried her into the house, careful not to knock her shoulder on the door jamb as I went. I set her down and she glanced about her, following the line of the cornice around the room and back with her head on one side; she seemed almost as uncertain as I was. Her attentive gaze took in the fittings for the gas light, then the fire surround, lingering on the cast iron acanthus leaves. She reached out and touched one with her fingers, then shook herself and in doing so noticed the flowers I'd placed upon the windowsill.

The lisianthus looked like exhausted rosebuds, their white petals tinged with pink, their delicate heads too heavy to support themselves. The same pink tinge flooded her face and she made an abrupt sound that was half of a laugh snapped off. She struggled for a moment with a number of abridged impulses: she took a breath to say something, she laced her fingers together and unlaced them, twisting her hands, then she hurried across to me with her arms outstretched and we fenced awkwardly: arm to shoulder? Hand to waist? Who goes where, and how?

We blundered into an embrace and she broke away only to kiss me on the mouth; my mouth, opening to demur, caught up unwittingly. When she pulled away, I found that I was burning. She held my face in her hands, subjecting it to the same cautious survey that she had the room.

"You — are — mine —" she said, with breathless emphasis, "And this is our house —" Her words came out on a sob and I saw in a flash that it was Ma whom she was jealous of, my old Ma, and I gave the same half laugh, gone ragged at the end, at the misapprehension of it, a laugh that had the unbridling of her and she kissed me again. Locked together, the two of us clambered up the unfamiliar stairs, stumbling and tripping against each other and we went flailing down onto the unmade bed, where my wife took time to teach me how close passion is to grief.

I felt awful when I told Ianto Pryce, laid off from the mine with the Silicosis, that he couldn't have the job as gardener's boy. It was only a few years since we'd been playing cricket together, but his batting days were over and his working days as well.

"But I've got two daughters, Ifor. Mouths to feed. The fresh air'd do me good, see?"

His face had a hand-crafted look, his features irregular: his nose bent out of shape from some fight or other, his mouth curved mournfully downwards. You could see the clay that he was made from, and the maker's mark. There was a slick of blue beneath his skin, a pronounced pallor on account of his illness. "Bit of digging…" he shrugged, the action triggering a fit of coughing. His smoking days were not yet over, the nicotine ingrained with the coal dust into the fingers that held his cigarette. "Nothing to it," he hissed. Down to his last breath, he sounded. "I could do the pruning, no problem."

"The thing is, Ianto," I began, "not sure your chest could take it, see? Out in the gardens in all weathers. It's a job for a young man. Gardener's boy…"

"I'm not that old —"

His point was unarguable. He'd not much more than ten years on me.

"I'm sorry, Ianto…"

You gave over the estate office for an afternoon so I could carry out the interviews, and I installed myself at the gate-legged table with some seed catalogues piled around me for protection. A motley assortment of locals trickled through, the Great Depression written in their long faces and their thin shoulders and their misplaced hopes and by four o'clock I was full of a great depression myself, at the impossibility of helping the people who were most in need — Ianto, and all the others — when a young lad came into the room a little too loud and a little too fast, so that he bumped into the table and sent my copy of *The Fragrant Path* flying. He stood stock still as I stooped to pick it up, pressing his hat to his chest, fingering the brim and as I righted myself and sat back in my chair he maintained his position, staring over my head at the wall behind me.

I ran my eyes over the list I'd drawn up. "You must be … Jenkins?"

He didn't respond. He stood there with a wide-eyed anticipation, which on closer inspection looked rather like panic, to me.

"So, Jenkins, tell me: do you know anything about plants?"

He passed the brim of his hat through his fingers. He had the blank, angelic face of a chorister as he took a deep breath

166

and opened his mouth, "I know about the Abelia Grandiflora, the Acanthus Hungaricus, the Acanthus Mollis, the Acanthus Spinosus, the Acer Campestre, the Acer Japonicum Aconitifolium and —" he said in a rush, his voice level and unpunctuated — "the Acer Palmatum Atropurpureum."

"Alright, alright," I interrupted him, wondering how long it had taken him to memorise his list and how far through the alphabet it extended. "Name me a plant beginning with W, then."

He took another dauntingly large breath, "There's the Wallflower, the Weigela, the Wisteria Formosa, the Wisteria floribunda 'Alba' — I can go all the way to the Zantedeschia if you want, Mister."

"I don't think there'll be any need for that," I said, blinking. "So, tell me about the Zantedeschia, how would you care for it?"

That set him off. "Commonly known as the Calla Lily, if you're talking about the Aethiopica varieties then it's a soggy soil they like, but the coloured hybrids love a sandy, well-drained soil with partial shade."

I was mesmerised: the boy was an automaton. "What about the — no, don't bother," I said as he inhaled mightily, ready to go again. "Which gardens have you worked in?" I asked curiously, as he looked too young to have any kind of experience under his belt.

"None," he answered promptly. "I learned it from a book." He had completed a full circuit of the brim of his hat and began to feed it back through his fingers in the other direction.

I was wracking my brains for something else to ask him. "Do you have any hobbies?"

My question seemed to make him nervous. He stopped looking at the wall behind my head and glanced towards the door. Then he read the label on the inside of his hat, frowning. I began to feel sorry for him.

"Things that you enjoy doing...?" I prompted, to help him out of his difficulty.

"Things that I enjoy doing?" His gaze was shooting all over the place; he seemed discomforted. "I've an interest in moths."

"Really?"

"One day I'm going to go to Scotland to see an Argent and Sable."

I felt a small pang when he said this — that glimpse you get of other people's dreams, and the certainty they have of their fulfilment. I wondered if he'd ever make it to Scotland, odd lad that he was.

"It's a Rheumaptera Hastata," he said, and I sensed another recitation was coming on. "A day-flyer, very rare. A priority species. The female has a wingspan of between an inch and a quarter and an inch and a half, with a beautiful livery —"

"Do you want to come and work for me?" I asked to forestall him and he looked round quickly, to see if I'd made the offer to somebody else.

I remembered visiting your father at the clinic. We drove there in the motor, Brown and me up front and you in upholstered seclusion behind us. He'd recovered something of himself, a semblance of how he was before the fire. The terrible caution was gone: we reached third gear, for a start. He seemed blinkered, barely looking to left or right, as if to do so would be to acknowledge present danger. He drove like someone who can sense the cross hairs of a sniper's rifle: onward, at speed. He'd done himself up so tight that no one could breach his defences. He appeared the same, he still had the face of an elderly boy, rounded and diffident, with his salt and pepper moustache and his moist eyes, but in fact everything about him was changed. It was disconcerting for him and the rest of us, his otherness. We all had a sense of it and nobody mentioned it. Sometimes, when I was with him, I felt like a bird hitting an unseen window. Goodness knows what he felt.

Thankful to have finished our journey, we parked at the far end of an avenue of lime trees, their sweet scent doused for winter. Punctiliously, Brown climbed down and opened the door for you. I saw you glancing up at what you were careful to refer to as the clinic, but which people in the village called the asylum, or worse. You stared uneasily at the metal bars on all the windows.

Your father was sitting in an armchair in the sun lounge of the house, a room set aside for visiting. There was a weeping fig and an aspidistra standing in an alcove, a collection of yellowing spider plants and a cactus or two lined up on the window sills and heat streamed up through metal grilles set in the tiled floor, so that the inside of the windows seemed to run with rain.

"Lillah!" your father exclaimed, half levering himself up from his chair so that the tartan rug covering his knees fell to the floor. "What kept you?"

"It isn't Lillah, Papa. It's Ella," you murmured, speaking of yourself in the third person, and I wondered if that was how you bore these occasional visits, at one remove. "Lillah's not — any more, she's —"

I hadn't known that Lillah was your mother's name.

"Sit! Sit!" your father said, clicking his fingers for me to bring a chair up next to his. He couldn't take his eyes off you. I set it down and he dragged it closer, then he glanced at the rug on the floor and up at me, so that I understood that I must pick it up and tuck it round his knees.

169

"At ease, at ease," he said, waving me to one side without looking at me.

"Actually," you said, "Griffiths has got some questions he'd like to ask you…"

At ease? I could hardly hear what you were saying, as the sound of my surname on your lips sent me into a kind of shock. Who was Griffiths to you? I pictured myself walking to the door, opening it and leaving the room without looking back. I'd settle beside Brown in the Daimler and we'd nurse the silence between us. He'd throw me a crossword clue: in Latin, I stumble over exercise that's self-absorbed, and we'd sit and mull it over and bide our time until we were ourselves again.

"Yes, sir," I said, not moving. "We're planning to re-plant the trees on the slope beyond the Drowning Pool…" I wondered if he knew about the fire and if he'd been told, whether he remembered.

"Very good, carry on."

I don't think he was listening. "Do you have any … suggestions … sir? Regarding the landscaping?"

"Lillah," your father said, gazing at you. He fumbled for your hand and held it to his cheek. Awkwardly, as though he couldn't make his fingers work because they were cold, or perhaps the joints were swollen, he then conveyed it, using both of his, to the inner edge of his thigh.

"We'd replace a number of the beeches, of course," I said slowly. "And oaks would do well, don't you think?"

He pressed your palm over the wasted muscle and held it there, then closed his eyes and let loose a long, inflected sigh. "What kept you?"

"Papa!" you said, under your breath. You slipped your hand free and tucked it out of reach beneath your arm.

"I don't know why I'm here," he whispered without opening his eyes, sixteen years in the madhouse scored into all the gullies of his face. A moan escaped from him; he started to rock, forward and back.

You twisted your head round and threw me a frantic look. "We need to go," you mouthed, then you said my name aloud, tremulously; not Griffiths, but my God-given name.

I hesitated, contemplating the ruins of a man. I felt a flicker of relief for my Dad and Glyn. They shall not grow old...

"It's time for us to make tracks, Papa." You made a small adjustment to the tartan blanket.

Still with his eyes shut, your father reached out a hand in your direction, searching the air for traces of you. He let it fall back in his lap. "Must you go so soon?" he asked with weary politeness, "Won't you stay for lunch?" Then as we walked towards the door, he added, "I've always been fond of elm trees, myself. Very pleasing to the eye."

I read that the Nazis were rewriting the Psalms to remove all reference to the Jews. There was altogether too much rewriting and too much removing going on, not to mention dark nights with long knives and on our side of the channel talk of massively expanding the RAF, so that we were starting to wonder where all of it would end. It was the summer of 1934, when Jenny and I went on holiday to Barmouth to celebrate my promotion.

We travelled on a Red and White Services coach — leather seats and chrome fittings and an advertisement for Robertson's Golden Shred marmalade framed on each side of it, feeling swoony with the excitement and the switchback ride through the Brecon Beacons. I wasn't sick, but I couldn't face my packed lunch. Jenny brought a copy of John Masefield's *Salt*

Water Poems and Ballads and she read to me as we bowled along, to take my mind off the lurching the motion of the bus and it felt like old times between us, whatever those old times were.

"Well, I'll eat that egg sandwich if you don't want it," my wife said, she of the cast-iron constitution, but she stopped with it halfway to her mouth at our first sighting of the Mawr estuary. The tide was out and we could see the slip and slither of the river nosing into the mudflats. Pine forests filled the clefts of the hillsides and the grey sky had a feathering of high cloud to act as a reminder that this was summertime, in Wales. Beyond that, silvered right to the horizon, was the sea, which neither of us had ever seen before.

We hobbled off the bus, stiff in our joints from so much sitting and made our way to the Balmoral boarding house on Marine Parade. Our room was five flights up at the back, with a view of rooftops and chimney pots that seemed incomparably urban and I half expected to hear a trickle of jazz being played through an open window, the sound of the saxophone and Elizabeth Welsh, singing. The smoky net curtains and sateen coverlet on the bed in our small room under the eaves were the epitome of sophistication to us country bumpkins and — earthly paradise — there was a flushing toilet on the landing.

After admiring the facilities we went scrambling back down the stairs and out into the town. We retraced the bus's route across the wooden viaduct, "The longest of its kind in the country," Jenny informed me, reading from the guidebook, her free hand tucked into my arm.

We leaned on the railing watching the interplay of tide and wind and current, the waves sheering away from one another, creating brief rivulets and crests that curled then disappeared. I bought us ices, chocolate for her and strawberry for me, to see how it felt to be a man with a girl on his arm.

"We'll remember this," I grinned, watching her lick her cornet, the guilty part of me aware of the need to store up memories that we could draw on later, as insurance. "Have a taste of mine," I said, to banish the thought.

That night I did what Jenny wanted me to do, an act of guesswork and compliance in an unfamiliar bed with the lights turned out. There were no stray notes of jazz reaching through the window, although I listened for them. I was conscious all the while of the presence of the ocean, bearing down upon our narrow stretch of coast.

There was a slight air of reserve between us the following morning. Jenny seemed subdued, which made me in turn more eager to please her and we found ourselves acting out being a couple away on holiday, inexperienced and uncertain of our roles. We chatted over breakfast about this and that: where to get our postcards, whether Fred Perry would win the Men's Final at Wimbledon, papering over any cracks which might appear with well-meant observations. Because it was a sunny day we decided on a trip to the beach, where we rented deck chairs just like proper grown-ups. Jenny had bought a bathing costume specially, made from fine-knit navy wool and I held her towel as she scuffled underneath it, tugging it on while preserving her modesty. I took off my shirt and rolled up my trousers above the knee and the two of us raced down to the shoreline, fingers glancing together, not quite holding hands.

Jenny braved the cold and went in up to her waist, "It's freezing!" she cried, squealing with laughter.

"Careful," I said, because neither of us could swim.

"Aie, aie, aie!" she yelped and from the vantage of her greater wetness, she started splashing me, faint-hearted in the shallows, giving me a proper soaking.

"Is this the height of your ambition?" she asked me later, when we were sitting on our rented deck chairs wrapped in towels, blue-lipped from the cold.

"Why not?" I replied, listening to the lazy soundtrack of people having fun. Two lads were playing leapfrog along the beach and I could hear them grunting with exertion; a father was teaching his daughter to fly a kite and the whiplash sound of its tail cracked above us as it changed direction with the wind. "Taking my wife for the holiday of a lifetime because I've got a job that means we can afford it?" I rolled my head to one side to look at her. "Why shouldn't it be?"

She didn't answer. She lay in the deckchair with the towel swathed right up to her chin, gazing upwards through the gauzy cloud to the glimpse of blue beyond. After a while, she reached into her bag for her book. It was an American novel called *Tender is the Night*. She found her place and read a page or two, then laid it face down in her lap.

"What do you think makes a good book?" she asked, not looking at me but out to sea.

I noticed a glint of green in the pale sand, like a small emerald. I nudged it with my toe. It was a piece of glass scoured by the ocean and I reached to pick it up, then made a study of its salty patina, tilting it this way and that in the palm of my hand. "Strong characters, I suppose."

"Yes…?"

"And it needs to be well written."

She waited, seeming to want more from me.

"It's got to have a gripping story. That's important… And interesting themes." I started thinking more about it, my interest caught. "The power to transport … to inspire…"

Jenny raised the novel to her mouth, breathing against the closed pages, making them fripp and whirr together. "What do you think makes a good marriage?"

I hesitated. I examined the piece of glass with its blunted facets, starting to formulate an answer about honesty and tolerance and respect, heedful that there may be a trick in the question. I flicked the glass high into the air and watched it fall, a shooting green star. In spite of my best intentions, I found it hard to speak about love.

"You don't know, do you?"

"Jenny —"

"I sometimes wonder if you'll wake up one day and see me for who I really am."

"I do see —"

She stood up and shook out her towel and brushed the sand from her bathing costume. I could feel the flitter of it landing on my skin. Clumsily she dragged on her dress and it snagged against the damp wool of her swimsuit.

I leapt to my feet, holding her by the arm to detain her. "Jenny, please —"

Pressing her fist to her mouth, she had to struggle not to blurt out all the things that she was thinking, then in the absence of words, she hit me with of the flat of her palm several times on my chest, swift and stinging blows. "You don't know what makes a good marriage because you can't feel, you don't know how," she cried.

I tried to gather her to me, "Hush, Jenny. Jenny — please," but she wasn't having it.

"Leave me alone —" she took a few steps away from me, her feet unsteady on the shelving sand. She swept her towel and book into her bag. "I'm going back to the boarding house. Don't come with me."

Shaken, I watched her go. The tide was in retreat and some seagulls came swerving down to the shoreline in search of the sea's leavings. My wife was wide of the mark, it wasn't that I couldn't feel: I was too full of feelings that I shouldn't feel, though how could I ever begin to tell her that? My trousers were almost dry and stiff with salt. I pulled my shirt on, fumbling with the buttons, then staggered into my socks and shoes. I stared the length of the beach to where her figure was disappearing into the distance, the velocity of her unhappiness leaving me way behind.

The rest of the week was spent in some sort of remission: we showed a kind of precarious courtesy towards each other. It took us ages to decide how we should spend our days, each of us deferring endlessly to the other's wishes, although a series of diffident negotiations helped us agree about a walk to Arthog Falls and we managed to spend an afternoon puffing through the sand dunes on the Fairbourne miniature railway with an approximation of enjoyment. The days passed wistfully and I found myself filled with unfathomable sadness.

One afternoon when Jenny was reading — F. Scott Fitzgerald seemed to have got right under her skin — I wandered into the town and bought some postcards and sat myself in a seafront café. "We're having the time of our lives," I wrote to Ma. "The Balmoral has all mod cons..." I dashed off a note to the Browns about the food and the weather and then I wrote a card to you all in the conditional tense, if only ... if only... I posted two of them, the third I left tucked into one of the wooden groynes on the beach and later I went back and it had gone.

On my way home to the boarding house I stopped at a souvenir shop and bought a present for my wife.

"Is it for someone special?"

I nodded and the assistant wrapped it up importantly in tissue paper. Five flights of stairs later, I tapped on the door to our room and peeked inside. Jenny was sitting hunched in a chair beside the window, not reading.

"For you," I said, tentatively. I handed her the package. "Go on, open it."

Tiredly, she undid the wrapping. Inside was a small bell made of white porcelain decorated with tiny pink rosebuds. It had *A Present from Barmouth* in gold letters on one side.

"It even rings," I said. "Try it and see."

Jenny gave the bell a listless shake and we listened to the tinkle of it.

I knelt on the lino beside her chair. A strand of hair had escaped from the nape of her neck and I tucked it into place. She turned the bell over in her hand, setting off the tiny china clapper, then she leant forward and placed it on the windowsill, adjusting it so that the lettering showed.

"A Present from Barmouth," she said, resting her head against my shoulder and we stayed like that for several minutes, looking out over the rooftops.

"I want to make you happy," I ventured. "That's the height of my ambition. You're all I've got, you know."

Chapter Fourteen

The great day dawned at last and Ted and Delyth tied the knot. After all the waiting and the saving, I think Ma was a little aggrieved that they chose to be married in a registry office: no chapel vows, no fairytale dress, everything plain and simple — Ted abhorred any fuss not of his own making. He looked well-scrubbed with his pale hair plastered to his head, though I couldn't help noticing that his great mastiff's frame put the seams of his suit under considerable pressure. My defensive, opinionated sister was in thrall to her new husband, hanging on his every, bullish word.

After the ceremony I kissed her on both cheeks. "I hope you'll be very happy together," I said and I found myself praying he'd be good to her, then wondered what kind of a husband I was myself, to offer up that prayer. Jenny, normally so restrained, put her arms around Delyth and held her briefly, without saying anything.

The wedding breakfast took place at the Fleece in Morwithy. There were drinks and a cold collation laid out downstairs, while upstairs the tables and chairs had been pushed back for the dancing. Most of the villagers put in an appearance and a number of grey-faced factory folk made it over from Mynydd Maen, so there was a good turnout and things became pretty lively once the beer began to take effect.

I tried to do right by Delyth's guests, greeting her friends and her new family and agreeing what a lovely day it was, but a bit of me was longing to retreat to the corner to nurse my pint, not being a great one for the chitter-chatter. I glanced across the room at Jenny, who was hard at work with one of Ted's elderly relations. Her new dress was a strange confection, made from lilac-coloured lastex silk — she showed me the label, it's the latest thing, apparently. There was a design of geometric pink roses at the waist and it clung in a way that I suspected made her feel self-conscious — she kept smoothing it while she was talking.

A few notes from a song I didn't know filtered down from above and when she heard it, my wife returned my glance, raising her eyebrows in an invitation to me to go upstairs with her and listen to the music. I was halfway through responding that I needed to finish my beer and circulate some more, all of this conveyed without a single word being spoken, for in some respects we knew each other intimately, when the door opened and you slipped unaccompanied into the pub, self-conscious in your own way, too.

You were abroad when Jenny and I were married and unable to fulfil the long established custom which dictated that the local gentry should stand the happy couple a round of drinks on their wedding day. The landlord hurried round and offered to take your coat, turfing Parry the Paint off his bar stool so you could have a seat and when you handed him two five-pound notes he touched his forelock to you, at a stroke making all of us appear inferior and ingratiating.

I knocked back the remainder of my glass. The bar seemed as close as a tight-fitting jacket and I could have done with some air. I ran a finger around the inside of my collar and moved a few paces towards the door thinking that no one would notice if I absented myself for a moment or two, when Ted's best man, a foreman at the factory, jumped up on a chair and shouted for everyone to go upstairs for the speeches and the cutting of the cake.

I fell into step with you — how could I not — as people drifted towards the stairs.

"I know that suit," you said appraisingly. You were carrying a gin and tonic and you took a sip from it, contemplating me over the rim of your glass.

"It's had a good few outings," I squinted down at it, "with me, and my brother before me, and our Dad before him. It's as close as we get to an heirloom in our family."

You smiled, tilting your head to one side, then mounted the staircase ahead of me, leaving a slipstream of gardenia in your wake that could easily have gathered me up after you, but I turned back at the last minute to look for Jenny, seeking the protection that she offered. Perhaps I already sensed the danger I was in. In the crush upstairs I found a place of safety between my mother and my wife.

Ted seemed overly serious for a man on his wedding day — I think he'd have launched into a speech about the socio-economic context of marriage during the first part of the twentieth century given half a chance, but he managed a few brief remarks about Delyth, saying that from the moment he first saw her, he thought she had the makings of a good wife. My sister stood beside him in her sober linen dress with matching jacket, a brooch of seed pearls which Ma had worn on her wedding day pinned to her lapel, her blunt face suffused and sentimental; perhaps she had inherited our mother's virtue of making a little go a long way.

When the cake was cut and the toasts were drunk, Ted's best man wound up the gramophone and the bride and groom opened the first dance together, Ted doggedly manoeuvring Delyth round the floor until the song was finished. He gave a plausible performance of a newly married man. I couldn't fault him, but I didn't quite trust him, it seemed just that: a performance, done, I hoped, for my sister's benefit and possibly for ours. Perhaps there's something about marriages — all that expectation — that makes a fellow melancholy as he gets older.

They changed the record and a few adventurous couples edged their way onto the floor. Jenny leaned against me, her feet tapping to the rhythm of the music.

"Another drink?" I asked, aware that she would like me to set both our glasses down and lead her off in the rumba, or whatever it was they were dancing. I'm a two left feet man, myself.

Ma's gaze rested meaningfully upon me.

"Or would you like to dance…?" I enquired doubtfully, scratching my head.

"Oh, Ifor — would you?"

"I — er — yes — why not?" I swallowed. "Though I'm not much good at this kind of—" but before I could finish Jenny had towed me to the middle of the room and put one of my hands on her shoulder and another on her hip. I stood there floundering for a moment.

"You put your left foot there, like that, then follow through with your right. Count the rhythm in your head, it helps. One, two, three, four. That's it… Now your left foot there again… One, two, three, four."

I tried the counting, I honestly did, but I was always about half a beat behind her. I tried to follow her instructions, but I was a bit of a clodhopper: my knees kept striking hers and I trod on her foot and in the end I started laughing, "I'm sorry, Jenny. I don't know my left from my right. You'd best give up on me…"

Instead, made uncertain by my laughter, she burrowed close and buried her head against my chest and we stood like that, shifting our weight to the music, more or less content to dance on our own terms. She grew heavy in my arms as she leaned into me and although I didn't feel the burden of her, I felt the care.

"Shall we —?" I asked, when Ted's best man changed the record, glancing towards the table where we'd left our glasses. She shook her head, holding me tighter, and we kept up our strange, conjugal swaying. Other couples started dancing and there was a press of bodies all around us, so that the smell of sweat and cigarette smoke and the cellophane tang of cologne wiped out any tell-tale traces of gardenia which might have put me on my guard.

Before I knew it, you tapped Jenny on the shoulder.

My wife, drowsy with the dancing, lifted her head.

"Excuse me," you said. "May I?"

Jenny blinked at you. "I'm sorry?"

"May I dance with your husband?" you said. It crossed my mind that you had had another gin.

"Oh." Jenny's arms dropped to her sides.

"I don't know anyone else here."

"I was going to sit this one out," I said, but you wouldn't take no for an answer.

"If you don't mind…" You slid between my wife and me and slipped your arms around my waist. I thought you must be very drunk indeed. I twisted to look back at Jenny, who stood on her own in the middle of the jostle, but then you leaned so close it felt as if we were merged together and I could think of nothing but your thigh against mine and the peril of our hips, touching, so that I doubted I had it in me to protect you from yourself, or from me, or to protect Jenny either.

You were like running water, rippling in my grasp. I forgot all about my clumsy feet: when you moved, I moved; when you arched, I arched with you. You wound me round the dance floor and for a moment I sensed how it might feel to be one flesh, one heart.

"Wouldn't it be heavenly to dance like this all night?" you said.

I answered you inside my head: yes to the dancing, to the closeness, to the changing pressure of your body again mine, to the aching subtlety of touch; yes to the holding you all night. I made myself listen to the music. I made that my lifeline. The song was about Capri.

"Have you ever been to the Isle of Capri?" I said, trying to tamp down the wild elation I was feeling.

"Of course," you looked up at me, your flawless face so close that I could taste your breath. "Mama and I went, on our travels."

"Tell me about it," I said, clutching for anything to say.

"Oh, you know, the usual — lovely beaches, fishing villages, blue sea — that kind of thing."

An image of the shoreline at Barmouth flashed into my head. In order not to look along the length of it, at the retreating figure in the distance, I scanned the wide reach of the room. Amongst the blur of shapes I caught a glimpse of clinging, lilac-coloured lastex silk.

You drew me to you, resting your cheek against mine.

"I don't think…" I pulled back a fraction.

"What don't you think…?"

"I don't think we should…" It felt like the beginnings of an admission. I held my tongue.

"What?" you pressed me. "Dance like this?"

I couldn't answer you. This was the stuff of which my dreams were made. Distantly I could hear the siren insistence of your whisper.

"Why not?"

"Because…" I said reluctantly.

"Everybody else is…"

I glanced sideways at the other couples. It was true. They were as interlaced as we were. "But they're not…"

"Like us?" your pupils flared black, your eyes glistening; "No, they're not." Then you said my name, Ifor, with the long history of wanting in your voice, so that I couldn't help myself, I placed my finger against your lips to stop you, an irresistible act of trespass, and suddenly the record ended.

On the walk home on that beautiful, bruising evening, my wife and I made our way back to Nanagalan through the unstable darkness, the night sky as volatile as we were, its blackness lanced, from time to time, with moonlight. I couldn't always see Jenny; I could hear her footsteps and was alive to the simmer of the air around her. Once, her sleeve brushed mine and she snatched her arm away as though I'd burnt it. I was seething in my own way, too; full of a kind of broiling joy, and guilt and mortification as well, but mostly the surging, breathless flight of happiness.

We followed the curve of the hillside down. At the sight of the big house biding its time in the depths of the valley, Jenny came to a halt. There was light enough to see the agitation in her features. She was chewing at her lip remorselessly.

"It isn't what you think," I ventured.

"What do I think, if you're such an expert?"

I hung my head. We walked a few minutes in silence until she stopped again, covering her face with her hands as if she were rinsing it clean with cold water.

"You have no idea of the daily hurt you do me."

"Jenny —" I said, her accusation winding me. "It was just a — dance. She asked me. She's my employer. I couldn't refuse her."

"Employer?" she exclaimed, turning on me, the sarcasm in her tone making me flinch, but I stood my ground, all that happiness leaching away as though some vital artery had been cut.

"I didn't mean to upset you," I began.

"In front of everyone — the whole village."

"It was just a dance —"

"I've never been so humiliated."

"It's not what you think…"

She took me by the shoulders, untenderly. "What is it, then? You tell me what it is."

"We've known each other on and off since we were both fifteen. There weren't any other young people on the estate. We —" I broke off. In the distance I could hear the intermittent thrum of the Daimler. High above the clouds parted, sending moonlight sifting down on to us, enough for me to see the acceleration of understanding in Jenny's expression.

"On and off…?"

"It's nothing," I said.

As the car's headlights threaded through the dark towards us, growing larger, she lowered her hands. It lumbered past and our heads swung round, as one: Jenny as stricken as if the vehicle had hit her, while I strained to see your darker shape in the darkness of the interior. You left lipstick on the tip of my finger when I pressed it to your mouth, which I couldn't bear to wipe away. Further down the valley the tail lights of the motor glimmered like hot coals; I watched until they flickered and went out.

"You see?" I said, struggling to keep the sadness from my voice. "How could it possibly be anything at all?"

I remembered how shorn and vulnerable the hillside seemed once we had cleared the remnants of the beech wood during the spring following the fire; how tender the folds of the landscape appeared, all revealed. I remembered how unprotected Jenny and I were, shorn and revealed in our own way too, the fact that she guessed my feelings underwriting every glance and every silence I could see you were a subject she wanted to come back to: she'd turn her head and draw a breath to speak, then look away and the quietness would thicken between us until it became too dense for us to penetrate. The closest she came was after one interminable evening meal, when we had chewed our way through our food and she was washing up. She stood at the sink with her back to me. There was a plate in her hand and she peered at it, scratching at some dirt with her nail. The scratching stopped.

"You and she," she said, her words sheathed in a whisper I could hardly hear. "Has anything —? Have you —?"

The cool March air in our kitchen heated with the shame of such a question. "No," I said swiftly.

She let the plate slide back into the sink, resting her hands in the water. She stood for a moment, considering my reply with her head bowed. "Will you?" she said, unable to swallow the asking.

"Jenny — it was just a dance, that's all."

From then on, we closed our embassies. We circled around each other, making small, barbed weapons out of jealousy and guilt. We slept in exile in our big bed.

It was at the time of the great replanting that Jenkins started as my boy. The restlessness contained in his wiry frame obliged him to walk on the balls of his feet: he seemed to be permanently on the brink of running off and I hadn't quite realised that my role would be to contain as well as employ him. That wasn't the only revelation that I had.

The first morning he turned up all clean and tidy and he stood to attention as though he'd been drilled, waiting for my instructions.

"You haven't had much practical experience, have you?"

"None, Mr Griffiths," he answered, blithe as can be.

"There's no need for any of that Mr Griffiths malarkey," I said mildly. "You can call me Ifor…"

"I can't do that, Mr Griffiths," he asserted, without explaining why. After a pause, I asked him what he would like to call me and following a brief and unlikely debate, we compromised with Mister and having settled on it, he used it all the time.

"It won't take long to show you the ropes."

"Yes, Mister."

My plan was to set him to work in the gardens while I attended to the new trees, so we were in the Herbar getting him started on planting out some of the hardy annuals that I had brought on in the greenhouse. We'd carried several trays of them across in the wheelbarrow, which was parked on the pathway close to the central ornamental bed.

"You'd best watch me to begin with," I said, as I showed him how to dig the holes and space them far enough apart to give the seedlings a chance to grow. Taking me at my word, Jenkins stood inches from me and made a study of my every movement.

"Fetch me that tray of Rhodanthe Chlorocephala, will you?" I jerked my head in the direction of the barrow.

He stood on one foot, then the other. I remembered him feeding the brim of his hat through anxious fingers at his interview. "Otherwise known as helipterum," he stated.

"That's the one," I said, housing my trowel in the earth.

"An attractive, long flowering bloom."

"It is."

"With…" he was staring at the wheelbarrow with wide, hectic eyes, "white flowers."

"That's right."

There was a pause. Jenkins clasped his hands behind him as though to draw a line under our discussion.

"Will you fetch them, then?"

There were trays of Ammi Majus, Nigella Damascena and Layia Glandulosa scattered along the path, all of them purest white. I watched him dart across with his distinctive, springing step, launching himself from one to the other. He looked at the Layia, then circumspectly in my direction, then he snatched it up and hurried back and set it down in front of me. After that he stood very close, watching to see what I would do.

I scratched my head. "I had other plans in mind for the Layia," I said carefully. "Perhaps you could fetch me the Rhodanthe?"

Jenkins face turned a miserable shade of red. He made a close inspection of the lacing on his boots. Thoughtfully, I sat back on my heels.

"Although the practical stuff's the easy part, really," I said. "It's all those long Latin names that get me."

He licked his lips. He started up a jiggle with one of his feet. I could see the energy rising like sap in him. I thought he might be off at any moment.

"Maybe you could help me with the complicated names and I could show you what the flowers look like? Match them up. We could work something out in that way," I said casually.

"Maybe." Jenkins was following the flight of some invisible insect through the air. I wondered if it was a moth that he was after, but I had a feeling he was searching for somewhere more comfortable to put himself.

"Let me fetch the Rhodanthe Chlorocephala for you to see," I clambered to my feet. "And you can tell me everything you know about it."

"They can be annuals, perennials, or sub shrubs," he said hesitantly as he followed me over to the wheelbarrow. He began to warm to his theme. "With simple, narrow, alternate leaves..."

"Like this," I lifted a clump of them to demonstrate. "Look — here..."

"...and daisy-like flowers," he said, which concluded the arrangement between us to the satisfaction of us both.

His Majesty's Silver Jubilee rescued us all, for a day or two, from our worries and our fears. The Prime Minister was too old and frail to contemplate what German rearmament might mean: what need did Adolf Hitler have of conscription, not to mention his own Luftwaffe? With the scars from the war to end all wars still livid, this was a question that most of us were scared to answer. The plans for the celebrations of the glorious reign of our King Emperor were a diversion from plans for a major civil defence exercise to teach us all how to use gas masks.

The parish council came up with a cracking programme: on the day before the jubilee there was to be a sports afternoon for the village children, followed by tea; then in the evening there was to be a pageant at the village hall describing the history of Morwithy. On the day itself, a service of thanksgiving was to be held in the parish church. You offered to hold the sports day and the teas in the grounds of Nanagalan as a thank you for the loyal support of the villagers at the time of the fire.

I'd hardly seen you since the night we danced together. Our next weekly meeting was cancelled because it was Easter, then all of us were caught up in the preparations for the jubilee, so you went about your business and I went about mine and perhaps both of us felt some relief. I saw you once, though: Jenkins and I, Tom Ten Bricks and some folk from the village were putting the finishing touches to the marquee on Dancing Green. Something made me lift my head — the leaf weight of your gaze upon me as you wandered over the grass towards us.

"Is everything going alright?" you asked, scanning the marquee. You had a tiny puppy with you, a whippet dog and you crouched down to make much of him.

"Reckon so, Miss Ella." I watched you playing with the little fellow, scratching his tummy as he lay on his back till he was in transports of delight.

"Good," you said, glancing up to see that my eyes were on you as your fingers worked the dog's sleek pelt. "You'll let me know if there are any problems, won't you?"

"Of course, Miss Ella."

You fiddled with the puppy's collar, not looking at me now, then with some sleight of hand on your part or the little fellow's, I could have sworn you let the dog go free.

"Damn," you said. "He hasn't had his inoculations."

Tom Ten Bricks and Gwilym Jones the Ancient exchanged glances at your blasphemy, then recollecting themselves they made minor, sanctimonious adjustments to a guy rope.

"He's not meant to be off the lead," you said, shading your eyes to see the kinetic perfection of the whippet streaking away across the garden, not much more than an impression of flattened ears, shoulder blades carving forwards and the piston effect of muscles working. You turned to face me with that artless, aristocratic helplessness I'd come to know.

"Would you like me to go after him, miss?"

You hesitated, looked in the direction of the men, then nodded. We set off and you followed me through the nut tunnel, each of us keeping a careful distance. "What's his name?" I asked.

"His full name is Bayard Clarion's Jasper," you said wryly, screwing up your eyes to peer into the distance. "I call him Jasper for short."

We lapsed into silence after that, scuffing our way through the long grass. I felt a heaviness in your presence I had never felt before. I was full of guilt at what had happened and resolve that it shouldn't happen again, yet these righteous feelings were tempered with anxiety that you might be feeling the same remorse and regret that I was, a prospect that would have finished me altogether. I kept my eyes fixed on the hummocky ground and walked a length ahead of you, without speaking.

From time to time you called out for your dog and then upon a reflex I remembered to scan the slope ahead. I could see the first green graze of spring in the branches of the trees cresting the hill and the sight of it caught my breath: the unfailing promise of renewal. It made me sigh out loud.

The dog's lead you were holding slipped through your fingers and you stooped to pick it up. "We were probably both a bit carried away the other evening." You straightened up so that your back was at an angle to me. You stood obliquely turned away.

"Probably…"

"Although it's not as if —" You dropped your gaze to the dog lead, running the leather through your fingers, tracing the grain of it with your nail. "I mean, we were only dancing…"

"Yes," I said, flinching as you used the excuses I had made.

You nodded, and then you started to fiddle with the chrome clip at one end. "It's not as if we were doing anything wrong."

"Wrong's different for different people," I began, thinking of Jenny, edging my way towards saying what had to be said, spelling it out for me as much as for you.

"One dance —" You gave the lightest lift of your shoulders, a thistledown shrug, but you didn't turn to face me.

"I'm a married man," I said.

You were still for a moment. "Yes." You began to coil the lead up tight, binding the leather round and round. "And anyway, I'm —"

"Yes." I didn't want to hear you list the differences between us any more than you wished to hear of my — attachment.

"And you're —"

"Yes," I said. "I am."

You nodded. "Well," you said. "No more dancing." You looked back at me over your shoulder; a slow, relinquishing stare. Then before we knew it, the little fellow was upon us; he'd crept up on us unawares. "Jasper," you cried, bending down to pet him and he licked your fingers as you fed him biscuits and you clipped the lead onto his collar, then scooped him up and held him in your arms.

The heaviness that was on me settled. No more dancing. I stood there, watching the puppy nuzzle against you, his snout following the scent of biscuit to your pocket, so that you laughed and whispered and tickled his neck and he gave a tiny yowl of pleasure that tore into me. The lonely rich buy things:

expensive clothes to wear, and motor cars, and houses, and holidays, and animals to love; that's how they fill the vastness, while the rest of us...

"Best be getting back to work, Miss Ella," I said.

How terrible the gaiety of the jubilee celebrations seemed: all that joy on display as we strained to escape what was coming to us. It made everything seem out of kilter: Jenny trying to mend her heart with hopeless glue and smiling as she did it, and me smiling back at her encouraging, compensatory smiles; you and I acting as if nothing had happened between us and wishing that something had.

None of it seemed real. There were three million people unemployed, Herr Hitler was leading us all to hell in a handcart and our response was to set the trestle tables for tea, whip out the bunting and have a party. Perhaps that's what has put the great into Great Britain, but it seemed peculiar to me.

The King had the measure of it more than the rest of us. He didn't forget the unemployed, or the disabled — he gave them pride of place in his special broadcast. He wasn't afraid to talk about the future, either. "Other anxieties may be in store, they may all be overcome if we meet them with courage, confidence and continuity." I thought about his words a good deal after, searching for those qualities in myself.

The garden was wearing its new spring clothes: the clematis was out and the white lilac which your mother had loved was beginning to unfurl. We'd marked proper chalk running lanes along the lawn in front of the marquee and everything looked tidy. Some of the women from the village, including my old Ma, were seeing to the last minute touches, arranging posies of flowers in patriotic colours on every table, and I needed to get hold of Jenkins. I wanted him to direct any cars which arrived to the designated parking in the courtyard, but I couldn't find him anywhere.

On a couple of occasions I'd run him to ground in one of the greenhouses, staring hotly at the trays of plants, mouthing information, so I was on my way to the kitchen garden to see if he was there, when I bumped into Brown. He'd volunteered to oversee the races and was heading for his dugout to fetch the starting pistol. He walked with an old man's shuffle as if he were wearing carpet slippers, although his shoes were polished to a shine you could see your face in.

"Ifor —" he said my name as if I were still a boy; I half expected him to reach out and ruffle my hair. He was the father I'd gained, not the Dad that I'd lost.

"You haven't seen Jenkins, have you?"

He shook his head. "Queer sort of a lad," he observed ruminatively.

"He's not so bad. He's a bit of a whizz at Linnaean Classifications — knows them all inside out and back to front. Puts me to shame." We fell into companionable step together. I shot him a sideways glance. "Everything alright for this afternoon, Mr Brown?" It was as close as I could come to asking him if he could cope, knowing as I did that he was more out of kilter than the rest of us, following the fire.

"Reckon so," he answered, noncommittally. I followed him into the dugout and watched as he reached up to the top of the wooden wine box shelving and lifted down a tin wrapped in some greasy gabardine. He unwound the material and opened the lid, then lifted out the gun which was wrapped, in its turn, in some wadding. "It's a Webley Mark One air pistol," he said. He wiped the wooden handle with his sleeve. "Should do the job nicely." He scooped up a handful of pellets and put them in his trouser pocket, then replaced the gun in its tin.

"Are you sure...?" I began, mindful that even the blow from a hammer could make him jump. I couldn't help thinking of him leaning against the door of the Daimler, with his hat fallen to the floor.

"I know how to handle a gun, for Christ's sake!" he snapped.

"Of course, of course — I didn't mean —"

He made small, offended adjustments to his shoulders, twitching them into place. He picked up the tin and tucked it under his arm. "Let's find this lad of yours, shall we?" he said brusquely.

Jenkins wasn't in any of the greenhouses and he wasn't in the potting shed. We made our way back through the courtyard. The door to the kitchen was open and the scent of sugar and vanilla hung on the breeze. Drawn by the smell of baking I strolled up to the door, although Brown hung back, glancing up at the clock tower. "Shall we grab a quick bite?" I suggested. "There's a good twenty minutes before the crowds start arriving and I haven't had any lunch." I began to wander down the passage, when I heard something that brought me to a standstill. It was Mrs Brown, her voice like raw silk, reading out a recipe.

"I'm going to take eight ounces of sweet almonds and pound them in a mortar with some orange flower water."

I stopped dead in my tracks.

"Then I'm going to add a quarter pound of bitter almonds for the taste, see...?"

In my mind I could see her silvery, dark hair coming loose in the heat of the kitchen, the plunge of her open neckline, her spectacles sliding down her nose. Oh no, I thought.

"And mix them with the whites of three well beaten eggs..."

There was a moment of silence, of stealth, of fingers being licked for their sweetness. It was broken by the sound of footsteps in the passage.

"Mr Brown —" I held out my hand to bar his way, shaking my head, but he barged straight past. I caught up with him as he reached the threshold. Mrs Brown was leaning with both arms on the table, her blouse unbuttoned, with her head thrown back and her mouth slackening. Beside her was Jenkins, his face fierce with concentration, weighing her released white breast with one hand.

Brown stood for a moment, taking in the scene. He seemed to be in retreat, although he didn't move a muscle: his gaze lengthened, he held the tin with the gun a little tighter — imperceptible signs of recoil. The quality of the silence changed and Jenkins swung round. He blushed to the roots of his hair.

"She was showing me how to make Ratafia biscuits," he stammered.

Mrs Brown briskly fastened the buttons of her blouse. "Is it hot in here, or is it me?"

I remembered the children racing. They stumbled through the egg and spoon race and the sack race and the three-legged race, but the one that I recalled was the hundred-yard sprint. They went hurtling by in a flash of white aertex, their stubby legs working, their eyes straining wide with intent, and the sight of them reminded me of the lines from the Bible about time and chance: that the race is not to the swift, nor the battle to the strong, and I thought of Brown, firing the starting pistol again and again without flinching, and the children running with uncomplicated clarity towards the finishing line.

Chapter Fifteen

I remembered the day that Jenkins was trimming the box hedges in the Herbar, while I was taking some cuttings from the philadelphus in the flowerbed at the edge of Dancing Green. I could hear a lamb bleating Mayday messages on some hillside further down the valley and the persistence of it made me raise my head to listen for a moment. Out of the corner of my eye I saw a sturdy figure bumping a pram down the drive. It took me a second or two to recognise my sister.

"Delyth?" I called.

She swung round at the sound of her name and even at a distance I could see that she looked distracted, a little askew. She was pushing a pram which she parked on the grass verge, kicking on the brake with her foot. Baby Gwyneth (not an Angharad or, to my old Ma's secret sorrow, a tiny Glyn) was five months old. Her mother hauled her out of her nest of blankets.

"What's up?" I abandoned the pot of cuttings I was holding on the lawn and hurried over to her. "Is it Ma?"

"It isn't Ma. It's Ted." The lamb was still bleating further down the valley. At the highest register in Delyth's voice I could hear the same demanding note. She angled her cheek for me to kiss and held out Baby Gwynne. "Take her, will you? She hasn't slept, she's teething and I need five minutes peace and quiet to think."

"Ted?" I exclaimed. My niece and I regarded one another with mutual alarm as Delyth thrust her in my direction.

"Oh, if he hasn't gone to Spain and joined the International Brigade," she snapped. "Is there somewhere we can sit? I'm worn out."

"He's what?"

Baby Gwynne's mouth curled then widened and a terrible squawking sound came out of it. She had dribble down her chin and phlegm on her upper lip. Tears now, too. I looked from daughter to mother in consternation.

"What does that fellow think he's doing?" Delyth asked. I followed the line of her gaze. In the Herbar, sensitive to signals of distress, Jenkins was standing with both hands covering his ears.

"You'd better come with me," I said. I took them to the tool shed and settled Delyth on the bench. "Perhaps you'd take her," I began, holding out her wailing offspring to my sister. "Just for a tick? While I put the kettle on?"

Delyth ducked her head to one side, "Give me a break will you, Ifor?"

With Baby Gwynne flailing on my hip, I took the kettle to the outside tap and filled it. I juggled my niece and the kettle and the primus stove and the matches. The gas went out. Gwynne's tiny body was convulsed with sobs. My sister ran her fingers through her hair with a ragged sweep, then held her head in her hands. "Jiggle her up and down," she said. "That sometimes does the trick."

"Shh, shh, shh," I said, jiggling away. "You'll make the tea then, will you? It's on the shelf up there." I took the baby out into the kitchen garden. Her crying came in snatches now, small shuddering afterthoughts. It stopped altogether when I introduced her to the scarecrow, a ramshackle old thing with a sacking face, a moth-eaten jumper and a pair of overalls Samuelson had discarded years ago. She was particularly taken with his hat, gripping it with her fat fists, seeing how much of it she could fit into her mouth. She nested into my arms and I was utterly undone by such flattery.

Delyth was sitting hunched in the tool shed holding a mug of tea against her chin, biting her thumbnail. She looked at us, unsmiling, as we came in. I inclined Baby Gwynne in her direction, but she shook her head, so I found an old crate to prop the little mite in and gave her a ball of garden twine to play with.

"He's in somewhere called Albacete," my sister said. "He just upped and went."

"When?" I said. "Why? What did he say?"

"Last Tuesday."

I remembered the sullen look of her when she was a girl and she could fill the house with her brooding. She took a sip of her tea, her narrowed eyes fixed on something I couldn't see.

"What did he say?"

She roused herself enough to sigh. "He said you have to fight for what you believe in. That it was a matter of conscience."

Gwynne had discovered that if she threw the ball of twine across the shed I would pick it up and give it back to her. She was putting the knowledge to good use.

"What did you say to that?"

She didn't answer. She bit her lip, holding it between her teeth in a tight white fold.

Absentmindedly I rolled the twine back towards the baby, but this time she ignored it. She was plucking fretfully at the air. "I suppose our Dad must have said something like that, when he enlisted."

"That was different, Ifor," Delyth said scathingly. "And anyway, look at the good it did him."

"You must feel..."

"I feel bloody angry with him, that's how I feel."

My eyes widened and I glanced in the direction of Baby Gwynne, who was grumbling away to herself. She'd got her thumb caught in the cuff of her matinee jacket and I leaned across and freed it for her. She let out a stream of unintelligible syllables, detailing her disgruntlement. I found an old flowerpot and put a few zinc plant markers inside it and rattled them around for her, a gift she accepted sceptically, on provisional terms.

"I told him straight. I said he had responsibilities, that he didn't have to fight, that he was making a choice." Delyth began. "He said he couldn't live with himself if he didn't go. That's what he said! I couldn't believe it. What about living with Baby Gwynne and me? He said it was a matter of principle. Principle? I said to him. You have to stand up and be counted, he said. Don't we count? I said. Me and Baby Gwynne? Don't we count at all?"

I was thinking how quickly love is twisted into grievance, my Jenny with her downturned mouth and her air of disappointment never far from my thoughts, when my sister paused for breath and burst abruptly into tears. "He wouldn't go if he really cared for us, would he? Oh, Ifor!"

I put my arm around her. "Shh, shh, shh. There now..." Baby Gwynne, daughter of two activists, soon came out in sympathy and sat in her wooden crate howling, until I picked her up and perched her on my knee, jiggling inexpertly.

"Let me have her," Delyth sniffed and then swallowed, reaching for her daughter and the two of them sat damply entwined, holding on to one another, the uncomprehending tears wet on their faces.

"Have you told Ma?" I asked, anxious to forestall more weeping.

"I've been putting it off. On account of Dad and Glyn and so forth...?"

I nodded. We weren't on intimate terms usually, but we sat side by side and she leaned against me and I laid my hand upon her knee in sympathy.

"She'll take it badly..." Delyth lapsed into thought, imagining of the lug of our mother's grief coming to rest on her own shoulders.

"He'll be back before you know it."

That evening Jenny came home and slung a canvas bag full of books onto the kitchen table. "I've too much time on my hands." She unfastened her coat, shrugged it off and laid it on the back of the chair. I understood what she was saying: between us we had found some of the companionability that comes from habit, although the lack of any children (the slow cessation of relations between us) was like a physical obstruction, a presence so huge that it pressed us up against the walls and into the corners of our life together.

"I'm going to do a correspondence course," she said. "I'm going to study the shelf arrangement of interdisciplinary works. I want a proper qualification. Then one day maybe I'll be head librarian."

On Thursdays she stayed on after hours at the library. "It's not all theory," she said a little breathlessly the first time she was late home. There was a sprinkling of rain on the shoulders of her coat. She brought the outdoors in with her — the dashed hope that comes with a wet April, the broken promise of spring, though she spoke with more animation than I was used to seeing in her. "We need to work on the practice as well. Make sure books on the same topic can be found in the same place. One of the other assistants is doing it with me."

She hung her outdoor clothes on the back of the door. I watched her loop her scarf over the hook, scattering stray raindrops onto the floor. "We're going be learning about synthesised notation next week. Did you keep some of the shepherd's pie for me?"

The news about Ted found its way back to Mynydd Maen in the winter of that year. He was under siege in a town called Teruel, fighting from street to street, ceding territory to the Nationalists one neighbourhood at a time. They were battling it out in blizzard conditions — we heard later that Ted was suffering from frostbite and hadn't had a proper meal for days. A man's principles can cost him dear; I knew that, in my own small way. He was holed up behind some makeshift barricades with a Frenchman and two Spaniards. It was the Frenchman who got a message to Delyth, after it was over. Ted was standing at a crossroads, his shoulder leaning into the corner of a building, steadying his gun. No longer the mastiff, his clothes hung loose on him, not holding any warmth. He swung round the corner, aiming without looking, cracking out a shot. There was a moment's respite as one of the Spaniards let rip some covering fire giving him time to reload, shouting at him, Rapido! Rapido! His fingers were blackened stubs; pus-filled, fumbling stubs paralysed by the cold and the cartridge was as slippery as ice. Rapido! Rapido! He dropped it. The metal casing landed soundlessly in the falling snow and he was stooping to retrieve it when the sniper got him. He didn't make it home to Delyth and Baby Gwynne; another of our dead we never buried.

Overnight, my opinionated sister went from knowing everything to being certain of nothing. She looked dazed. She couldn't take in anything we said to her. She made Baby Gwynne into a bundle that she held in her lap like the last possessions of a refugee. She had to be reminded to feed and change her.

"What? Yes. In a minute."

She drank endless cups of tea, fresh leaves each time, the only comfort we could give her. It wasn't that she stayed with us for a few days; she was stranded with us, marooned in shock and disbelief.

One night, I woke to the sound of terrible violence being done. Dredged from sleep, I went racing into the front bedroom we'd given over to our guests thinking she must be killing the baby, but she was lying on the floor beating her fists and her forehead against the wooden boards, as though grief was something she could destroy with her bare hands.

"Stop it!" I flung myself onto my knees beside her, "Delyth! For goodness' sake! You'll do yourself an injury, stop it!"

"It hurts. It hurts so much..."

"Stop it!" I caught her by the shoulders and hauled her up so that she was slumped against me. "There, there. Shh. Hush now."

She gave a small, exhausted convulsion and the silence gathered close in broken fragments. Baby Gwynne rolled over in the bottom drawer we'd made into a makeshift crib and risked a timid cry. After a while I helped Delyth into bed and tucked her daughter in beside her and fetched a cold flannel compress for her poor, swollen eyes, then I sat with them until they were both asleep and for several minutes more, although I was worn out by the glimpse I'd had of the aftermath of love.

The next morning my sister, depleted and a little shaky, insisted on going home to Mynydd Maen to the rooms she'd shared with Ted. "Not sure what I'll do when I get there, mind," she said. On her brow a raised, red bruise was flaring yellow at the edges. "The factory's had a whip around, all the lads from his old works, to tide us over. I could always take in washing, I suppose." She ran her thumb along the handle of the pram, a sad little gesture tracing the brightness of the chrome. "Like Ma," she whispered.

I walked with her up the drive and slipped a tenner into her pocket, a few bob short of two weeks' wages, but it was the best that I could do.

"Ifor, I don't need charity," she began, retrieving the note and holding it out to me with a flash of her old, contestable spirit. She hesitated. "Perhaps I do," she said, tucking it back into her pocket. She stood on tiptoe and pecked me on the cheek, learning to be grateful, learning to be alone, then she looked down the road in the direction of the village, turned the pram around and set off on the long journey home.

My mother aged about ten years when Ted died. She had the gnarled lean of trees in a hedgerow at the mercy of the wind, her hair a startling widow's white, her flesh thin clothing over angular bones. I couldn't quite suppress a feeling of irritation that she'd let herself get so ancient, as though it were an oversight, as if she could have done something about it if only she'd paid more attention. Don't go growing old, Ma, not you.

At your suggestion, ("Out of respect for your loss, Ifor. It's the least that I can do.") Brown drove us in the motor to Ted's memorial service at the plain-spoken chapel in Mynydd Maen. With no body, and no grave, soberly we committed to him to memory.

"You'll come in for tea, won't you?" Ma said when Brown deposited us at the door of the cottage in Morwithy.

Jenny fingered her wristwatch. She watched the chaotic progress of the Daimler down the road and out of sight. We were all of us slightly shaken by the journey. "The thing is, I've got studying to do…" she said evasively.

"On a Friday?" I said in surprise.

"Oh, there's always, you know, work to put in. If you're going to do something…" She looked the length of the road again, and the rest of the saying hung in the air.

"Do it properly," Ma supplied without thinking, rooting in her bag for the door key.

"I'd better —" Jenny gave me a tense smile — "go, then. If that's alright."

"Alright," I said.

Ma served tea in the parlour, not in the back room, so I should have realised something was afoot. She used a veiny cane to walk with and insisted on carrying the tea things and a plate of cake as well. She wouldn't have any help from me. That tea took a long time to make.

She levered herself down into the armchair and we sat without speaking for a while, thinking about the service, waiting for the tea. Jenny, studying on a Friday? I shook my head, then slid the cosy up the side of the teapot so that I could lift the lid.

"Shall I give it a wind, Ma?"

While I was busy stirring the pot and pouring the tea, Ma heaved herself up out of the chair, her joints snapping with the effort, so that she could reach the family Bible down from the top shelf in the alcove. She dropped back down rather more quickly than she'd anticipated and sat for a moment with her head leaning against the anti-macassar and her eyes shut. "A merry heart doeth good like a medicine, but a broken spirit drieth the bones," she murmured. "That's what they say…"

"You've the least broken spirit of anyone I know."

"I've got the driest bones, mind," she said, arranging herself more comfortably in the chair, tugging a cushion into the small of her back. "Poor Delyth..." she straightened the book on her knee and opened it, sending some pieces of paper sifting onto her lap. "There'll be some mending of the spirit for her to do before she's right again."

"What have you got there, then, Ma?" I asked.

"The family safe. If anything happens to me ... well, you know ... when it happens, it's all here." She picked up a few of the sheets and let them fall. "Stuffed full of everything, it is. Your birth certificates, the letter telling us you got into the grammar school, Delyth's Cyclist badge from the Girl Guides. Oh, she was so proud of that. Don't know why I've kept those —" She dropped some newspaper clippings and a yellowed knitting pattern on to the floor. "Then there's the telegrams," she said.

I could see what was coming.

The paper was cracked along the folds and after all these years the ticker-tape message was lifting off the page and curling at the edges. It's strange how something so slight and small can knock the breath out of you. In an instant I was a nine-year-old lad again, the steam in the kitchen clearing round us as our world tilted on its axis and sent us reeling. Ma opened her mouth to read what was written but she stopped before she could get a word out, pressing one hand to her breastbone. After a moment she handed me the telegram so I could read it for myself. She was discreet in her grieving, locking Delyth and me out and herself in. From the corner of my eye I could see her twisting the wedding ring round her finger. Our Dad, killed in action at Messines.

"There's one for Glyn as well."

"I know."

The whites of Ma's eyes were shining. "Your father could have made a special case, as an agricultural worker he could have asked for an exemption. But he wouldn't." She blinked fiercely. "He wouldn't do it, silly bugger. Not for me, not for any of us. 'Doing my duty,' that's what he said. 'For King and country.'"

Once again I was a lad staring along an empty lane, waiting for a turning back that never came.

"Your brother lied about his age," my mother said.

I didn't know that. With a sharp intake of breath I bowed my head.

"He couldn't join Kitchener's army quick enough. He was only fifteen." She stared at the telegrams, touching the corner of one so that it lay in alignment with the other. "That's all you're left with," she said. "That, and a watch, and a Bible." She faltered. "And a penknife, too."

"Finish your tea," I said, my heart beating hard in my chest. "Or it'll go cold."

She nursed the cup in her hands, not drinking, regarding me through the steam. "Promise me…" she began.

All of us knew the war was coming, would come, at some point. Germany and Italy had signed some malodorous pact between them. The Foreign Secretary had warned Hitler that we would fight to protect Belgium. We knew.

"I'm thirty, Ma." I said uneasily. "They won't want an old fellow like me. And I'm a land worker, to boot."

"Promise me," she insisted. "Promise me on the Bible."

"Besides, it may not happen."

"With Ted gone now, as well." She closed the Bible and held it out to me. The weight of it was too much for her wrist, thin as a twig in winter, and I had to catch it to stop it from falling.

"I can't lose you as well," she said. A glimpse of my dad's knife, raised aloft, flashed between us and part of me wanted to curl myself into a ball and lean against the warm, forgiving wood of our back door and forget about the lot of it. Instead, I thought of the men who downed their tools and kissed their wives and quit their homes, their goodbyes flung backwards after them or never spoken, their valleys left, their farms neglected, their jobs taken by others; no more cricket, no more pale ale, no lengthening shadows on a summer's evening, no scent of wood smoke in the autumn, no frost-sketched breath on a freezing morning, no more hot and tarry tea, no freshly laundered sheets, no more pedalling uphill for the swooping abandonment of the downhill ride, no walks to Withy End in the slanting light, no more Nanagalan, no more you.

Would I lay down my life for a principle like my Dad? Like Glyn? Would I? Would I give up everything I loved — everyone who loved me — when my turn came? I felt the weight of the Bible in my hands and Ma's gaze upon me and when I glanced up, there were tears in runnels on her weathered cheeks so I knelt on the floor beside her chair and put my arm around her and I could feel a pricking in my own eyes as well, for the dead that were lost, and the lives of the living that were taken too.

I swore on the Good Book to give my mother ease and she wiped her face and gave me a wafery kiss. "Keep yourself safe for me, Ifor, there's a boy."

Chapter Sixteen

I remembered the weekend of Jenny's conference. We were lying back to back in bed reading when she told me about it. I was on the last chapter of *To Have and Have Not* and she had the latest Dorothy L. Sayers.

"Oh, I think I forgot to mention," she said, turning a page, "there's a conference in Nottingham at the end of the month. Proposed Improvements to the Dewey Decimal Classification in British Public Libraries."

"Nottingham?" I said, still reading.

"I think I should go."

"It's a heck of a way."

Jenny rested her novel on the coverlet and glanced back over her shoulder in my direction. She took a moment to answer. "It's over a weekend. There's a couple of colleagues from work..."

"I don't know much about Nottingham."

"It's where D. H. Lawrence was born," she said automatically, turning back to her book.

"I never finished *The Rainbow*. It was a bit — I couldn't get to grips with it, somehow."

"We thought we'd go up on the Friday before."

"Of course," I said.

"So that we're fresh."

"Which colleagues?" I asked as an afterthought.

"My boss Marjorie and one of the other assistants."

"Oh yes?"

"Emlyn Ellis. He's doing the correspondence course as well. I think I'll stop now." Jenny slid her book on to the bedside table and reached to blow out the candle.

I flicked the remaining pages through my fingers. There were more than I thought. I wondered if I should save it till the following night. "You've got to keep up with your studies," I said counting how many there were until the end.

I worked late in the estate office on that Friday, catching up with the accounts. I'd just got all the receipts into little piles and had plunged myself into the arithmetic, when you popped your head around the door.

"Haven't you got a home to go to?" You came fully into the room. "I saw the light was on."

"I won't be long," I said, scribbling down a sum on a piece of scrap paper before I forgot it. I raised my head, then made a slight, involuntary sound at the sight of you. You were dressed formally in something long and velvety, the greenish grey of undergrowth at dusk, your hair the last shaft of sunlight, shining gold.

"I'm just going out," you said, adjusting the lie of the strap of your dress. Your shoulder looked so white beneath it. Briefly, you leaned against the wall. "My old friend Nicholas is back," you added, as though a polite apology was in order, as though you knew what it would mean to me.

"I've just been going through the bills, checking payments. The quarterly accounts."

"He was posted to India a few years ago, but now he's come home," you explained, waiting.

On the desk in front of me was an invoice for copper sulphate solution. I stared intently at the figures, thinking hard about paying it on Monday, concentrating on the need to do so.

"He's having a party to celebrate. Half the county's invited," you went on, relentlessly informative. I don't think you meant to be unkind. I don't think you did.

"Wasn't he...?"

"His family's estate adjoins Nanagalan. We used to go to the pictures together, that sort of thing. Our parents were quite keen..."

I could recall every detail of him: his broad back, his thinning, sandy hair, his arm stealing round your shoulders; you, acquiescent in the flickering light of the cinema projector. "I think you did mention him." I picked up the invoice and put it down again. "I'd better get this finished..." I said, gesturing towards the receipts, scattering them over the blotter as I did so.

"Mrs Ifor must be wondering where you are," you said finally, rippling yourself upright with an arch of your back.

"She's away on a course this weekend." I was stooping to retrieve one of the bills which had fallen on the floor so I couldn't see your face, but I could feel the atmosphere changing for a moment, the invisible threads of comprehension pulling tight.

"Oh," it was the softest registration of sound, no more than a mouthing. "Well," you murmured. "Brown will be waiting..."

"Have a good evening, Miss Ella."

I went home to the cottage when I had finished my reckonings, my brain seized up with all the sums. The light was on in the dugout when I went past and strains of some music from the wireless trickled into the darkness, the louche melancholy filtering through the courtyard. I knocked on the garage door thinking to nod in for a minute or two, but Brown didn't hear me, or perhaps he didn't want to. He'd be in there tinkering with something to pass the time until he had to collect you, his pipe on the go, a cup of tea cooling on the workbench.

I didn't want to think of you in your ferny evening dress at Nicholas's party.

When I got in, I put a couple of logs in the stove and heated some water to fill the zinc tub: having a proper wash with water that wasn't already filmy with other people's soapings was a rare treat and I sat curled like a clam, steamed pink, listening to the resinous spit of the apple wood burning, taking time to adjust my bearings to account for the solitude. Jenny and I defined one other in such detail: the great truths between us being unspoken, we addressed the smaller issues exhaustively and without her it was as though I had been decompressed.

There was too much air to breathe and I felt light headed. I towelled myself dry and dressed, putting on a clean shirt. Upstairs in our bedroom I opened the window, leaned out and listened to the silence. Brown had shut up shop and I was conscious of the sibilant shift of leaves in the breeze and the rustle of a fox: night sounds, the absence of birdsong.

I went downstairs, tipped my bath water down the sink and heated up some soup. I thought about Delyth in her aloneness: no proper mooring, just Baby Gwynne to cling to and I decided I'd put my freedom to good use and go to Mynydd Maen to see them over the weekend. I washed the dishes, drank a glass of milk and spread yesterday's paper on the kitchen table. The Duke of Windsor, as we must call him now, had married Wallis Simpson. There was a photograph of the two of them looking slightly stunned at what they'd done.

212

I don't think I heard the motor. I was idling my way through the news and I reached for an apple, polished it on my sleeve and was thinking about eating it, when there was a knock at the door. I stood up to answer it, the apple still in my hand.

You were standing on the threshold in your dress the colour of twilight, holding a bottle of Nanagalan Blanc de Blanc carelessly by the neck. "I was just passing..." you said with an awkward smile.

I glanced behind me on a reflex. The column of light from the gas lamp shone thinly, seeking out angles. My glass stood empty on the table. The room seemed homely enough to me, I liked the sparseness of it; I didn't want to see it through your eyes.

"May I come in?"

I didn't stand aside and hold the door wider. I stared down at the apple, turning it over in my hand, feeling the russet skin. "It's nearly eleven o'clock..." I knew that letting you into my empty house at a late hour on a June night would be as good as — I stopped, so constricted by a sense of propriety I couldn't even risk the thought. "I won't bite," you said. There was a hint of derision in your voice.

I switched my gaze to your face. The excitement of the party was still in the ether around you, an echo of the dancing, the witty exchanges, the drinking. You seemed agitated and it struck me that you might be as unmoored and as lonely as my sister. A poor little rich girl in the darkness on my doorstep with her bottle of champagne. I could see that you were shivering and as I felt the cool of the evening closing in, I shivered too.

"I was just..." I said warily. This was the last — the only — line of my defence.

"I'll go, if it's not convenient —"

"Don't go!"

"If you've got something more pressing..."

"No." I felt slightly out of breath, as if I'd been running and running to get here. "There's nothing pressing."

"May I come in, then?"

You slipped into my kitchen and gazed around you, blinking. I closed the door and leant against it, then exhaled with slow precision. Everything seemed too ... acute. It was like physical pain. I stood without moving because I feared that anything I touched would burn me.

"Will you open this?" You held out the bottle. "Or shall I?"

I took the bottle, ripped off the foil and unwound the wire. The cork eased out with a breathy sigh. "I've only got half-pint glasses," I apologised, rinsing the milk from one, stretching up to get another from the shelf.

"Just the ticket," you said, reaching for some champagne with more effort than was required, so that the movement carried you in an indistinct arc to the chair that I'd been sitting in. You dropped down onto it. "We can drown our sorrows." You looked across at me. "I'm not drunk, Ifor, but I would quite like to be."

I sat down carefully in Jenny's chair. "What sorrows, miss?"

"Oh, you know, the usual kind." You took a sip of your drink, and then another. You scanned the newspaper lying open on the table, then loosed a small mewling sigh, putting your glass down and propping your head in your hand. You touched the photograph of Mrs Simpson with your fingertip. "And they lived happily ever after," you whispered.

"What sorrows?"

You paused for a moment. "The thing is, Ifor, I'm not ... accountable ... to anyone. That's what I find hard." You seemed to consider what you'd just said, as though the

214

admission had slipped out without you quite realising. "That must seem strange to someone like you." You lifted your head and subjected me to a brief scrutiny. "I expect being accountable is something that you hate."

I shrugged. I rolled the wine around my glass, watching the bubbles rising to the surface, tiny beads in flight.

"And because of that," you said, "it can feel as if nothing has much ... meaning." You drank again, for longer this time. "There. Now you know my darkest secret." You gave me a brittle smile. "So you must tell me one of yours in return."

"My secret..." I could have told you that I loved you, there and then. I wish I had. It's the things we don't do that we regret the most. "My secret is that I don't really believe in happy ever after." I regarded you, levelly. "There."

"What a pair we are." You sighed a small, regretful sigh. "It's awfully bright in here, don't you think?" you observed, looking from one side of the kitchen to the other. "What do you believe in, then?"

I stood up, fetched a candle from the drawer beside the sink, put it into an old earthenware candlestick that Jenny's parents had given us and struck a match. "I think I believe in making the best of what you've got. Or trying to, at least." I leaned forward and lit the candle, then turned the gas lamp out. I extinguished the match. The half-light feathered round us as the candle flickered into life.

"And does that work?" you asked. "Is it something I should try?"

Your silhouette washed in soft shadow across the distempered wall, so that your presence in the room was everywhere. I stood, susceptible and still, taking you in.

"Some of the time." One of Ma's sayings flashed into my mind. "Any fool can have a miserable life. It takes a clever man to lead a happy one."

"And you're ... clever?"

"I was a grammar-school boy," I answered dryly.

A spill of wax ran down the side of the candle. You checked its passage with your fingernail. "So you and Mrs Ifor are happy, are you?"

I was still holding the match. I pinched the head of it between my fingers to see that it was cold and put it on the table. "I think you know the answer to that." I half turned, meaning to sit down in my wife's chair, but you caught my hand and held it in both of yours. I could see a pulse beating in the vein at your temple, frail and blue.

"He tried to kiss me tonight. Nicholas. I had to excuse myself and he was in the corridor waiting for me, after. He said he knew I wanted it. That a woman, living on her own, must have needs..."

I was on my knees beside you. "Are you alright? What did he—?"

"The man revolts me." Hesitantly, you rested your head on my shoulder until I could feel the curve of your cheek against my neck. My arms described the space around you. I wasn't going to touch you. I wouldn't let myself touch —

"Will you hold me for a moment?"

A tremor went shooting through me, the lightning strike of conscience. I laid a faltering hand against your hair. "I..."

"That's what's left for unmarried women of my age: the opportunists, the gropers. Not you," you breathed, as I retreated a fraction. "Not you." We leaned close for a minute, for another minute, lost in the eddy and slip of each other, our bodies inclining together, time sliding past us in soft currents. I closed my eyes to have the learning of you better.

"At least we're not dancing," you murmured and I gathered you to me in spite of myself. You tilted your head back, your eyes swimming beneath their lids and all I could think of was your quickening pulse, the whiteness of your neck, the soft meld of you and me. You brushed your mouth across mine, and so began the gentle articulation of lip and tongue, the long, drawn out syllables of a kiss. We were disclosing ourselves with slow languor, weightless in each other's arms; we were elsewhere, we were other, we were in flight, we were falling.

"Show me how," you whispered, touching the buttons of my shirt, undoing the first, then the second. "I've never..."

I opened my eyes and for a moment I was dazzled, like some woodland creature caught in the beam of the poacher's torch. You were glistening, the candlelight gleaming on your skin and in the lustre of your hair. Hardly knowing what I was doing, I broke away. "This isn't right —" I said. "I'm sorry. We shouldn't be — we can't — do this."

You kissed me again in answer, a brief, obliterative kiss.

"We mustn't," I said, putting you from me, holding you at the length of my arm. I bowed my head. "I've made promises. Promises I have to keep."

"But what about...?"

I watched the redness of your mouth as you spoke, the mesmeric shapes your lips made. I had enormous difficulty in hearing what you were saying.

"What about this? What about — us?"

"There can't be an us. There mustn't be. I'm married. You'd be finished if we were found out. Your reputation —"

You shrugged your white, white shoulders.

"And there's Jenny," I said, "I have to think about her."

"Ah," you whispered, "Jenny." You reached unsteadily for your glass. "Mrs Ifor. Is it like this when you and she —?"

"We don't," I said swiftly. "That side of things never really — worked, between us. We haven't — for ages. We don't." You took a sip of champagne and I couldn't help thinking that only a minute ago I had been the drink you drank. I swallowed hard and reached behind me for Jenny's chair, then sat down heavily.

"I suppose that's some kind of consolation." You dipped your finger into the wine then ran it broodingly round the rim of your glass. "You can sound a note, apparently," you said, "If you know how. You can make music." Your mouth turned down. "Though I don't seem to have the knack."

"What do we do now?"

"I suppose we do nothing." There was a slight turbulence in your voice as you spoke, a squall you had to master before you went on. "That's what we seem to be saying. It is what we're saying, isn't it?"

I couldn't answer. I pictured Jenny in some draughty hall in Nottingham trying to better herself, jotting down the lecture notes with her usual proficiency. She had taken to wearing glasses for reading and I imagined her pushing them back to the bridge of her nose as she listened to the speaker. I could see her bent over her exercise book writing at such speed that the words threatened to unravel and the earnestness of the image was worse than any reproach that she could level at me.

I cast my gaze way back to the young lad out drinking at the Fleece with Mr Brown on the night before his wedding. I'll be a good husband. I've made up my mind. I will. The buttons of my shirt were still undone and I remembered you undoing them and the song that had sung inside me then fell silent.

"You were right to ... draw a line. I shouldn't have thrown myself at you. I've had a beastly night." You stood up abruptly, "I've probably had too much to drink, in any case. It's an occupational hazard if you own a vineyard." I saw you straighten your shoulders, assuming the poise you had acquired at finishing school all those years ago: the cool politeness, the defensive grace. "It won't happen again." You crossed over to the door and opened it. "Good night, Ifor," you said tiredly as you let the latch fall shut behind you.

My wife came home from Nottingham radiant with all the learning, her face flushed and alive. She told me about the lectures and the seminars at great length, looking sideways at me to see if I was listening and I was listening, to remind myself of the choice I'd made, to blot out the rasp and whisper of what had happened, which hissed like static in my head.

I watched her as she was speaking and for a moment her ardour was reminiscent of the earnest, myopic girl that I first met and I felt the current of emotion that was seething inside me switch and shift: the cataclysmic desire I had for you colliding with the remorseful affection I felt for my wife. It wasn't that I didn't care for her. I cared enough to stop myself from having you, to stop you from taking me. That's how much I cared. So I listened and I told her about my trip to Mynydd Maen and said I'd finished the quarterly accounts. I neglected to mention that I had given up a fundamental part of myself — a dream rendered derelict: the windows broken, the roof stoved in and all the people gone.

"Jenny —" for a fraction of a second I thought that perhaps I could tell her; that the gulf between you and me could become the demarcation of a better, fuller married life; that we might knit up the threads of communion which had worn so thin.

I could feel the passing speculation of her gaze as her eyes rested on me for a moment. "I'm fair worn out," she yawned with an indolence I hadn't seen in her before, or hadn't noticed. "Think I'll turn in early." She mounted the stairs, and as she climbed the last few treads she started humming and I could hear her cross the landing and close our bedroom door behind her.

I remembered the evening that Brown died. He'd been the teacher of my younger self, my pathfinder, my drinking companion, my counsellor, the repository of everything I knew about music, about the wider world. He was the father I should have had and lost. He was my friend in both need and deed and the night he died almost had the finishing of me.

There had been a heaviness about him, a profound aura of distraction, and it became harder than ever to rouse him from his thoughts of an evening.

"Do you fancy a walk up to the Fleece?"

"Not tonight, my boy."

"How about a drive over to Newland?"

"I don't think so. Thank you for asking."

"Whist, then? Or cribbage?"

Mostly he was rooted to the wireless, the Murphy A3 on full volume straining every valve because he was becoming hard of hearing. He'd sit forward in his armchair, leaning close to the grey grille silk, shaking his head at the way the world was turning. The crisis in Czechoslovakia got right under his skin — the German army just walking in and helping themselves. Before we knew it, we were up to our necks in civil defence exercises. Parry the Paint put himself forward as the new air raid warden for Morwithy and all of us had to troop up to the village hall to collect our gas masks and the Home Office handbook about what to do in the event of an attack. I was sat in the dugout with Brown the night that the Archbishop of York led the nation in prayer: if we are called to suffer in a just cause we must be brave and constant.

He took terrible offence at that. "The man that doesn't know what he's saying. We've been brave. We've been constant. We don't need to take lessons in just causes." He rubbed one eye with the heel of his hand. "We fought the war to end all wars, chum," he said, addressing the wireless bitterly. "Beg pardon, my boy," he sighed, slumping back in his chair so that dust from the horsehair stuffing rose into the air.

The last time I saw him alive he was striding across the courtyard, fulminating. I was with Jenkins and we were wheeling a barrow full of sand over to the kitchen garden, in order to make sandbags to place around the glasshouses. Brown was striking his forehead in frustration and my lad flinched and skittled sideways with the wheelbarrow.

"Idiot woman!" Brown growled. "She could have brought the whole house crashing down around our ears."

"Anything the matter?" I enquired.

"My wife is a liability. Talk about the frailer sex!"

"If you could to make a start on the sandbags..." I said to Jenkins, who was concentrating on taking up the smallest amount of space possible, systematically reducing his own volume by a fidgety series of tucks and squeezes. "What's happened, Mr Brown?" I asked when we were alone.

"I was going to ask her to get some rich tea biscuits for me — she's going into town later — and I only walked into the kitchen to find the inestimable woman, wearing her gas mask, on her hands and knees, with her head in the oven. For goodness' sake! She said she was testing the mask out. She said she didn't want to get caught out by the Hun. I said she could have blown us all to kingdom come. What if I'd been smoking my pipe when I came in?" He was lathered with it, as hot under the collar as I had ever seen him.

Parry the Paint organised a civil defence exercise for the whole of Morwithy and we were under strict instructions not to allow a single beam of light to slip between curtains or through doors. Perhaps the depth of darkness was too much for him.

We were on our way to bed when Mrs Brown came running into our cottage in her night clothes, screaming. She was clawing at her face with her fingers, with her nightdress whipping round her. "Help me, God!" She bent over double, clutching herself, clawing her face again, rocking her whole body.

We stood aghast, then in alarm Jenny ran upstairs to find Mrs Brown a dressing gown, as though that could protect her against unfolding tragedy. "Stay here," I said, dashing out into the courtyard.

"The blackout!" Jenny shrilled. "Close the door!" but I could see that it wasn't the blackout which was making her panic.

There was a darkness inside the dugout undiluted by the thready light from the stars overhead. I stood on the threshold, gripping the doorframe, trying to distinguish one looming shape from another — the shelving, the table, his armchair — and I could already detect the slippery, ferrous, salty smell of blood. I dragged the door shut behind me and snapped the light on.

A spurt of blood and matter glistened on the far wall. I was transfixed by the arrested violence of it, taking in the red spew thinning into rivulets, the pale cusp of a fragment of bone caught in the mortar of the whitewashed brickwork and I kept staring at the wall, not willing to look elsewhere, not willing to look.

He was sitting in the armchair all akimbo, as if the force of the blast had lifted him up and then dropped him, not very tidily, so that he was slumped over to one side. He had changed out of his overalls into what he used to call his civvies, and his shoes with their neatly tied double bows shone as though he had polished them shortly before he shot himself. It was the sight of his shoes that had the undoing of me. I started shaking my head, then found that I couldn't stop. I stood with my hands clamped over my ears like Jenkins, trying to block everything out.

From the corner of my eye I could see the Webley Mark One air pistol on the floor beside his chair and I inched my way towards it. I would have stooped to pick it up, but then I thought about the police and stopped in my tracks. Doctor? Coroner? Priest? Where do you turn when your friend has killed himself? Standing this close to him I could see the extent of the blood, scarlet and copious, thick as jelly, and I found that I was trembling. I noticed that his hand was crooked anyhow and I straightened it, then with a feeling of trepidation I took it in mine and it was still faintly warm, so I cradled it for the comfort thinking that I had known and not known that this might happen. Poor Mr Brown, damaged by the war and then imperfectly repaired, holding back the great tide until he couldn't hold it back any longer.

I thought about him doing the crossword and bowling beamers at me by the hour in the wildflower meadow; I thought about the dignified cuckold, the old soldier felled by the fire in the beech wood, the approximate driver, and for one absurd moment I opened my mouth to tell him how terrified I always was on those careering voyages in the back of the motor and caught off my guard I glanced at his face.

I have an image of my friend that effaces all my other memories of him. I have an image of my dear friend that I just cannot erase.

The police arrived and then an ambulance. It was an Austin 18 with two-tone livery — I found myself making a note of the fact the way Mr Brown would have done, taking refuge in detail in order to blind himself to what was happening. At some point Mrs Brown must have wrested herself free from Jenny's care because there was a commotion at the entrance to the dugout and I could hear her sobbing, "I never thought … I never thought he actually — I mean, he said it sometimes, but I didn't think —"

The recollection of her upending herself for Samuelson year after year and reading out her wretched recipes to all comers made me boil with anger. I had to restrain myself from elbowing through the surrounding throng and taking issue with her: "That's because you never stopped to think. You never stopped —" I remembered the blistering arguments we used to hear over spilling from their cottage, Mr Brown shouting out his desperation so that she would hear it.

The police sergeant had come from Monmouth. He was a stocky fellow, tired at the end of a long shift, who seemed to be inured to the procedures involved and had doubtless seen too much over many years of service. He cleared his throat with a compassion that seemed a little weary. "You said you thought it was an accident, didn't you?" he asked with emphasis.

Mrs Brown drew a breath to answer before I realised where the line of questioning might lead.

"Yes," I did step forward then. "He cleaned the pistol regularly. It must have … gone off … by mistake." I spoke as firmly as I could.

Behind me in the dugout I could hear the circumspect tread of the medics and the burr of their movements. Somebody was taking photographs, turning Mr Brown's dead body into an exhibit. I had to bite my lip to steady myself.

"We were talking just the other day. He was full of plans — for the cricket next year, for lots of things. There's no question —" I didn't want him to be branded a criminal. I didn't want him to be buried in unhallowed ground, by the crossroads in the village where the bodies of past suicides were supposed to lie, with no mark to show their resting place. I wanted everything right and proper for him, with hymns and blessings and prayers and respects paid and all the Christian consolations to speed him on his way. "I was a colleague of his," I said, by way of explanation. There was a catch in my voice. Talking about him in the past tense filled me with a grinding sadness, terrible and familiar: the tectonic shift of grief which changes the world so that it is never quite the same again. "It was definitely an accident."

They covered his body with a sheet once they had worked through the formalities and they drove him away in the ambulance. The doctor gave Mrs Brown a sedative and Jenny put her to bed in our spare room. At one point I glimpsed you speaking to the police sergeant. We were hampered by sorrow, all of us; moving uncertainly, gauging the weight of it. Some young constable was given the job of cleaning the blood from the dugout wall and I offered to help him — my own last rite — but he wouldn't let me. I went home and Jenny made me a mug of hot milk and I sat, unhoused, staring at the surface of it until a skin formed, and she put her hand on my arm and said that she was sorry.

After work the next day, stumbling through the vineyard checking the grapes for ripeness, I went and sat in the dugout. The blood-soaked, varicose old armchair was in the corner of the kitchen garden waiting to be burned on the next bonfire, so I perched on my stool the way I always did, alert to traces of him in the air, with the sense that everything good had turned bad, that everything white had turned black, his presence, like a photographic negative, turned to absence.

I switched on the wireless, lowering the volume by degrees. Mr Chamberlain had just arrived home from Germany and was speaking from the foot of the aeroplane steps at the Heston aerodrome. He was carrying an agreement he had signed with Herr Hitler and promised us peace for our time.

Hharvest time that year seemed so mechanical, with no real sense of satisfaction at the gathering in. I was thrown off-course by Mr Brown's death, his poor tumbled body always in my sight and as autumn flamed into the valley, the leaves looked bloodied on the trees. I couldn't find a place for myself. Wherever I was — at home, in the tool shed, in the vineyard — I didn't want to be. I felt untethered and utterly at a loss.

A pall of November mist lay over us and the nights began to close in around Nanagalan. I had forgotten that bereavement could be so peremptory in its comings and goings — anything could set me off: the Sunday hymn singing, a glimpse of the motor in the garage, seeing the first robin of the winter busy with its beaky gleanings in the kitchen garden, just about anything would have me burying my face in the crook of my arm, cuffing away my own grief's gleanings.

Jenny was good to me in those troubled months. In her quiet way she accompanied me through the days of mourning. It was like being orphaned all over again. I couldn't grasp what had happened, I couldn't make sense of it and she was gentle with me in my bewilderment. I think she was as shocked as I was and we passed each other on the stairs going up to bed, or in the kitchen making breakfast with the same numb expression on our faces. I became used to the slight touch of the comfort she tried to give me: a hand on my shoulder, a glance in my direction when the spate was on me.

"The busy heart?" she'd say, reminding me of the Rupert Brooke poem from our courting days. It was a kindness that reached me from a distance, but it was a kindness that reached me. She'd look at me with a downward turn of her mouth that was almost a smile, as though she were in some way culpable, as though she would have changed things, if only she could.

We made it through that disconsolate winter and into the quietude of early spring. With the first stirrings of the garden I had fleeting moments of hope that the worst would soon be over and that 1939 would bring some promise with it, or at least some respite. In chapel at the Easter Service, washed clean with prayer on my knees before God, I had the first real intimation of remission. All shall be well, and all shall be well, and all manner of things shall be well. I took some early daffs up to Mr Brown's grave, safe in the embrace of the churchyard wall, and I looked at the inscription on his headstone and discovered with a pang that he was called Wilfred. I stood there for a while with my head bowed, thinking of all the other things about him that I should have liked to have known.

The storm which had the shaking of Mrs Brown blew itself out soon enough and she began taking herself off to the Fleece of a Friday evening.

"For a port and lemonade, just the one," she said, but each week the jet brooch she wore in memory of her late husband was pinned to her collar at a jauntier angle. "It's for the company," she said over her shoulder as she set off up the drive. "That's all."

She found some company rather quickly, all things considered. Within six months of Mr Brown dying she had the butcher from Llancloudy under her flaky spell and I tried not to picture her reading aloud to him about black pudding faggots, caul fat and stout gravy.

When the new Mrs Hughes moved away from Nanagalan after a whirlwind romance, you shut down more rooms in the house, engaged a part-time cook and at one of our weekly meetings you told me you were going to learn to drive.

"I'm also going to grow my hair long and let birds nest in it, clothe myself in the wedding dress I'm never going to wear and seal myself up here in mouldering splendour, growing a little madder with every year that passes. You can't say I'm not planning ahead."

You kept me at arm's length with your brittleness. It was when you were in pensive mood, glancing at me at then looking away, opening your mouth to speak and saying nothing, that I could almost convince myself that things were as they had always been between us. We avoided any kind of awkward acknowledgement by being cordial, by taking a polite interest in aspects of each other's lives which had no meaning. We were so successful that sometimes I wondered if I had dreamed that we kissed each other on a June night, the gasp of your lips parting at the touch of mine.

When you said that you were learning to drive, you neglected to mention that Nicholas had offered to teach you. One unfurling, sap-filled afternoon in the spring, I was mowing the lawn on Dancing Green, lulled by the reach and retreat of the lawn mower and the green spume of the cut grass when I heard the sound of an engine — not the hiccoughing lurch of the Daimler making a cautious descent, but something lighter — with torque, I suppose, and sophistication. Looking up I saw an open-topped blue sports car skimming down towards the house. You were driving, with your hands braced against the steering wheel and your hair, escaping from a scarf, scattered like largesse in the wind. From here it looked as though your eyes were tightly closed. You skidded to a halt in front of the Herbar, making Jenkins, who was planting rose trees, dive for cover.

"Steady on, old girl," said your instructor, guffawing. He was in the first sprawl of middle age, his sandy hair reduced to a few strands, sporting more moustache than was strictly necessary as if to compensate. He had the studied casualness which the rich spend money to acquire: the artless cravat, the open-necked shirt, the blazer just so. "Jolly good show, though. How about a spot of reversing?"

I continued the precision engineering of my stripe of lawn, making a study of both of you together. It was like watching a film with the sound turned down so that all your gestures seemed exaggerated, your expressions too pronounced, the two of you performing for each other the larger than life "driving lesson". I fought to keep the line straight as I imagined Nicholas, salivating, pressing himself up against you, and you, hurting yourself in his tight embrace.

In April, when Germany denounced the mutual assistance pact that Mr Chamberlain had signed with Poland, the government introduced conscription and called up men aged twenty and twenty-one for six months' military training. Jenkins became more precipitate than usual, rushing from job to job in a state of high alert and he started working on a new list. When I first met him he recited the names of flowers to me. Now, if I came upon him unawares clipping the box hedges in the Herbar or pruning the spring flowering shrubs, he was whispering about weaponry under his breath, "...the Thompson M1928, the Thompson M1928A1, the Bren light machine gun, the Lewis gun, the Vickers K machine gun, the M2 Browning machine gun, the Lee Enfield bolt action magazine fed repeating rifle..."

"You've missed some, back there," I said indicating a straggling tuft of box. "You need to keep your mind on the job, my lad."

He jumped up, nervily. "Yes, Mister?" he said, looking at something just beyond my left shoulder.

"You need to think about what you're doing," I said mildly. A scent of resin rose from the clippings. In the distance I could hear the crow of a cock, snared on the valley breeze.

"I'll be doing my bit, soon, that's what I'll be doing," he said, rising up onto the balls of his feet, readying himself for action. "I've had my papers."

God in heaven, I thought. I glanced at the boyish set of Jenkins' head, his snub nose, his freckles. He looked barely old enough to be in long trousers. He looked as though he'd still have conkers in his pockets and scabs on his knees.

"You'll be doing important work here, growing food and suchlike, if the war kicks off."

"But what if my country needs me?"

"You don't have to go, not if you're working the land."

"I'm going to do my bit," he reiterated, dropping back down onto all fours and resuming the clipping of the hedge. As I set off for the vineyard to remove some of the early side shoots from the vines, I could hear him mouthing the names of different kinds of hand grenade.

Nicholas appeared to be giving you more driving lessons then you really needed, or so it seemed to me.

I remembered thinking, after a while, that Jenny took the death of Mr Brown harder than the rest of us which, when I thought about it, didn't quite add up, as the two of them were never close. She looked withdrawn and her kindness began to have a vague abstraction to it, as though it had become detached from any real sympathy. I came home one evening and she was cleaning my best boots, slathering on the blacking then polishing them until stray bristles flew from the brush.

"That's my job. You don't have to do that."

"I was doing my own," she replied, panting a little with the effort. "And anyway, a good wife should look after her husband," she said, buffing the leather to a shine and I thought then that she had been a good wife to me, that between us we had reached an accommodation.

I washed my hands and sluiced my head and neck under the kitchen tap. Lately, her studies — she was doing some sort of certificate in advanced librarianship — seemed to take up more and more of her time and when she came home she was often so exhausted she would lie on the bed for half an hour, although when I looked in on her she was frequently staring up at the ceiling, her jaw tense, not sleeping. I thought the polishing and the mending — sheets turned sides to middle, buttons sewn, elbows patched — were some kind of reparation for her being late so regularly, or absent even when she was here.

Then, out of the blue she started preparing elaborate meals, kneading pastry, making batter — and the sauces! What on earth is a béchamel sauce and why would you want to cook it on a Wednesday?

"You don't have to —" I'd begin, "Simple food ... like we always ... you know ... is fine by me," and she'd shake her head and start whisking, or stirring, or folding in (the phrases we were learning) even faster.

One day I came home from work and she was in the kitchen, standing at the table resting her weight on her fists, her head slung low as if the burden of it were too much for her to support any longer.

"I'm five months pregnant," she said, without looking up. "And Emlyn won't leave his wife."

I was halfway to hanging my jacket on the back of the door and I halted, wondering if I should loop it over the chair instead, because suddenly I didn't seem to have the energy to reach the hook. The jacket was a tired old thing that I'd had for ages, made from some kind of waxed canvas that was wearing through in places. After a moment or two I folded it over my arm, smoothing it flat. It seemed oddly empty of me.

"Who's Emlyn?" I said, glancing over at my wife. She lifted her head, tipping it right back then arching her spine as if she were in discomfort and the intimacy of the action was shocking, in a way, something I felt I shouldn't have seen. I took a step back. I couldn't locate myself in my own kitchen.

"He's my lover."

"You're pregnant?" I would have looked at her belly then, but she sat herself in her chair and folded her hands in her lap.

"We've been lovers for two years and friends before that."

"Emlyn?" I held my jacket to my chest as insulation, hugging it close, resting my chin against the material while I tried to think. The shoulder was splitting at the seam and the cotton was fraying. "When's it due? The — baby?"

"We work together at the library. It's due in October."

"This has been going on for two years?" I said, trying to make sense of what she was telling me. I sat down abruptly. "I … I don't know what to say."

Her hands weren't folded in her lap, they were resting against her stomach, and I was conscious of the fluttering communion between her and the baby — the searching, reassuring pressure of her fingers. I could feel her gaze upon me, her face tilting this way and then that in contemplation. "If I didn't know better," she said, "I could almost believe you cared."

I shook my head, sorrowfully. "I do care. That's the whole point. I've always cared."

Jenny raised her eyebrows at that.

My mouth was inordinately dry and I wanted the cleansing respite of a cold glass of water, but I didn't seem to be able to find the vigour to stand up and cross to the sink. I felt as if all my vital strength had been taken from me. I stared at Jenny, imagining her as a stranger I had just met to see what I would make of her if I didn't know, and the longer I regarded her the less familiar she seemed to me.

"What's sauce for the goose is sauce for the gander," she said. "Don't look at me like that."

"Sauce for the goose?" I could hear the geology of shock and disbelief and shame and anger in the harsh seams of my voice and I didn't know how to soften it. Her air of preoccupation over recent months — over years, over years — was starting to make sense. When I looked carefully, I could see her altered state in everything about her: in the rounding of her cheeks, the knot of her black hair that was loosened and glossy, the motherhood bloom of her, all of it made new and differently and not by me.

"I do care," the words, when I repeated them, had the same truth they had always had for me. I wanted her to know about the damage she was inflicting.

"You never loved me, Ifor. Let's not pretend. It would insult me if you tried to pretend."

I thought of Brown's words. Fond isn't worth the paper that it's written on. It seemed that he was right. "Perhaps not as you wanted me to." I said. "I've always thought we were quite alike, you and I. Quiet souls; bookish, and so forth." I felt as if the stuffing, the breath, everything, had been knocked out of me. "Two years?" I shook my head. There was something to mourn in that time and I, so inured to grieving, hadn't realised.

"If you had given me a single sign. If you had shown the faintest interest," she said, leaning forward with vehemence. "But all you thought about was — what was it you called her? — your employer."

I made as if to stand up, thinking of cold water, thinking of fresh air, thinking my wife is pregnant with another man's child. "At least I've been — loyal."

I placed my head in my hands, as if I could contain my thoughts, as if I could protect their thin bone casing. That June night, you at the door with your champagne, you in this room, you in my arms. The stammer and choke of abstinence: of not touching, of not undoing, of not sinking then lying then holding then having. Your shadow on these walls flickering all around me, and all the while Jenny had been spreading her legs for her librarian.

"He won't leave his wife. He's told me. He's made it very clear," she said, her voice for the first time beginning to falter. "He has two daughters, and a job, and a life that he … doesn't want to give up."

She pressed her lips together, but couldn't stop them trembling. I saw the brimming in her eyes, pent tears on the brink of overflowing.

"It's not being enough," she whispered. "For anybody. That's what —" She rounded her shoulders, hunching herself forward. I watched a teardrop being absorbed by the cotton of her dress, although I hadn't seen it fall.

This was territory that I, the less-loved son, the surviving second best, could understand. I reached into my pocket and found my handkerchief, then handed it to her gently.

"We love each other. We just can't ... be together," she wiped her eyes, folding the handkerchief in upon itself. "So now you know."

The freedom that her words dangled before me was a wound I hadn't thought to sustain. "What are we going to do?" I said. "You and I?"

Wearily, she handed me back the handkerchief. "I don't know," she sighed. "That rather depends on you."

For better, for worse, I thought, to have and to hold from this day forward — such rigorous and unrelenting promises. "I'll stand by you," I said shortly. "Of course. If that's what you want." I started pulling on my jacket. I wanted some air. I wanted some time to think.

"Ifor —?"

My fingers were already on the latch. I glanced back at her. "Yes?"

She looked at me searchingly for a moment. "I'm sorry," she said.

I remembered walking all the way up to Long Leap, the fusillade of my heartbeat making me dizzy. If there was sanction for Jenny and Emlyn, then why not for Ella and Ifor? I was wanton with the thought of you and me. I was reckless with plurals. Us. We. Our. I could hear the keening sound of blood pounding in my ears. Oh my Ella, my Ella. Part of me wanted to go hammering over to the house, bursting with this extenuating news which could change everything, which offered absolution. Things would have been so different, if only I had.

The next time I saw you was at our weekly meeting. I'd made up my mind that I would explain everything and I had been awake for half the night, lying in bed beside Jenny, planning what I would say. Over and over again I pictured you hearing what I had to tell you, that we had licence of a kind: your hand fluttering to your neck, your pupils dilating before your eyes slurred shut as I kissed you. For all my weight of years, in some ways I was a green lad still.

You were working away at your desk with the thin northern light at your back. "Please sit," you said, although normally I took my place without you asking.

I sat in my usual chair, suddenly wary. A pulse ticked at the base of my throat and my breath felt tight in my chest.

"I've had a letter from the Ministry of Agriculture and Fisheries," you said without preamble. I should have felt a prickle of alarm at this, but I was studying your expression intently, trying to work out if the edge I sensed in you was anger or anxiety. There seemed to be a polite brutality to the way that you were speaking. "They're sending me six girls from the Land Army." You picked up the letter opener from your desk and turned the slim sheath of it over in your fingers and your nails were as translucent as the mother of pearl. "As part of the preparations for the war…"

"Well, that's good news," I said uncertainly, "Isn't it? It means we'll be able to expand…"

"It's so the men can start training, for when the time comes." You appeared to scrutinise me and the blue of your dragonfly eyes was cooler than I was used to. "For when the war comes."

"Of course," I said. "That makes sense."

"It means," you said, switching your gaze to the still life painting on the wall behind my head — the dead birds, the plucked fruit, the clay pipe, "It means there will no longer be … a position … for you at Nanagalan."

It seemed as if I was falling from a great height and I kept falling and the ground never came any closer. From a distance I could see you run your finger round a string of pearls you were wearing, as if they were constricting you, as if, for a moment, you couldn't breathe.

"You can keep the cottage, of course," you said, swallowing, "for the same rent. But it means that you'll be free to enlist."

"What do you mean — enlist? What are you talking about?"

"We must all do our duty," you said and the words on your lips were a punishment and I shook my head in disbelief at the reproof, your lips that I had pictured kissing. "The Land Girls will be arriving at the end of the week."

"But I'm an agricultural worker," I began and as I spoke I thought of my old Ma and the promise that I'd made her and whether the breaking of that promise would be the end of her. Then I thought of Jenny, stranded in our marriage with someone else's baby. "I could claim an exemption."

You placed the letter opener on the blotter and drew a pile of correspondence towards you. "I can't imagine you'd do that," you said, as if that settled the matter.

237

"No." I felt as if I'd been struck from behind by a blow that I couldn't have anticipated. "Don't think I don't know about duty," I added as an afterthought. I levered myself up out of the chair. I felt dazed and I blinked to try and focus my eyes in the lamenting, northern light. Then, wakening too late to the urgency of the situation, I asked, "Has something happened...?"

You took a letter from the top of the pile and started reading. "I'm expecting a telephone call in a moment," you said without looking up. The paper in your hand was shaking.

I had often wondered how men said their goodbyes and took their leave of everything they loved, and now I had the answer. They say very little and they go as quickly as they can and like my Dad, they don't turn to look back.

"You're the one with all the news, in any case," you said as I reached the door. There was a serration in your voice, the drawing of a sharp, uneven blade. "I heard from the vicar that Mrs Ifor is expecting a baby. My felicitations to you both."

I stopped in my tracks. I would have answered you. I would have put this terrible misapprehension to rights, although I was still so stunned I could hardly form the words. I was on the point of turning round to explain everything: about Emlyn, about Jenny, when the telephone started to ring.

Chapter Seventeen

I was sent for military training to a depot near Newport. At the age of thirty-two I was considered too old for frontline action, though they put me through eight weeks of PT and digging weapons pits, for which, it was observed, I had a natural talent: all those years and years of gardening not entirely wasted, though I would have given anything to have been planting out a new border at the edge of Dancing Green — I'd had a mind to create a camellia hedge for you between the garden and the drive, something I would never have the chance to do, not now.

When we weren't digging and doing star jumps, press-ups and square bashing, we were at lectures. I went to bed each night with my mind full of maps and compass bearings and drill movements and military law and the theory of small arms fire, but my heart was full of you and the possibilities we had squandered; it was full of my old Ma too, and even Jenny's baby, whom I might not live to see. My past in echoes, which like the lost songs of Nanagalan I could almost hear, if the wind was blowing a certain way and there was time to stop and listen.

We were given twenty-four hours' leave before we sailed to France. I sat through the final lecture about petrol and carburettors, thinking that Brown in his oily overalls would have made short work of the subject, but our chap made a right meal out of it: on and on and on he went, with no sense that we were soldiers who had homes to go to. Then it was a long queue to see the MO for a shot of tetanus and a shot of typhoid, before we were given our passes.

I went to visit Delyth and Baby Gwynne first, because they were closest, Gwynne stomping around the confined flat barking orders to her dolls like some tiny sergeant major. She eyed me speculatively, through Ted's pale lashes, weighing me up as suitable material to join her alphabet class. "Sit in the corner over by there and I'll be with you shortly," she said, reserving judgment.

Delyth had volunteered to join the WAAF and was learning to type, so we were all of us doing our bit. "It's good news about Jenny, you must be —"

I was still watching my niece, waiting to see if I passed muster. "Yes," I said, keeping my voice level, "I'm very pleased. We both are."

"Bad timing, though, what with the war and things…"

"You could say that."

My sister had cooked a Patriotic Pudding in honour of my departure, a grey entity made from grated potato and oatmeal with a tiny speck of jam and we pushed it around our plates for a few minutes.

"I'm sorry, it isn't very nice," she said with a grimace.

"It's … tasty. I'm just not very hungry. Army rations. They've been feeding us up, getting us ready for the fight."

"Don't you anything foolish, will you, Ifor?" she blurted out. "Don't get it into your head that you have to be a hero. We can't afford…"

"No." Our family's brief roll call of names remained unvoiced between us. "I know." I finished my tea and set the cup back in the saucer. "Best be getting along then. There's Ma to see, and…"

"Ifor —?" There was a detaining note in Delyth's voice. "Before you go, I wanted to ask, you see —" She wasn't looking at me. She was making a ferocious study of the little

Lloyd loom table she'd set the tea things on, working at the weave of the beech stems with the pad of her thumb. "There's someone on the RAF base, a mechanic, wants to take me to the pictures." Her movement stilled, her eyes straying to her daughter who was pressing palm prints of Patriotic Pudding onto the window panes, making overlapping, sticky patterns. "Would it be very wrong?"

"Nothing wrong in going to the cinema," I answered, stealing a look at my sister's upturned, earnest face.

"Because of Ted?" she persevered. She bit her lip. "I don't want to be disloyal … to forget him…"

"Then don't forget him," I said, struck by the simplicity of other people's problems. Mindful of the time, I stood up and my sister rose to her feet as well, "But take your happiness where you find it, because it can be very hard to find."

She stood beside me, nodding, twisting her fingers round each other, "And it would be much better for little Gwynne, in the long run, to have some kind of father figure — wouldn't it?"

"Delyth!" I said, landing a soft blow on her upper arm. "He's only asked you to the pictures — don't you be getting married yet."

I don't think I'd ever seen my sister blush so deep.

I sat on the bus to Morwithy, watching the landscape lose its blackened, industrial angularity and soften into curving green. I saw the first snowdrops of wartime, unrationed, along the banks next to the road. When I climbed off the bus beside the covered market I walked back to the edge of the village to pick some for Ma, a whole fistful as a peace offering.

It was late afternoon and the cottage was dark as widows' weeds, no light shining in the window, no fire burning in the grate. I walked up the path to the front door, my footsteps slowing, my hand reluctant on the latch.

"Ma?" I stuck my head into the parlour, then looked in the back room and the kitchen. "Ma? It's me!"

I climbed the stairs, listening to the familiar creak and ease of each tread. I remembered the sound — the comfort — of my mother's footsteps as she came up to kiss me goodnight, the distracted rustle of her apron, the carbolic scent her movements revealed, the loose silk weave of her skin against my cheek, the roughness of her hands as she tucked the sheet beneath my chin.

"Ma?" I tapped on her bedroom door before I went in, glancing at the flowers I had picked; they seemed poor recompense. "It's me."

She was lying on her side in bed, her arms and legs bent as if she were in the act of walking away from me. There was a momentum about her even as she faced the wall, so that I wasn't sure which of us was doing the leaving. Her eyes were shut and her breathing shallow. I touched her shoulder and she stretched her head back then opened her eyes and blinked as if she were coming up for air.

"I've brought you these," I said. "It's me."

"Ifor?" she exclaimed, turning, attempting to lever herself up on her elbow.

"I've brought you these," I held the snowdrops out for her to see. "Are you not well?" She was struggling to sit upright and I placed the flowers on the table beside her bed, so I could plump the pillows for her. "There," I said.

Ma considered the breathless little blooms I'd brought and then glanced in my direction, as though there was a connection between the flowers and me that troubled her. She searched my face. "Is it you?" she asked, peering at my uniform, and for a moment I wondered which one of us she meant — my father, my brother, or me. Her hands were resting on the bedclothes and she stared at them as though she'd suddenly remembered they were there. She fumbled with the buttons at the neck of her nightdress, touched her dishevelled hair, but the effort seemed to exhaust her and she subsided into the pillows. "There's tea in the kitchen," she said, her eyes closed. "You'll have to light the stove, though."

The house was freezing, the flare of condensation turning to frost on the windows. It wasn't like the iron grip of winter out of doors, the cold had a domestic delicacy: the ice inside was thinner. I lit the stove downstairs to make some tea, and later I carried up a shovelful of hot coals to warm the grate in her bedroom.

"Are you not feeling well?" I said again. Her sunken features belonged to somebody I barely knew, some old lady in a photograph, an ancestor from long ago, not my Ma. Her cheeks weren't ruddy with the steam from the washing, the hoar fronds of her hair no longer curled in ways she couldn't predict or curb.

"I'm tired," she said. "That's all." The weight of the cup was too much for her to hold and it slipped in her grip, splashing some tea onto the bedspread. "We'll never get that out," she wailed in alarm. "It'll never come out." I held the cup to her mouth for her and she took a tiny sip, but wouldn't drink any more.

"Are you eating properly?" I asked. I had seen a shrivelled apple in the bowl downstairs and the heel of some cheese in the larder. She chose not to answer me, closing her eyes, breaking off negotiations. "Delyth comes to see you, doesn't she? With little Gwynne?" She didn't answer that either, crumpling into something smaller in the bed. "And Jenny...?" I mentioned my wife's name uncertainly.

She reached out her hand at that, groping for mine. "I'm glad about the baby," she whispered. "You took your time."

"We'll call it Glyn if it's a boy," I said, "And Angharad for you, if it's a girl." I smoothed her swollen knuckles with my finger, tracing the long hawser of each tendon, the blue corrugation of her veins, then I pressed her hand to my mouth to guard my secrets. "I couldn't keep my promise," I said, after a moment. "About enlisting. I couldn't be a man and keep my promise."

Our hands still locked, she let them fall one way, then the other, shrugging off all the things that might have mattered once.

"I will come back, though. That's a promise, Ma. I'll get home, whatever it takes."

I stayed beside her until she was fast asleep, the sound of her breathing as familiar as my own, my heartbeat a memory of hers, then I banked up the fire in her grate and loaded the stove downstairs with coal and drew the curtains to keep the night at bay. I found a glass and put some water in it for the wilting snowdrops, which I placed beside her bed. I stood looking down at her, with only the flickering embers to light the room: the mother who had loved me so and not loved me enough, then I stooped and kissed her forehead one last time.

Parry the Paint had done a good job with the blackout, for the village was in darkness and I blundered home to Nanagalan by the weak light of indifferent winter stars. I knew the valley though, and had the glimmer of the house to guide me. I could see the shutters were up in all the windows, which meant that you must be away somewhere. My boots sounded loud on the drive as I passed the Herbar's waist-high wall. Scotland, maybe;

though the truth of the matter was that I had no idea where you might be and my heart tightened in my chest at the thought.

The old clock chimed the quarter and as I rounded the corner and walked beneath the arch, I could just make out my ancient Beeston Humber propped up in the corner of the courtyard. For a moment I thought of cycling back up the valley, straining forward with the night in my face, through Morwithy and onwards, keeping going, keeping going.

Jenny was expecting me, but I knocked on the cottage door, all the same, a guest in my own home, a visitor to my old life.

"Good gracious," I said when she answered, though I had schooled myself for the sight of her. "I'm sorry. I didn't — it's just that you're…"

She dipped her head. "Only a few weeks to go now."

"Yes." I said. "I didn't mean —"

"Come in," she said.

There seemed to be a convention, only just established, that we should have no physical contact, so navigating my way past her swollen size and into the kitchen was an awkward manoeuvre executed with diffident politeness. Both of us were relieved to reach the table. She'd made a stew from some root vegetables and I wondered, briefly, if they were ones that I had planted months ago.

Jenny ate mounds of it. "Got to keep my strength up," she explained. "And besides, you can't waste anything, these days."

I slid the food around my plate. There was so much that could have been said, but we continued in silence, glancing at each other from time to time, then glancing away, and the weird impropriety of us dining together seemed to be hard to overcome.

After she'd told me about the baby, one afternoon when there was a break from training I made my way to the Book Lovers' library. I hadn't been for years — Jenny always brought home any books I wanted — and I removed my hat with an instinctive respect for all the learning and stood in the entrance hall staring at the notice board. Having come this far, I wasn't sure I wanted to go any further. There was a sign saying, "Drimpton Potato Day, 7th February", the minutes of the most recent WI meeting and an advertisement for something called Music and Movement with Angela. A woman came through the swing doors carrying a basket and I shrugged my jacket around my ears and peered more closely at the patchwork of announcements. There was an open letter about obtaining quotations for the repair of the library notice board, which was said to be exhibiting the familiar symptoms of condensation, a stained pin board and a sticking lock, although it looked alright to me. I felt full of the mercy of the world's small preoccupations.

Eventually I did go in, the grind of the turnstile as I passed through disrupting the library's particular peacefulness — the quietness of endeavour, the receptive hush of industry. I glanced around me, searching out my wife. Neon lights hung on long chains from the ceiling, shining the beam of knowledge into every dark recess. Jenny was sitting at the central desk, talking on the telephone in an undertone, an expression of bored impatience on her face. "Perhaps I could get back to you ... yes ... yes ... by Wednesday ... yes."

I'd imagined skulking in the corner of a stack, getting my bearings, scenting my rival while I was still upwind of him, but when it came to it I walked straight across the room in open view. The back office was partitioned from the main library, its window made from reinforced glass whose frail wire intersections chequered my first sight of Emlyn.

He wasn't what I expected, not some dark-browed, rumpled sybarite in glasses, the intellectuality palpably rolling from him. He was a thin-haired clerk in a suit as threadbare as my own, typing up a reference card on an old machine. From time to time the type bars clashed together and he squinted upwards and released them. I could see ink on the ends of his fingers.

I heard the scrape of a chair some distance behind me and Jenny saying my name with an urgency that managed not to breach the protocol regarding noise levels.

"You can't go in there."

Until that moment, I wasn't sure what I planned to do. The type bars clashed and Emlyn reached to untangle them, lifting his head absently when they proved intractable. He must have caught sight of Jenny because I saw his face — alter. I wouldn't have seen it if I hadn't been on the lookout: it was not much more than a softening in his bearing, of tension fleeing as a glance was held a second longer than it might have been, and in that instant I couldn't find it in myself to dislike him. He was about to resume reading what he had written on the reference card, when he noticed me.

"You can't go in there," Jenny planted herself between me and the door, "It's private," but my grip was already closed around the handle. "It's Staff Only, Ifor. Don't cause a scene." I paused only to make my intention clear, then I opened the door. "Look — we can talk about this at home."

Emlyn was scrambling to his feet and a pile of files tipped over, scattering across the floor. He eyed them for a moment, weighing up the indignity of scuffling after them. He let them lie. Instead, he straightened his tie and fastened the button of his jacket and when there were no other adjustments he could incorporate, he offered me his hand to shake. "You must be … Mr Griffiths?"

I stood there, sizing him up. After a beat, he held his hand out further. I gave a single nod then I took it and we shook.

"I was just … passing," I said.

"Going abroad soon, aren't you?" he observed, after a longer pause.

"I believe so."

"I've got a medical exemption," he said. "Tuberculosis. When I was younger."

"Oh," I said.

"Getting ready for the off, are you?"

"Yes."

We stared at one another. We seemed to have covered everything. Under the guise of scratching his head, he shot Jenny a glance and she tugged at my sleeve.

"Ifor —?"

"I'll make sure —" Emlyn said. "I'll keep an eye —" he swallowed. "While you're gone."

I sighed at the thought of him, the intimacy they seemed to share so ordinary, and in its way so enviable. I pushed my plate to one side. "I'm not very hungry. I'm sorry." My wife and I were long past speaking of our infidelities and our disappointments, but they were present at the table with us and through the clearing up after the meal.

"Would you like some hot milk? I'll be having some…"

I shook my head. "Jenny —" There was one thing I needed to say. "If anything happens — to me — you will look out for Ma, won't you? There's Delyth, I know, but she's not that close and…"

She was pouring the milk into a cup to measure it and then into a saucepan. She had her back to me.

"Only she didn't look too special, when I called by today."

After a moment's hesitation, in which I imagined her weighing up her debts and obligations, she nodded, and the two of us stood there waiting out the time it took for the milk to come to the boil.

"I hope things go well," I offered, "When the baby comes. You will let me know...?"

"I've made up the bed in the spare room for you," was all she said in reply.

I lay awake under the eaves and it seemed to me I heard every quarter that the clock told, those bleak and sonorous measurements sounding through the night. I couldn't sleep. Coming back to a place so haunted by memories had rather stumped me: caught between then and now, I felt that it was me who was the ghost.

I remembered the months we spent tucked up on the German border while Adolf and his bully boys were busy in Poland. They were relatively pleasant, if one can say such a thing. The RAF jockeys practised fighting high overhead in French skies that looked uncannily like English ones and when Jerry had a spare moment he'd drop propaganda leaflets down on us, which our corporal had us gathering up for use in the latrines. Some of the officers clubbed together and imported a pack of beagles so they could go hunting, but there was a shortage of foxes and the French authorities wouldn't let them bring live ones in from England.

Time, not the Hun, turned out to be our greatest enemy and we fought continually against boredom, discomfort and more physical exertion than most of us were used to, not to mention rotten army food. The sort of diversions we could look forward to were a nineteen-mile march in full kit with a mock battle at the end of it. There were some fine men in my platoon, but only one of them — a Welshman called Cadwalladr — appeared to be able to shoot.

If you had asked me at that point, I would have said I'd had a good war.

Then, out of the blue one April morning, I received a tight little note from you written to me care of the colonel of the regiment — an old friend of your father's. It is the cruellest month. I stared at your handwriting, at the loop you made of my name on the envelope. I used a knife to open it because I didn't want to tear it. The single sheet had a deckle edge and I ran my finger apprehensively along it.

"I hope this finds you well. It seems congratulations are in order — Mrs Ifor, delivered of a healthy girl," you wrote. The sting came in the postscript. "I expect to have some news of my own, in the fullness of time." I inhaled the thick, kaolin scent of the paper, searching for gardenia; I tried to picture where your hand had touched the page. "Wallet litter" is what they call the personal effects they find upon dead soldiers. I didn't want your letter to be wallet litter. I was in an agony about where to put it for safekeeping. I read it over till the expensive glaze grew thin, in a torment at what your news might be.

Everything happened so quickly after that. At the beginning of May the Germans invaded the Low Countries and within weeks they were fighting on the Somme as if it were 1916 all over again, with all the lives still lost and the years between still lived, but none of the lessons learned. We had learned nothing: the Allied armies were avoiding rout in the same Belgian villages and on the same rivers as they were twenty-six years ago — Brussels fallen, Paris in danger, everything exactly the same, and we were supposed to be heroes crusading to save the civilised world.

Our lot were part of the scramble towards Arras: cut off Jerry before he reached the coast, that was the plan, though in the event it turned out to be not one of the best laid ones: instead of two infantry divisions we had two infantry battalions. You can work out the shortfall for yourself. It was the Frenchies who saved us, gave us the cover to withdraw, when we had come all the way to France to save them.

I tried to forget the eight-mile march we had along roads congested with refugees just to reach the battle's starting line; that there was no time for us to study our orders or to do any reconnaissance. I tried to forget about the shelling coming from a nearby wood, or what it was like to be pinned down by heavy machine-gun and mortar fire. I tried to forget all of that. I tried to forget about hand to hand fighting in cornfields; about out-dated weapons and lack of ammunition and radios that do not work; about dead civilians, about the confusion and the terrible, terrible fear as forty thousand Tommies who didn't make it to Dunkirk were taken prisoner by the Nazis, and we kept falling back and back and back, until we reached the Brittany coast at St Nazaire and couldn't fall back any further.

Chapter Eighteen

I was picked up by a trawler in the end. A Frenchie leaned over the side, stretching his hand out to me, but I couldn't get a hold. I kept slipping from his grip like a piece of soap, there was so much oil all over me. He grabbed me by the seat of my pants and hauled me on board. I lay on the deck for a long while, the dry wood warm against my cheek. I shouldn't have lain there all that time. I should rot in hell for doing that. I should have leaned back into the water and grabbed a small memento, something, anything to identify the dead man who helped me cling on to life; something to send to his mother or his wife. But I couldn't move. I just couldn't move. I let him float away as I lay there, remembering that this was a June afternoon and the sun was still shining; trying to believe that I was safe.

There were twenty or thirty of us on the fishing boat, some with broken arms or legs; many with bullet wounds; one man with the flesh melted from his face; the least of us coughing our guts up. When I did move, it was to vomit shiny black strings of oil over the side. The Frenchie trawler took us to one of the destroyers. The man with the melted face didn't make it and we left a couple of other bodies behind with him. There was sweet tea waiting for us and a sailor held the mug for me while I drank. He said we'd be going home on the *Oronsay* and when I started to shake, he put his arm around my shoulders. "It's alright, mate. You're going to be alright."

The wounded were carried from one ship to the next like parcels. I didn't want to go on the *Oronsay*, sister ship of the *Lancastria*, damaged herself, with no bridge, already listing. It hurt my hands to hold the rope rungs of the scrambling net, but nobody complained as I inched my way up the side of the liner. One of the ratings helped me up the last few feet and found a space for me on deck. He unlaced my boots and tugged them off, removed my sodden trousers and wrapped a blanket around me, using one of the corners to wipe my face. The lad was half my age, yet he tended me as if I were a small boy. I couldn't stop shaking.

A young naval officer made an announcement. He said that England was four hundred miles away, that we had no escort, a ten-degree list to port, no bridge, no food, and that the Captain had broken his leg and had only a handheld compass and a sketch of the coast of France to guide us by.

I survived it; I survived all that: the sinking, the rescue and the return, because I hoped that you would be waiting for me, if only I could get myself home.

The Red Cross greeted us at Plymouth. I had my boots and a blanket and nothing else. A nice young lady gave me a pair of trousers and a shirt and directed me towards the holding centre. People from the town were lining the streets from pity, or curiosity, or to look out for a loved one. Someone pressed a tin of corned beef and a ten bob note into my hand. A young girl held out her autograph book for me to sign.

I didn't follow the dazed line of men to the depot. I kept on walking; listing myself a little because I couldn't quite believe the ground was firm beneath my feet. At the station I bought a ticket. The steam from the train swamped the platform and I could hear somebody shouting, and I thought I was back in the water with the smoke all around me, with the body of my unknown comrade in my arms and the dead scales of the silver fish rising to my face, and the person who was shouting was me.

It was evening when I came back to Nanagalan. I walked from the village through the valley and it was as if I was already dead, or dreaming; the landscape veiled in the twilight, but every curve of it known, every dip and hollow a part of me. The vines had gone, though. I could see that much. And the flowers in the Herbar had that winded look that comes after the first frost, not in the heartbreak of high summer.

My boots slurred the gravel in the drive and for a moment the dark horizon tilted. "I'm home," I said to steady myself. I could see the wall of the summerhouse like a prow, rising through the dusk. I leant against it, shaken, when being back here should have made me feel so happy. I twined my fingers through the wisteria and held on.

I made my way inside. The greenish scent of the stonework was like kelp and the Delft tiles were downy with damp. There was a crack in one of the windows — I made a note to tell Jenkins, and then stopped myself. I sat for a long time, breathing crystals onto the cobwebs, remembering the glass glitter of your face the first time I saw you.

I steeled myself. I had come back almost from the grave, my only thought to say I love you, that I have always loved you. I walked round the edge of the Herbar, with the clamour of leaves in my hair. A watchful moon gleamed above Long Leap. I reached the house and looked up. The blackout was drawn, no slit of light to warn a man, to put him on his guard. The stone façade was faintly warm and all I could feel was remorse and I didn't know why.

At the corner of the building I stopped and peered round. I could make out several pallets piled up in the centre of the courtyard, a tractor at one end, with the plough disengaged, its blades shining propeller-bright. I felt incalculably cold walking into the yard, having endured so much yet still so unprepared.

There was a blue sports car parked up close to the house, and as I walked across the gravel I could hear the voice of a man and the forced sound of your laughter, floating down from an open upstairs window. The blackout whisked apart, and Nicholas looked out.

"Of course there's nobody out there, you funny little thing. Now don't be such a goose…"

I froze midstride and then I said your name, out loud, just once, " Ella —" It's been my grace, that I have always loved you, but I knew that I'd come to the end of all my blessings.

I stood there, thinking where on earth I could fall back to now — falling back and falling back, with no end in sight. From the corner of my eye, I glimpsed Brown's dugout, then our cottage and I thought of Jenny and her daughter in safe oblivion inside and wondered if she'd have her mother's dark hair and earnest myopia, and I wanted so much to wish them well.

I turned to go. My feet were heavy and slow, as if I were wading through water. "I am with thee, and will keep thee in all places whither thou goest." I retraced my steps past the Herbar, the scent of rosemary was sharp on the summer air and I stopped to breathe it in. "I will not leave thee." I hesitated, waiting to see if the half-heard songs of Nanagalan would sing for me, but though I closed my eyes to listen better, I couldn't catch the echo.

"Ifor —"

I started walking. By straining my eyes through the shadows, I could see that Dancing Green had been ploughed over. Digging for victory. The first peas were coming on, and rows of what must be beans were planted where the cricket pitch had been.

"Wait! Ifor, wait! Don't go!"

I wondered if the Land Girls had thought to sow some beetroot and whether there were radishes and globe artichokes ready to harvest yet. It was the time of year for rhubarb and perhaps a few late asparagus. I could have bent down and scooped some of the good Welsh earth into my hand, but the road to the village stretched ahead of me and I had half the lumber of a lifetime in my head to carry with me. Then I thought of my Dad, heading off to the war without ever turning back and I twisted my head around to take one last look at the valley that I loved.

It was then that I saw you, running up the hill towards me, waving, calling out my name. When you reached me you were panting with the effort and you put your hand to your chest to calm your breathing.

"I wanted to tell you," I said. "That Jenny's baby isn't mine. She's been having an affair. But I never got the chance."

You were gazing at me, the consternation on your face visible in the pale, immaculate moonlight. I must have looked like a man come back from the depths, crusted in sea salt and blackened oil, my skin burned in places, wild-eyed, the carnage I had seen still trailing in my wake. The twist of a sound came out of you. "I married Nicholas," you stammered.

For a moment I wished I was drowned at the bottom of the sea. "I've always loved you," I bowed my head. "And I've never been able to say it."

Your hand flew to your mouth and I could see the glint of a ring on your wedding finger. "I suppose I was blind with jealousy when I heard she was pregnant. I was so — I had no right, I know, but I…"

I reached out for you and put my arms around you.

"I wanted to hurt you —" you said, with a sob. "That's the truth. What a mess. What a terrible mess…"

"It doesn't matter. Nothing matters. None of it."

"I've loved you too. I've always loved you," you said. "But you know that."

I held you close. There were tears on your cheeks and I wiped them away with my thumb and then at last I kissed you. I felt as if the waters were closing over my head again, but it was a different kind of drowning and when I breached the surface, I could almost believe that the valley was alive with ancient voices and that I could hear them singing: "I will bring thee again into this land."

A NOTE TO THE READER

Thank you so much for choosing *The Line Between Us* — I hope you have enjoyed reading it as much as I enjoyed writing it.

Most people are familiar with the sinking of the *Titanic* in which fifteen hundred and seventeen people were drowned, and some have heard of the *Lusitania* which sank with the loss of eleven hundred and ninety-two souls. These two disasters are reputed to be among the worst in British maritime history, but until recently few people have known about the fate of the *Lancastria*, a Cunard liner requisitioned by the government to rescue the straggling remnants of the British Expeditionary Force from St Nazaire after the mass evacuation at Dunkirk. The ship was bombed by enemy fighters off the coast of Brittany and as nobody could be certain about the number of refugees who were on board, it is difficult to say how many died when it went down, but the lower estimates suggest around four thousand men.

The sinking occurred just as France capitulated to the Nazis and Marshal Pétain signed an armistice with Hitler, such a devastating blow to the Allied cause that Churchill felt the nation should be spared further bad news and slapped a D Notice on the subject, forbidding any reference to what had happened with the threat of prosecution under the Official Secrets act.

This meant that the men who died on the *Lancastria* and those who managed to survive the horrifying ordeal never received any acknowledgement of what they had been through and the sacrifice they made. In June 2015 on the seventy fifth anniversary of the disaster, following years of campaigning by veterans and their supporters to ensure that the loss should be officially recognized by the British government, a tribute was formally made in parliament, where it was announced that the French government had agreed to give the site of the wreck, still lying in the shipping lanes outside St Nazaire, legal protection.

This novel is a small and personal tribute to the bravery of those men.

Any help in spreading the word about books is always profoundly welcome and I'd be thrilled if you took the time to review *The Line Between Us* on Amazon and Goodreads — it can make such a difference. If you would like to find out more about my work please visit **www.katedunn.co.uk** — and you can always follow me on Twitter: **@katedunnwriter**.

Sapere Books is an exciting new publisher of brilliant fiction and popular history.

To find out more about our latest releases and our monthly bargain books visit our website: **saperebooks.com**

Printed in Great Britain
by Amazon